JOHN L. DeBOER

SKELETON RUN

Skeleton Run
Copyright © 2015 by John L. DeBoer All rights reserved.
First Print Edition: March 2015

ISBN-13: 978-1-940215-45-7
ISBN-10: 1940215455

Red Adept Publishing, LLC
104 Bugenfield Court
Garner, NC 27529
http://RedAdeptPublishing.com/

Cover and Formatting: Streetlight Graphics

CHAPTER 1

Late February 1995
Richmond, Vermont

J EANNE FAVREAU KISSED HER EIGHTEEN-MONTH-OLD son and put him in his crib for the night. Exhausted from her long day at Bolton Valley, she flopped into her own bed across the room. Sufficient snow on the popular ski resort's slopes kept the snack bar busy on Saturdays. At least she had the next day off. She quickly fell asleep.

The baby cried, and Jeanne's eyes snapped open. No light crept through the blinds. She turned on the nightstand lamp and glanced at the clock radio: 10:15. *Crap!* She stepped to the crib, where Timmy stood gripping the side rail and emitting unhappy squawks.

"What's the matter, sweetie?" Jeanne lifted him over the rail and held him to her shoulder while checking his diaper. Dry and empty. Then she felt his forehead. Hot.

Oh, Christ! Another ear infection? Probably. With a sigh, she carried Timmy into the bathroom and took the bottle of Tylenol suspension from the medicine cabinet. She closed the bathtub drain and turned on the water. She went into the small kitchen and deposited him into his highchair, where he rubbed his right ear with a fist.

"I know, Timmy. You don't feel good," Jeanne cooed, "but Mommy will make it better." She opened a cabinet drawer, got a spoon, and poured the liquid Tylenol into it. The pediatrician had said he could have a full teaspoon. Unfortunately, Jeanne had become experienced dealing with ear infections. After successfully getting her child to take the medicine, she picked him up and returned to the bathroom.

***

From the back seat of the Toyota Land Cruiser, I gazed out the window at the passing forest. Though clouds intermittently obscured the face of the half moon, enough light bathed the landscape to provide a contrast between the smooth, untrampled snow and the skeletal stands of hardwood trees rising above it.

My buddies and I had taken full advantage of the good conditions on the slopes, and with the end of the season looming, we wanted to double down and continue skiing into the evening under the lights. But our social director had another idea in mind.

Alan Granger chuckled as he piloted the SUV down the Bolton Valley access road. "Hot babes in a hot tub. Doesn't get any better than that. Didn't I tell you? Stick with the Grange if you want to party? Bring your swim trunks just in case? I'm definitely going to give that Tammy a call tomorrow." Tall and lanky, with a shock of unruly dark brown hair, a handsome face, and a gregarious personality, Granger was well known in our high school as a chick magnet. And starring as a wide receiver on the football team hadn't hurt.

Bob Kretchman, sitting next to me, grunted and took a gulp from his beer can. With his intimidating size and ferocious tackling exploits for that same team, his nickname of "Crushman" had evolved naturally. He scratched his scalp through his blond crew cut. "Yeah, it was fun. But I can't see us taking this any further. They're college chicks, dude."

"Get me one of those Buds, will you?" Granger said. As I reached into the Styrofoam cooler behind me, he continued, "What difference does a year make, Crush? In seven months, we'll be in college, too. So we lie a little to get laid. You know, like we usually do." He laughed again.

I popped the can and handed it to our driver.

"What about you, Jimmy?" he asked me. "Going to give Green Bikini a call? You two seemed to be getting it on pretty good."

I smiled, thinking of those luscious tits practically rubbing against me as we "got to know each other" in the spa's swirling water. The girls, Pi Beta Phi sorority sisters, were sophomores at the University of Vermont, all from out of state. They were staying in the ski condo belonging to the parents of Granger's date for the weekend. Unfortunately, the father and his wife were also there, so we had to confine the frolic to the public hot tub. But we'd all said we would like to get together again in the near future—hopefully to take our newfound "friendships" to the next level.

"The lighting helped," I replied, "since I don't look *ancient* like the rest of you guys. But I don't think my face could pass for a college stud in the light of day."

Tom Webster faced me from the front passenger seat. He twiddled his index fingers in his cheeks and grinned. "Mr. Dawson, she'd just think you're cute. Go for it, man. Sometimes you gotta go for the long ball." The team's quarterback turned his broad shoulders back to the front and nudged the driver with his elbow.

"Amen to that," Granger responded.

"Hey, Jim," Kretchman added, "you can't always dance your way through the line. Somebody like me could be waiting for you, stop you in your tracks."

I laughed at the ribbing, since I was used to it. They had been my friends since grade school. Though in good shape, able to hold my own in the weight room, and certainly not short in stature, I was the "little" kid among them and the youngest by four months. Not to mention my young-looking face. "Well," I said, returning the linebacker's grin, "if there's a *hole,* I'll be sure to find it."

"Good one, Jimmy!" Granger laughed and took a pull from his can.

"And," I said, "you seem to have forgotten that ninety-five-yard touchdown run I made against Essex. The *Burlington Free Press* certainly thought it was noteworthy. Didn't the article say it was a school record? And how about those two—I repeat, two—kickoff returns for TDs against BFA? I can go *long,* too." I gave him a light punch in the arm.

"Yeah, you're a legend in your own mind," Granger said over his shoulder. "Anyway, those girls do open up some possibilities."

The car came to a stop at the bottom of the hill before turning right onto US 2. The exit for I-89, the route we'd take back to Burlington, lay just a few miles ahead.

———— ✦⟨⟩✦ ————

At eleven p.m., after bathing Timmy in tepid water, Jeanne checked his temperature again with the rectal thermometer. *103.6!* His fever had risen a full degree. Listless and lethargic, Timmy was no longer crying. Not a good sign.

She placed him on the bed while she quickly dressed and put on her parka. Then she wrapped a blanket around Timmy, picked him up, and went out the trailer door. Along with her child, the decrepit singlewide was all she had left to remind her of her ex-boyfriend, who'd run off as soon as she revealed the positive pregnancy test.

She secured Timmy in the rear-facing infant car seat of her beat-up Yugo and then drove out of the trailer park. The medical center in Burlington, just twenty minutes or so to the west, was her destination. Richmond didn't have a hospital. *But that's what my baby needs, and soon.*

———— ✦⟨⟩✦ ————

The heavy beat of Meat Loaf erupted from the Land Cruiser's CD player as snowflakes began to hit the windshield.

Granger turned on the wipers. "Where the hell did this come from?"

"Some freak snow flurry," Webster said from the shotgun seat.

"More like a freakin' storm."

I leaned forward to peer through the windshield. The headlights' illumination reflected back at us from the fluffy crystals. We appeared to be the only car on the road, so playing Follow the Leader wouldn't help us pick our way through the wall of white. Roadside lights were non-existent.

"Better slow down," I said. As Kretchman had implied in his metaphor, I was usually the cautious one. I preferred to call it the "voice of reason."

As the car rounded a turn, Webster yelled, "Watch out!"

At the same moment, I saw it as well. A dim red glow penetrated the heavy snowfall directly in front of us. A car's taillight.

Granger tromped on the brakes, but the SUV skidded on the slick asphalt. "Oh, Jesus!" he shouted, and we all watched helplessly, knowing a collision was unavoidable. The heavy Land Cruiser slammed into the rear of the much smaller car, sending it careening off the road and into a stout maple tree.

"Shit!" Granger regained control of the SUV, pulled onto the shoulder, and put the car in park but left the engine running. He scrambled out of the vehicle and headed toward the stricken sedan, his open parka flapping.

The rest of us followed. Snow crunched beneath my boots as I hurried to the car. The initial shock of the collision became full-blown panic as I feared the worst. The Yugo's right headlight had escaped damage and sent its beam onto the cornfield beyond the tree. The front of the driver's side of the car had received the full force of the impact. Snow continued to fall, its insulation imposing an eerie quiet. Except for our heavy breathing and the slight tick of the Yugo's engine, no sound reached my ears.

We gathered around Granger and looked through the shattered driver's side window. Faint light from the moon revealed a young woman pinned to her seat by the steering column. She wasn't moving.

"Are you all right?" Granger spoke through the window as he tried and failed to open the door. No response came from the woman who appeared to be, at best, unconscious. "Bob, give the door a try."

While Kretchman put his bulk into the effort, I went around to the other side and opened the front passenger door. The dome light came on, illuminating the woman, and my fear became real.

The collision had driven the dashboard assembly, including the collapsible steering column, into her chest. Her unblinking eyes stared ahead as if expressing shock at the sudden catastrophe. Med school was still more than four years away for me, but I didn't need medical training to diagnose the obvious.

Still, I felt for a pulse in her cool, lifeless wrist. "She's dead," I announced.

"Oh, my God!" Granger wailed. "What're we going to do?" He banged his fist on the roof of the car. "Shit!"

From behind me, Webster said, "Look in the backseat, Jimmy."

Though I'd thought my despair couldn't get any worse, it climbed to a new level.

Webster opened the rear door, and I leaned in. The infant car seat lay askew but still restrained by the seat belt. The child in it was motionless, eyes closed. *Oh, Jesus, no!* I put my ear close to the baby's mouth, and the sound of rhythmic breathing rewarded me. *Thank God!* I didn't see any apparent injuries. Granger and Kretchman came around the car.

"I think the baby's okay," I said as I backed out and stood upright. "Call 9-1-1 on your car phone, Al."

"Yeah... all right... good idea." He started for his car then came back to us. "Oh, man. We should think about this first. I killed somebody, for Christ's sake! Vehicular homicide is what they call it." He shook his head. "I'm in big trouble, guys."

"It was an accident," Kretchman offered. "Bad weather conditions, slippery road. That car came out of nowhere."

"And it only had the one taillight," Webster added. "We'll back you up, man."

"Except they'll say I was going too fast for the conditions, since I rear-ended her. Slam dunk there. And I was drinking. Unlike you guys, I'm eighteen, so I'm screwed both ways. I'm not allowed to drink, but legally I'm an adult. I am totally fucked!"

I couldn't argue with that assessment, and apparently, the others couldn't either as indecision paralyzed all of us. I glanced at the baby. We had to do something for it and soon.

"Even if I can stay out of jail and my old man doesn't disown me, there goes law school. Think I could get into Georgetown or any other top school with this on my record?" Granger put his hands on the sides of his head. "Oh, man. What am I going to do?"

"So let's get the hell out of here," Webster said. "You gotta make that call because of the kid, but do it when we're on the road and keep it anonymous."

"I think the cops can trace those calls," Granger replied. "Can't take that chance. I need to find a pay phone."

"What about the baby?" I asked. "We can't just leave it here. If something happens to—"

"Uh-oh, car coming," Kretchman said.

I looked to the east. The trees lit up from an approaching car that had not yet rounded the curve. We watched as the car came into view and then reached our location. I held my breath, but it continued past us without even slowing.

Maybe the snow had obscured the driver's view. Maybe something else had distracted him. Maybe he had issues of his own and didn't want to get involved in our problem. Whatever—his appearance on the scene emphasized our precarious position.

"We better get going before a Good Samaritan or a state trooper comes by," Granger said.

"The baby?" I asked again.

Granger looked at the sleeping infant. "He's got a warm blanket." He reached in to tuck the wool fabric around the kid. "It's not that cold. Gotta be above freezing." He gazed at the sky. "And the snow is letting up." The panic in his eyes told me whose welfare he was really considering. "The kid'll be okay. He's not even crying, Jimmy. I'll call 9-1-1 as soon as we hit town. Twenty minutes, tops." He headed to the Land Cruiser. "C'mon, guys, let's book."

Kretchman must have sensed my hesitation. "Jimmy?"

I didn't know what to say.

Webster grabbed my arm. "C'mon, man. I don't like this any better than you do, but we're all in big shit here. Al's right. This is the only way out for us."

It wasn't right to just up and bolt, leaving the mess behind us. Okay, it was Al's mess, really. But Webster had a point. We were all involved. Even though I had only been a bystander, I wasn't innocent. I had been drinking, too, had even given the driver a beer. Because of us, a woman lay dead, and her baby had lost its mother. A terrible thing.

Guilt was one thing. I'd have that regardless. Suffering real-world consequences was another matter. In the short term, I'd be grounded for sure. But I could imagine how this incident could forever mar my reputation. I'd be one of "those boys"—the drunken teenagers on a joyride who killed a woman. And Al, my buddy, was right. He would be in a shit-pot full of trouble, legal and otherwise, if this got out.

Self-defense and loyalty finally won the debate. We could do nothing for the woman now, and the baby would be fine, I told myself. I leaned in once more to check the baby and made sure the blanket was secured around his sleeping form. I closed the door and said, "Okay, let's go," then followed the others to the car.

CHAPTER 2

"ONLY TWO MORE WEEKS." MICHELLE grabbed my arm as we walked along Church Street Marketplace. "I can hardly wait."

We had shared an Italian meatball grinder at Bove's and were now strolling it off in the four-block pedestrian mall in the heart of downtown Burlington. The warm, sunny day augmented our good moods. We had finished the last of our final exams at the University of Vermont, and it felt great to be free again.

I patted the hand clutching my arm. "Yeah, I'm looking forward to it. Kinda sad, though, our last summer at Silver Bay."

"Maybe not, Jim. Someday, I'd like to have our own place on Lake George."

I grinned at her. "Now that's an idea."

"Why not? We both love it there."

"Well, it's fun to think about. But we have a long way to go before that can happen. And who knows where we'll be then?"

She frowned and pursed her lips. "Always Mr. Practical."

"Gotta be, babe."

"Where is that go-for-it guy who first attracted me back in the day?"

I chuckled. "Still here, Mish. Just older and wiser."

"So you say." She gave my biceps a hard squeeze.

Our introduction had occurred just after classes started for our freshman year. There was an almost corny, movie-cliché quality about it. I had noticed her in French class. Hard not to, really. She was a stunner—shoulder-length dark hair framed a face I considered exotic-looking, suggestive of some Asian influence in her ancestry; a trim but curvy figure; great legs coming out of Bermuda shorts. About five six, I estimated.

We had just left the Waterman Building that fateful afternoon, she just ahead of me, when she stumbled on one of the steps. I reached out to grab her as the notebook she carried flew from her hand. Having prevented her nasty fall, I picked up the three-ring binder and handed it to her.

"Thanks," she said, smiling. She shook her beautiful head and chuckled. "I guess I wasn't paying attention to where I was going. Michelle Conway." She stuck out her right hand.

"Jim Dawson." I shook it. "I think we have French class together."

"Yeah, I thought you looked familiar." She smiled again. "Well, thanks again, Jim." She turned to go.

Go for it. She's a babe! "Uh, Michelle, maybe I should walk you to your destination. Wouldn't want you to fall if you get distracted again."

She squinted at me for a moment then laughed, a light musical sound. I liked it. "You know, I think I'm already distracted again. Good idea. I'm headed to the student center for a snack. Will you be so kind as to escort this clumsy damsel across the treacherous campus, Sir Galahad?"

I executed a campy bow. "It would be my pleasure, dear lady." I took hold of her elbow, and we successfully negotiated the remaining steps before heading to the student center and the start of our relationship.

Now, two and a half years later, we had pretty much diagrammed out the next few years ahead of us. Marriage next summer, then med school in the fall for me while she supported us as a grade-school teacher.

And this summer would be our third, and last, summer working at the Silver Bay YMCA conference center and retreat. Located on Lake George, the thirty-two-mile-long jewel in the Adirondacks, it lay only sixty or so miles west of Burlington, in upstate New York.

The pay wasn't much, but meals and lodging were included. And one couldn't ask for a better work environment. As with all the young men and women employees, college students mostly, we were assigned a variety of jobs. I mainly worked in the boathouse, lending out kayaks, canoes, and mini-sailboats to the guests. I also helped maintain the clay tennis courts and gave the occasional lesson.

Michelle organized activities for the young kids, freeing up their parents for their own pursuits. Her other chief responsibility had her at the beach as a lifeguard.

Images of Silver Bay flitted through my mind. The lake's crystal-clear blue water, the shuffleboard courts and the archery range, the softball games, enjoying a treat in the evening at the ice cream store. It truly was an idyllic place for a family vacation, where the opportunities for recreation abounded and where adults could enjoy themselves as much as their kids could.

As we neared the entrance to a clothing shop, a young woman pushing a stroller came out of it. We stopped to let her get around us, allowing us a good look at the sleeping baby in the carriage. I stared after the stroller as it traveled toward Pearl Street.

"Jim? Something wrong?"

I came out of my semi-trance and turned to Michelle. "No, honey. I just thought that baby was cute, is all."

She stared at me as if trying to read my mind, something she was pretty adept at doing, actually. "You're not thinking of moving up our timetable, are you?"

She hadn't divined what the baby had really stimulated, so her question didn't compute for a second or two.

"Because I thought we'd decided that," she went on. "We have to wait until after med school, remember?"

"Sure, Mish. Of course. We'll have plenty of time to start our family." I smiled. "The baby *was* cute, though." I kissed her, trying to disguise the ache in my gut.

That snowy night on Route 2 had come back again, as it often did over the intervening years. Aside from learning the child's name through newspaper stories following the incident, I knew nothing else about the kid. What happened to him was a mystery. "C'mon, let's go down to Waterfront Park. Such a beautiful day."

She gave me what I called her "Mr. Spock stare" again, and I knew I'd been made. But she didn't know the real reason for my angst. And she never would, if I could help it. I had no idea how she would react, and I felt no need to find out.

We were blocking the entrance to the shop, so I nudged Michelle gently past it. She put her hands on my cheeks, forcing me to look into her eyes. "I want to have a baby, too. If you really think we can manage it, maybe we can work it out. I could take a leave of absence from teaching, then later we'll find a good day care…"

I grabbed her hands from my face and held them in front of me. "Honey, you're the best. But our original plan was the right one. I know that. I really do. Now let's go to the park and talk about getting ready for Silver Bay."

She nodded, but I knew that she knew that I knew I had failed to convince her. Being the trouper she was, she changed the subject as we walked toward College Street. "What time are we going to meet the guys tonight?"

I'd almost forgotten. Granger and Kretchman were back in town for their summer breaks from college, and we were supposed to meet them and their dates for dinner at the Dog Team Tavern. Webster's year at Dartmouth had also ended, but he was due to start an internship at a securities firm in Boston, so he wouldn't be joining us.

The guys. Another reminder of that terrible night. More pangs of unease shot through my midsection. "I told them we'd meet at six." We turned right on College and headed down the hill to the park at the edge of Lake Champlain.

"Tammy will be there, of course." Michelle frowned.

That Tammy. The girl in the hot tub who had attracted Al that night. Michelle didn't like her, thought she was too self-centered.

"Mish, they're a couple." I nudged her with my elbow, trying to keep things light. "Like us."

"Not really like us." She grunted. "Too into themselves. Both of them."

"You like Sheree, though, right?"

16

"She's nice, but what she sees in that Goliath, I'll never know."

Bob Kretchman and Sheree Stallings *were* like us, in that they were also unofficially engaged. The Crushman, a second-team All American linebacker at Syracuse, hoped for an NFL career. Sheree, a year behind us at Burlington High School, had dated Bob since our senior year. Rather plain looking but vivacious and sweet, she attended Champlain College here in town.

At least the presence of the women tonight would distract us from the unwanted memory. Or so I hoped. But now I couldn't get my mind to move away from it.

Whap! The sound of the newspaper hitting the front porch below my second-floor bedroom window had startled me, though I had been awake for a while, waiting for it. It was the Monday morning following the "incident."

I rushed downstairs, afraid to find out but compelled to know. I brought the paper in and stood in the foyer, scanning the front page. Nothing. But in the Local section, I found:

Woman Dies in Crash

Vermont State Police report finding a car that had crashed into a tree along Route 2, just outside of Richmond on Saturday night at about 11:30 p.m. The driver, Jeanne Favreau, a resident of Richmond, was taken to Fletcher Allen Health Care in Burlington, where she was pronounced dead. Surviving the crash was a male infant, name and exact age unknown at press time. The circumstances of the apparent accident are under investigation.

So the kid did make it.

Relief that our cowardly flight had not caused the child's death flooded through me. That would have been unbearable to live with. The mother, well, that was an accident, I told myself. We could do nothing about it now except hope we wouldn't be caught.

For the next two weeks, the other guys and I sweated it out. We thought of fingerprints too late, but Granger assured us that would only work if they suspected us. There were no sets of our prints on record. The trampling of the snow leading from the road and around the Yugo would indicate more than one person had gone to the crash site, so the cops probably figured whoever made that anonymous call was one of those people.

The only thing directly tying us to the accident was Granger's car. That motorist who drove past us could have read about the crash and remembered seeing a Land Cruiser parked there. And there was the damage to the SUV's front bumper. Granger had told his old man he had a fender-bender in the ski lodge's parking lot, and got the car fixed right away. But the Land Cruiser could doom us.

A follow-up article in the paper raised the prospect of a second, unknown vehicle involved in the crash and mentioned Granger's anonymous call to 9-1-1. So the cops were looking for us.

Unable to concentrate on schoolwork—or anything else, really—we each waited with dread for that knock on the door. It never came.

As Michelle and I approached the lake, I wondered whatever became of that child.

That same day
Las Vegas, Nevada

Wendell Logan stood at the window of his top-floor office in the Phoenix, staring down at the Strip. Cars that looked like toys from his elevation had stopped, obeying the regulations imposed by a traffic light.

Regulations. He smiled at the word—so important in the building of his empire. Regulations had finally wrested control of this town from the mob, allowing men like himself—Kerkorian, Wynn, Adelson—to move in. Just as ruthless, perhaps, as Luciano and his successors but with a veneer of respectability and, of course, a history of conforming to "regulations."

He turned from the window and sat at his custom-made rosewood desk. As with everything else in his brand-new hotel and casino, the furnishings of his control center—the bridge of the ship that was Logan Enterprises, Inc.—bespoke class.

As he looked at stock quotes on his computer screen, the subject of rules and regulations wouldn't leave him. Like its namesake, his latest venture had risen from the ashes, as it were, of the demolition of one of Sin City's landmark hotels of yesteryear. Only a few of the old places that had flourished in the '50s and '60s were left. And he had his eye on those, too.

Obeying the rules got him into the game, but they seriously affected his bottom line. The ability to bend them to his advantage— or better still, to eliminate them—was a crucial asset for a man like himself to have.

He'd found it relatively easy to get local and state politicians, the ones who made some of those laws that increased his costs of doing business, to go along. Well-placed dollars in their hands could save him countless more. Washington, DC, however, where the real power resided, presented a much more formidable challenge. There, lawmakers not beholden to him could put a serious hurt on his financial picture. A well-meaning bill here, a self-interest amendment there, and with the stroke of the president's pen, Logan would then have agencies he'd never heard of looking over his holdings, putting up even more hoops for him to jump through.

The fifty-year-old billionaire sighed and ran fingers through his black-dyed hair, thinking of his effort six years earlier to get a seat at that table. He'd cast considerable bread upon the waters then, expecting significant access to the coming second Bush administration. *If only the putz had stuck to his principles.* But no, the man raised taxes, and the voters stated their disapproval that November. Maybe they just wanted a change. Whatever.

Logan shook his head and looked away from the computer screen that wasn't interesting him, anyway. But now there were rumblings about another Bush with his eye on the White House, H.W.'s son. A cocky young man, "Dubya," as some were calling him, talked a good game. But Logan saw the plain-speaking, first-term Texas governor as merely a front man for others, those needing a vehicle for their own agendas.

Nothing new about that. Altruistic motivations of political campaign drivers were rare in his experience. A candidate groomed by the movers and shakers to represent their interests was a fact of life. Only a very few aspirants for the greatest prize in politics had the ambition and spirit to pull their supporters with them rather than being pushed from behind, the voices constantly whispering in their ears. And from what he was able to learn, Logan did not count George W. Bush among that small number of independent idealists.

He picked up the telephone and pressed a button on the console. "Mark," he said to his second-in-command, "what's the latest news from Austin? Any more talk about a presidential run for Bush?"

"A definite maybe. Still just under-the-radar stuff, though. Can't afford to be more overt. He's gotta win re-election first."

"Any problem there?"

"Not really. Bob Bullock has brought him along nicely. With that old pol, who not only is the lieutenant governor but a *Democrat,* on Bush's team, Garry Mauro doesn't stand a chance. That's the consensus."

"Is Rove the main strategist?"

"Appears to be."

"See if you can set up a meeting with him. Let him know I'm interested in getting onboard. We can send the plane to pick him up, comp him to a suite here."

"I assume you're not talking about the re-election campaign."

"You assume correctly."

"Okay, you're the boss, but I remember the last time. And another Bush?

Logan laughed. "Gore is no Bill Clinton, Mark."

"Right. I'll let you know when I've got something lined up."

Logan disconnected and sat back in his chair, gazing idly at the Picasso on the wall across the room. *The President of the United States not only taking my calls but wanting to please me. On the advice of someone like Karl Rove, of course. Wouldn't that be something?*

CHAPTER 3

That same day
Vermont

THE DOG TEAM TAVERN HAD been a landmark for decades. That evening, its parking lot was full as usual, but I found a space, and Michelle and I walked to the entrance. After the host confirmed we were the first of our party to arrive, as was the custom we selected our entrées from the chalkboard in the small waiting area and then went into the bar, where we snagged a table large enough to accommodate the six of us.

"That's one of my favorite shirts," Michelle said, referring to the blue golf knit I'd selected because I knew she liked it. "Matches your eyes."

I smiled. "And your blouse matches the envy green the other women will be when they see you."

Though she rolled her eyes, I knew I'd scored. But it wasn't hyperbole. Michelle was one fine-looking woman. In addition to her sleeveless, light-green cotton blouse that didn't hide her generous bust, she wore mauve shorts that showed off her long swimmer's legs. Silver hoops dangling from her earlobes bracketed a model's face.

As I was admiring Michelle's features and thinking for the umpteenth time how lucky I was, a server appeared. "Hi, folks." She set a bowl of the restaurant's signature horseradish/cottage cheese dip and a basket of rippled potato chips on the table. "Can I get you something to drink?"

I looked at Michelle.

"Gin and tonic for me," she said.

"Make that two." We had celebrated Michelle's twenty-first birthday in April, so she was safe. With my legal-drinking age still four months away, I had my fake ID ready just in case.

The young waitress, who could have been a freshman at Middlebury College, squinted at me briefly. "I'll be right back with your drinks," she said and left.

Apparently, my face had matured enough to pass muster, at least to an underclassman. I scooped some of the appetizer onto a chip. "Hungry?"

"Famished!" She loaded a chip of her own and plopped it into her mouth. Michelle had a healthy appetite, one not confined to food. Our sex life was yet another item on the plus side of my "relationship" column. There weren't any listings on the other side, actually. Well... maybe one. Although she knew Granger and I had been buddies for years, she didn't get the bond we still had. But if truth be told, her perceptions of the guy were not far off the mark. "You *are* going to be nice to Al and Tammy, tonight, right?"

She frowned but quickly changed it to a smile. "Why, of course, Jimmy. I'm always the epitome of civility." She drew an air halo above her head.

"Good, because here they are." I stood to greet them.

Alan Granger, dressed in navy slacks and a white polo, looked as if he had just come from a GQ photo shoot. Tammy Litchfield, clutching his arm as if she owned it, wore a thin-strapped fuchsia sundress with enough of a neckline scoop to hint at serious cleavage. Her skin exhibited a tan that seemed more appropriate for a resident of Florida—which she wasn't—than for one exposed to the northeast sun this early in the season. Hulking Bob Kretchman and the diminutive-by-comparison Sheree Stallings followed behind. After we did the greeting thing and sat, the server took their drink orders.

Tammy was attractive, and I couldn't be blamed for looking. Well, Michelle undoubtedly would. But Tammy's allure was more aggressive, if that was the right word, while I classified Michelle's appeal as elegant, more subdued. Tammy had medium-length blond hair of a shade that must have come from a bottle, according to Michelle, and blue eyes set just a tad too far apart, Sophia Loren-like. And she had the full lips of that Italian actress as well. About five nine and well put together. She and Granger did make a handsome couple.

Granger had told us he would call the girl he met in the hot tub that infamous night, and he did about two weeks later, when the risk of our getting caught appeared to be over. After their first date, during which he successfully played the college-man role, his confident ego urged him to take a gamble. Surprisingly—to me, not him—the revelation of his true age didn't faze her, and the rest of us had to endure his bragging over the next several months.

Sheree, though a rather plain brunette, more than made up for it with a bubbly personality that attracted everyone she met. I could see why the laconic Kretchman, usually uncomfortable in mixed-company social gatherings, was drawn to her. She could carry the small-talk conversation load, allowing Bob to just nod and smile and occasionally utter something like, "That's right."

"Pedro's pitching tonight." Granger took a sip of his martini.

Michelle shook her head. "That's fascinating news."

"What?"

"Is that all you guys can talk about?" Michelle was smiling, but she was serious.

Despite her promise to be good, trouble might be brewing. Better nip this in the bud, I decided. "Beats the weather, Mish." I chuckled. "Hey, we're jocks. What do you expect?"

She sipped her drink and didn't respond.

"How about politics, then?" Granger grinned. "We could talk about Bill Clinton."

"And Monica Lewinsky, I suppose. Ha! You Republicans. Be careful what you wish for. Impeach Clinton and you get Gore. Is that what you want?" Michelle looked at him with defiance in her eyes.

Sheree made the time-out sign and laughed. "Okay, people, politics is definitely out! I want this to be a fun evening. You boys can go back to discussing the Red Sox or whatever, while we girls can talk amongst ourselves about less controversial things, like the best places to have destination weddings."

Thank you, Sheree!

"Uh-oh. That sounds dangerous." Granger winked at Kretchman.

"I like that idea." Tammy shot her lover a smirk.

"Gentlemen, we've gone and done it now," I said. "How about a compromise, Sheree? We won't ask Bob if he and Donovan McNabb can get Syracuse to a national championship next year, if you don't conspire to drag us to Hawaii as groomsmen for your nuptials."

"Hawaii! That would be perfect!" Sheree grinned at Kretchman, who covered his face with his hands and groaned.

<hr />

After the usual gut-busting meal at the Dog Team, we returned to Burlington to walk it off at Waterfront Park. Then we sat on benches and looked out at the lake, the lights of the marina reflecting off the dark water. The sun had set over the Adirondacks more than an hour earlier, but a temperature still in the mid-seventies kept us comfortable.

Granger suggested we all get together at Burlington's North Beach the next day for a swim and a picnic.

"We're in," Sheree said for her and Bob. "Sounds like fun."

"And I just bought a new swimsuit," Tammy offered.

Michelle poked me with her elbow. "No doubt a bikini," she muttered softly.

"Your body can't be beat, babe," I said in an equally quiet voice.

"What are you whispering about?" Granger leaned over from his bench. "Are you in or not?"

I chuckled. "Sure, we'll be there."

After deciding who would bring what and establishing a rendezvous time, Granger said, "I'm looking forward to it. I didn't want our weekend to be over already. Still got a lot of catching up to do. So we'll see you guys tomorrow." He grabbed Tammy's hand and helped her to her feet.

Bob and Sheree, who had come in Granger's car, also stood. The evening was over, at least the date part of it. But Granger had told Bob and me when the girls went to the ladies' room at the Dog Team he wanted to discuss something later without them.

As we headed to my car, Michelle asked, "Back to the apartment?"

I checked my watch. "Frank is there now. And I'm a little tired. But he's leaving town in the morning, so we'll have the place to ourselves tomorrow night."

"Okay."

I drove her to the Tri-Delt sorority house and walked her to the front door. "Pick you up tomorrow at eleven." My goodnight kiss must have been more perfunctory than I intended because she gave me a pout with those soft lips that I loved.

"You're not going to the apartment now, are you?"

"No." *How does she do it? The girl must be psychic.*

"You're going to meet the guys for a few beers, right?"

I laughed. "Guilty as charged. What gave me away?"

"Hey, Jim, I don't care. Go do that male-bonding thing. Just don't get wasted, okay? As Al said, the weekend is just getting started."

"I'll be good, I promise." I kissed her again and left.

The three of us sat at a table in Champ's, a downtown sports bar. A '70s local Golden Gloves champion owned the bar, but the name also alluded to the legendary Loch Ness-like monster reputed to be a denizen of Lake Champlain, given the cute name "Champ."

Multiple TVs around the room were tuned to either *Baseball Tonight* on ESPN or the NHL playoff game between the Washington Capitals and the Buffalo Sabres. Alas, for us chauvinistic fans of regional pro sports, those Capitals had knocked out the Bruins in the first round, and the Boston Celtics didn't even make it to the NBA postseason. So there wasn't much fan interest among the other patrons, and the room was fairly quiet.

Two of the three pool tables had games going, and about half of the barstools and tables were occupied. After the server delivered our draft beers, I turned to Granger. "So, Al, what is this big *thing* you wanted to tell us tonight?"

"Yeah," Kretchman said, "what's with the mystery?"

He arched his eyebrows. "Ever wonder why Tom seems to have one excuse or another whenever we and our significant others decide to get together?"

I knew why Webster couldn't make it to our reunion tonight. "You mean that job opening that came up in Boston? He told me he had to grab it."

Granger nodded. "Yeah, maybe that was legit. But what about the other times?"

"We saw him at Christmas and Thanksgiving. Spring break, too, as I remember," Kretchman said. "What are you getting at?"

"Sure, *we* saw him—the guys. Can you think of a time when he joined us for a date night?"

I thought for a moment and couldn't come up with an example. "So he couldn't get a date and didn't want to be a fifth wheel... seventh wheel, actually. What's the big deal?" I gave Kretchman a "what's he talking about?" look, and he shrugged.

Granger took a drink then slowly set the glass on the table. He stared down at it as he said, "I think Tom's gay."

Kretchman choked on his beer. "No way! Tom?"

We had known Tom since grade school. He had been our team's quarterback. We'd undressed together in locker rooms, had taken group showers with him. There never had been a hint he played for the other side. "What do you base this crazy theory on, Al? That Tom doesn't date all that much?" I shook my head. "What about Debbie Fincher? He went out with her all senior year. They were King and Queen of the prom, for Christ's sake." I looked at Kretchman for support, and he nodded.

"So where is Debbie now?" Granger continued.

"Tom went to Dartmouth; she went to Middlebury. Life moves on, you know?"

Granger picked up his beer and took a sip. "Somebody else went to Dartmouth, Jim. Somebody who is now sharing Tom's apartment in Hanover. A *he*, not a *she*."

"Big deal. I have a male student sharing my place, too. Does that make me gay? And how do you know this, anyway?"

"You know I called him last week to see if he could join us tonight. That's how I found out about that job thing in Boston when I talked with him. But his roommate answered the phone when I called. Remember Steve Fine?"

Now I knew the origin of Granger's suspicion. Steve Fine—cheerleader, president of the Glee Club, active participant in school play productions. Though he had not come out openly, it was well known throughout the school where his sexual orientation lay.

"Steve is living with him?" Kretchman asked.

"Yup."

"Jesus."

"Okay," I said, "Steve is probably gay. Probably. But hell, Tom knew him. We all did. They both went to Dartmouth. Natural for them to hook up."

Granger pursed his lips.

"I mean," I said, realizing my unintentional pun, "it's natural for two hometown boys to share an apartment in a new place. I'm not willing to agree with your verdict yet." The operative word was "yet."

The accuser finished his beer, caught the attention of the server, and pointed at the table. "I could be wrong. Just wanted to talk to you about it."

"Jesus," Kretchman said again as he stared at his glass.

I took the last gulp of my beer. Its taste had become stale. "So what if he *is* gay? He's still Tom, right? Our buddy? It's not like he's going to put moves on us."

"Do you have any gay friends, Jim?" Granger asked in a tone that implied the question was rhetorical.

"Not that I know of."

"Neither do I." He shook his head, lips tight, as if that fact revealed a sad truth.

"But it's not because I'm homophobic. It's just never come up. Different social circles, I guess."

"Right. Look, I'm not a gay-hater, either. But this changes things for me, you know? He doesn't fit in our group anymore. You heard the girls talking about weddings. Yeah, they were fooling around, but I know you and Mish are going to get married. And Crush and Sheree look like a done deal. Tammy? News flash—I think she'd be right for me. So that leaves Tom and his *boyfriend* on the outside looking in. I'm sorry, but that's the way I feel."

I sighed as the server returned with our second round. After she left, I said, "I'm not going to shut Tom out, Al, even if I know for a fact he's gay. He's my friend and will continue to be. What do I care if he can't get *married* like us? We're adults, about to start our careers. Live and let live, man." I turned to Kretchman. "What do you think, Bob?"

"I don't know. I think we should find out for sure, though. He's our buddy, like you say. We should be able to come right out and ask him."

"You're right, Crush," Granger said. "That's what we should do."

"And if he admits it? Then what? 'Sorry, Tom, but you're no longer our friend because you don't fit in'?" I shook my head.

"Yeah, Al," Kretchman said. "It's not like we're all going to end up living in the same neighborhood, having backyard barbecues with the wives and kids. We might be scattered all over the country."

Kretchman had just put his finger on what, I realized, was Granger's problem. He did see us as the Four Musketeers, together 'til the end, and now Tom threatened to break that bond, that image he had. I was about to say something to make light of it and thus soften the blow when Granger held up his hands.

"Okay, guys, you win. I surrender." The smile he gave as he said it, though, did not reach his eyes.

"Hey," Kretchman said, "we're not fighting with you, man. It's a shock to me, too. But we've gotta—"

"I know. I guess I just got carried away, thinking of us as a permanent team, sharing our lives indefinitely, our kids growing up together like we did." Granger shook his head. "Stupid, I know. Sorry about that. My nostalgia for those childhood days took a hit, and I shouldn't have put my bummer on you. You're right. We're not those kids anymore."

Kids. The afternoon incident with the baby carriage came back to me. Michelle was out of the loop. I had to talk to somebody about it. "No, we're not. But we did have those days, and one of them in particular I'll never forget."

"Which one?" Granger grinned, apparently glad for the change of subject. Then his smile turned into a frown.

"Do you ever think of that night, Al?"

"I try not to." He looked away toward the pool tables.

"Bob?"

Kretchman took several swallows of beer before responding. "I have nightmares about it every once in a while."

I glanced around to make sure there were no potential eavesdroppers then leaned across the table. "Me, too. I wonder what happened to that baby. Did a relative take him in? Did he end up in an orphanage or a foster home? There didn't seem to be a father around, from what I gathered from the paper. He'd be four or five now."

Granger stood, looking pained. "Hey, it's over, okay? It happened. What good does it do to dwell on it? Nothing we can do about it now." He pulled his wallet from a back pocket. "I'm sorry I brought up Tom's gay thing, but you guys are bumming me out even more. I've had enough of this negative shit for one night." He took out some bills and put them on the table. "Want me to drive you back, Bob?"

"I can drop him off, Al."

"Okay, see you tomorrow." He left, looking like the air had been sucked out of him.

I turned to Kretchman, who frowned with discomfort. "So what happens in *your* nightmares, Bob?"

CHAPTER 4

August 1998
Las Vegas

The meeting between Wendell Logan and Andrew Donaldson took place in the living room of Logan's office suite. Donaldson, Logan learned, was a recent addition to the Bush campaign staff and the one who had accepted the invitation to meet and discuss Logan's financial support. Logan had wanted the more experienced Karl Rove, but he'd take what he could get. The two men sat facing each other in matching burgundy-leather wingback chairs.

Logan sipped his bourbon as he assessed the serious-looking man. Much too staid for a man of only thirty-four, Logan mused, but politics *was* serious business. He'd checked the young man out and came away impressed with his political résumé. Dressed in a navy blue pinstripe over a tall and trim frame, he had combed his dark-brown hair straight back, giving him a Gordon Gekko look to complete the image of a man who could get things done.

Donaldson had barely touched the Wild Turkey in his tumbler while they had engaged in small-talk niceties. "Drink okay?" Logan asked his guest and glanced at his chief of staff, Mark Elliot, who stood unobtrusively by the bar across the room—a shadowy figure like the Al Neri character in *The Godfather*, standing in the background, ready to do his boss's bidding.

"Fine, thanks," Donaldson replied and, as if to confirm, took a small sip.

"So Bush appears to be a lock for a second term?"

"In politics, Mr. Logan, nothing is certain. But the governor should win re-election, yes."

"It's Wendell. May I call you Andrew?"

"Andy would be fine."

"Andy, I'll be frank. I don't have many interests in Texas, and who resides in the governor's mansion doesn't concern me much. But it's an important state electorally, and I have reason to believe your client will make a run for president."

"You think?" Donaldson managed to crack a smile for the first time.

"I've heard the rumors." Logan lifted his glass toward the other man. "Floated by you and your staff, I presume."

Donaldson shrugged and twirled the ice cubes in his glass.

"And I know about the conference George Schultz put together earlier this year. Likely to see if Bush has what it takes to be a presidential candidate."

"You've done your homework."

Still being coy. Logan smiled. "I've got my contacts."

"The governor is focused now on re-election."

"'Now' being the operative word. I understand. That would be step one, naturally. It's step two that interests me."

"Hypothetically, of course, that would be the primaries."

"Yes. And that's where I think I can be of assistance. With the front-loading of the primaries these days, a fast start by a candidate is essential, obviously. Before he begins to look like a winner and everyone then jumps on board, organization—and that means money—is crucial." Logan shook his head. "Listen to me, lecturing to an expert in these things. But my point is that I'm offering to contribute to the cause at that stage in the game to ensure momentum is established."

Donaldson sipped his drink. "Let me be frank, too... Wendell. I'm in the politics business. That's how I make my living. What's your interest in Governor Bush becoming President Bush?"

Slapping his free hand on his knee, Logan laughed. "Why do people back candidates, Andy? Sure, you get paid as a consultant, but you're not just a hired gun. Based on the campaigns I know you've been involved with, ideology is important to you. I haven't seen you work with any liberal Democrats. I'll just say my philosophy matches yours. Not only do I not want Gore to continue Clinton's disguised socialism, the other potential Republican candidates don't appeal to me. And I'm already familiar with the Bush family."

"The governor's father," Donaldson said. "Yes, I'm aware of your support during his re-election campaign. I was in high school at the time but did door-to-door volunteer stuff. I thought we'd win."

"That makes two of us," Logan said. "Who do you figure will be the strongest opponent?"

"Hypothetically?"

"Of course." Logan expressed a knowing smile.

"McCain."

"I agree. And if your client does run for president, when South Carolina rolls around, that's where I can help. With my operations in Hilton Head and Charleston, I know a lot of people in that state, including some folks in Columbia who could be useful." At the mention of South Carolina, Logan noticed a spark of increased interest in Donaldson's eyes. "The Palmetto State in your column couldn't hurt, right?"

Donaldson peered into his glass for a moment before responding. "I think the Governor would win Iowa. New Hampshire is iffy. South Carolina would be key to get that momentum you mentioned. Do you have something specific in mind, Wendell?"

Ah, so he's no longer speaking in hypotheticals. He's interested. "I know the state, Andy. Grew up in Florence. If it looks like Bush and McCain at that point, I think I can make a difference there. Let's leave it at that. Are you interested? Or do you already have more than enough oil money to get your boy to the White House?" Logan grinned. "If he decides to run, that is."

Donaldson grinned back at the potential benefactor. "I'm here, aren't I? A campaign can never have too much money or influence. Any support you could give would be appreciated if that time comes."

"Good." Logan put his glass on the small table next to him and stood, extending his right hand. Donaldson stood to shake it. "You have my chief of staff's number. When you feel the time is right for me to get into the game, call Mark, and we can work out the details. Meanwhile, I'll see about getting my legal ducks in a row. Wouldn't want to violate any FEC rules. At least overtly, would we?"

"I hear that. Thank you, Wendell." They shook hands again.

"Enjoy the rest of your stay, Andy." Logan turned to his aide. "Mark, see to it that Mr. Donaldson gets some chips for the casino." Smiling, he turned back to the strategist. "Maybe you'll get lucky. And that would be my first contribution."

After Donaldson left with Mark, Logan replenished his drink and sat in the armchair, mentally reviewing the meeting. Though hardly a political strategist, Logan did know the importance of the primary schedule. With ever more states trying to move their contests up in the calendar, early victories could establish a *fait accompli* and propel the candidate to the nomination.

If Bush won Iowa, a victory in South Carolina would mean at least two wins out of three, and Logan, after his organizations were up and running, had an idea for them to implement. He smiled as he thought of his plan. *McCain won't see it coming.*

April 17, 1999
Burlington, Vermont

Of Vermont's four seasons, spring held a special place in the hearts of its residents. Winter did have its moments of stark beauty, but when its cold fingers were finally pried from their hold on the land, when the threat of still one more snowstorm appeared to be over and green buds started appearing in the branches of maple trees, most felt a sense of relief. They've made it. Away into storage went the parka, the gloves, the wool toque. One of my chores growing up was lawn duty, and spring meant reversing the positions of the snow shovel and the weed trimmer on that hook in the garage and getting the lawn mower ready for action again after a long hiatus. As the growing season began once more, a feeling of renewal infused most of us.

But spring could also have its dark side. Most people thought depression, augmented by housebound "cabin fever," would be at its worst during the Vermont winter. But statistics pointed out that Vermonters, like the inhabitants of other northern climes, committed suicide in greater numbers in the spring than during any other season. Contrary to popular belief that such winter milestones as Christmas or New Year's were responsible for triggering most of those tragedies, it was the spring that reigned supreme in this regard. There are scientific theories that focused on light as being the culprit. Longer days could change the levels of certain chemicals, like serotonin and melatonin, in our bodies. Yeah, maybe. But I thought there was a simpler reason at work. Feeling miserable during the long, harsh winter would be understandable. "Of course I'm depressed now. But let me survive until spring, and then I'll see if I feel better." And for a number of those who didn't see improvement, it was the last straw.

But at the start of this warm and sunny day, I certainly had no depressive thoughts. An event was to be held that would decide Bob Kretchman's future, and we gathered at Champ's to share the moment with him. It was the first day of the NFL draft, and we were excited for our friend.

Sheree Stallings had a stake in the outcome, so she joined us. And the group included Tom Webster this time. The rest of us had decided that if he wouldn't tell, we wouldn't ask. But he must have known his "secret" was out. We'd known each other since childhood and had played poker together numerous times. If we didn't know each other's tells by now, we never would. It was apparent to me, and it must have been to Webster, that his presence among us had subtly changed the group dynamics. But we all ignored the elephant in the room.

We'd arrived just prior to the start of the televised "show," which was pretty boring, actually, except for Kretchman's part in it. And it would be a while before that important announcement came. But we had beer to tide us over as we waited, sitting at a round table near one of the TVs.

"So, Bob," Webster said, "what do you think the chances are you'll get picked in the first round?"

Kretchman looked at him and chuckled. "What do I think my

chances are? That's original. What are you, some over-clichéd sports reporter?"

Webster shrugged. "Sorry."

"Hey, man, I was just kidding. My agent says deep second round is more likely."

"Agent? Jeez, Bob, you're already a pro!"

"Well, you know. Gotta have an agent. That's the way it works. What do I know about contracts?" He looked at the nearest TV screen. "Crouch got picked number one. McNabb went second." He sighed. "Donovan was hoping to be the first pick."

"What team are *you* hoping for?" I asked.

Kretchman looked at Sheree before responding, "The Pats would be great, but hell, I'll be happy with any team that wants me."

Our server, a cute girl named Vicky, replaced our empty pitcher with a full one. She wore a red "Champ's" T-shirt and black short-shorts. "Want anything to eat, guys?"

"Wings?" Granger proposed, looking at us. When we voiced no objections, he said, "How about one order of hot wings and one order of plain, with the sauces on the side?

"You got it," she said and left.

"Bob, listen," Sheree burst out, pointing at the TV where two pundits were discussing their guesses about upcoming selections during the "dead" time between announcements.

"Kretchman? The Syracuse guy?"

"Yeah. Not a lot of linebackers out there this year. With Franzoni making noises about retirement, the Lions have a need at that position, and Detroit has two picks in the first round."

"You have a point. But my sources tell me it'll be Chris Claiborne out of USC. Kretchman won't go until the second round."

"We'll see, kemo sabe. All right, I see that the Redskins have just taken Champ Bailey, cornerback from the University of Georgia."

"First round, Bob?" Sheree said. "That would be great!" She grinned. "Maybe we could have that wedding in Hawaii after all!"

"Yeah, man." Webster punched Kretchman in the shoulder. "First round means big bucks." He grimaced. "And living in Detroit can't be that bad."

"Ha! Real funny. Look, guys, like I said, it'll be the second round if I'm lucky. Anyway, I know what I'll probably be doing later this year. What're the latest plans with you bozos?"

Granger said, "Unlike you, we won't actually be employed yet for quite a while. I've got law school, and Jim has med school waiting." He looked at Webster. "You're going for an MBA, right?"

"Yup. At Tuck School of Business. I can stay right there in Hanover. And then I've got an in at Bailey and Stokes in Boston. So," he added with a smirk, "while Bob is paying the bills by tackling quarterbacks—ouch!—and you and Jim are still in school, I'll be having two-martini lunches and smoking cigars with rich clients."

Kretchman chuckled. "In your dreams, turkey."

"What about Steve?" Granger asked the future financier. "What's he going to do?"

Webster's smile disappeared as the mood at the table suddenly chilled. *Damn it, Al!*

"Steve?" Webster responded, deadpan.

"Steve Fine. Your roommate," Granger said with a slight edge to his voice. He wasn't smiling, either.

Webster stared at him for a moment. "He's no longer my *roommate*, but I understand he's enrolling in an acting school in New York. Why do you ask, Al?"

"No reason, really. He was our classmate at Burlington High, and I know he was living with you. I was just curious."

As Webster continued to stare at Granger, I saw his jaw muscles working. Fortunately, the server returned at that moment with our beer and food, breaking up the uncomfortable silence.

We poured refills and sampled the wings, grateful to have something to do to change the atmosphere. Even the normally effusive Sheree was quiet.

Webster took a swig from his beer mug and then set it down on the wooden table with a loud *thunk*. "Look, I'm gay, all right? Let's get that out in the open, finally. Thanks, Al. At least you had the courage to stop pretending. Or maybe you're just pissed off."

Silence reigned again at the table, allowing the TV to be heard.

36

"For the ninth pick, the Detroit Lions select Chris Claiborne, linebacker from the University of Southern California."

"There goes Hawaii," Sheree said. She dipped a wing into the barbecue sauce.

"Told you." Kretchman sipped his beer.

Granger held up his hands. "Tom, I'm not pissed, okay? Well, not exactly. But I mean, we were buddies and teammates, right? Why couldn't you tell us?"

I wondered the same thing when Granger had first raised the issue, but it wasn't difficult to divine the reason.

Webster put his head back and closed his eyes for a moment. Then he took a deep breath. "Man, I didn't know... not in the beginning, when I was a kid, of course. Then in middle school, I suspected something, but I didn't want to believe it. All those queer jokes... that couldn't be me. I wasn't one of those limp-wristed swishy guys. So I denied it. Then when I was going out with Debbie, I knew. I think she realized it before I did. By that point, all of us were going our separate ways, and I figured, why rock the boat? Why create a big scene? I could only imagine what reactions I would get from you all. So call me a coward for not being on the level with you guys. But our friendship mattered a lot to me, and I was afraid I'd lose that."

His sad expression begged for understanding, and I stepped in. "We're still buddies, Tom. I'm glad we've cleared the air." I laughed. "It wasn't easy pretending."

"Amen to that!" Granger said.

"Yeah, you can stop acting. You weren't any good at it, anyway," Webster said with a rueful smile. "But let's keep it among ourselves for now, okay?" He looked at each of us in turn.

"Sure, no problem," Granger said. "You're not thinking of going into politics, are you?"

Webster frowned. "Politics? Hell, no. Why?"

"Because I think I am." He caught my eye. "And we already have one secret we don't want to get out, right? We'll just add this little one to it."

"A politician, Al?" I arched my eyebrows. "What's with that?"

"Oh, I don't know. Just an idea I've been toying with. I've always been interested in politics, as you all know."

"That's for sure!" Kretchman rolled his eyes.

"What's this secret you're talking about?" Sheree glanced at Granger and then at her fiancé.

I'd forgotten about Sheree, and Granger with his big mouth had just let the cat out of the bag.

"Uh..." Kretchman began before Granger broke in.

"Just some prank we pulled on Halloween a couple of years ago, Sheree. Harmless, really, but kind of stupid, you know? Might not look good on a C.V."

"That's for sure." Webster eyed Granger.

Clever, Al. He had already prepared this explanation to be used in a situation like this, I figured. Good thing.

"So tell me about it, if it's harmless." Sheree appeared concerned.

"Honey," Kretchman explained, "we all agreed not to divulge it. Swore an oath, in fact. Sorry."

Sheree stared at him, frowning. Then her face lightened. "Some blood-brothers thing, and I'm not an official member of the club." She smiled. "I get it."

Maybe what she "got," I thought, was that Bob couldn't tell her in front of us, and she'd get it out of him when they got home. Granger's face wore a worried expression—for good reason, beyond the obvious. When it came to a politician's background, there was no such thing as a statute of limitations.

CHAPTER 5

G RANGER HAD SUGGESTED THE THREE of us fly to Boston in his plane to see Tom Webster. It was a convenient arrangement. Years earlier, Kretchman said that the "Four Musketeers" could end up scattered all over the country, but it turned out Webster became the only outlier. As Bob and I waited at Philadelphia International Airport for Granger to arrive, I thought back on how our lives had reached this point.

We hadn't seen Webster in years. Before Granger, Kretchman, and I left Vermont to pursue our careers, we continued to get together with Webster as a guy thing on occasion. We didn't include our wives, and he didn't bring a boyfriend. Then the rest of us moved south, and he stayed in Boston, working at some big-deal financial firm. The opportunities for reunions with him petered out after that. Even at Christmas, when the rest of us traveled back home to see the folks, Webster stayed in Boston. I wondered if his coming out as gay had done something to the relationship with his parents. Well, his father, anyway.

After a successful football career with the Philadelphia Eagles, Kretchman retired and now owned a popular restaurant called Sacks, near the stadium. He and his wife, Sheree, lived across the Delaware River in Cherry Hill, New Jersey.

I had originally planned on a surgical career, but I changed my mind during the pediatrics rotation in med school. Perhaps the memory of that helpless, orphaned boy so long ago played a role in my decision. Perhaps, because Michelle and I moved up our long-range plan, it was the birth of our twin boys my junior year. Whatever, I chose to be a pediatrician. Following a residency at Children's Hospital in Philadelphia, I joined a four-physician practice in Villanova, Pennsylvania.

And then there was Granger. After law school at Georgetown, he was offered a position with the prominent Philadelphia law firm of Litchfield, Boone & Prescott. No big surprise there. Tammy Litchfield was the boss's daughter, after all, and marrying her naturally gave Al a sizable leg up on the competition.

Six years and two high profile, personal-injury-lawsuit victories later, Granger became a partner in the firm. And that was when he began his political career. First came a stint as a state senator, then three terms as a U.S. Representative. And now, at age forty-one, he was in his third year as the Republican governor of Pennsylvania.

Because the six of us all lived reasonably close to each other, we used to get together several times a year. Since Granger became governor, though, visits with him and Tammy became few and far between. Which was fine with Michelle.

The Gulfstream G650 landed at Philadelphia International Airport from Harrisburg, and Granger ushered Kretchman and me into the luxurious jet. As the pilots were doing whatever they had to do prior to takeoff, Granger took us on a tour. Wide, beige-colored leather seats extended on both sides of the aisle, each with satellite communication access. In the midsection, two such seats sat on each side of a small conference table. A forward galley had granite countertops, polished wood for the pantry door and refrigerator door insert, and both a convection and a microwave oven. There was even a private stateroom.

Twenty minutes later—time enough to settle in and have Bloody Marys prepared by the flight attendant—we were airborne.

It was a trip we'd rather not take, but it was likely our last chance to see our teammate. Of course, we had to go.

The phone call had come three days earlier. I had just seen my last patient for the morning. I put my feet up on the desk and opened the *Journal of Pediatrics*. My intercom buzzed, and the receptionist announced she had a Steve Fine on the line.

That caught me up short. The last time he had been in my thoughts at all was that day at Champ's almost two decades earlier. I'd had no contact with him since high school. *Could this be a class reunion invitation?* "Hey, Steve. It's been a long time. What's up?"

"Tom is sick. He's in bad shape, Jim."

"Webster?"

"Yes. He's in Doctors Hospital in Boston."

"Man, what's wrong with him?"

Silence for a moment, then, "AIDS."

AIDS? Jesus! "Oh, shit!"

Fine sighed. "Exactly. He called me about a year ago, after he developed some weird pneumonia. That's when they made the diagnosis. He wanted to know if I was okay."

"I thought you were, uh, no longer together."

"I hadn't seen him in years. But the incubation period can take quite a while, as you know. I think, though, he was just reaching out to me. We had a real... bond, Jim. But when he started fooling around in college, well, I had to leave."

"Does he have a... partner now?"

"No, he lives alone. I've been taking care of him the last couple of months. He didn't want me to call you, but I know what you guys meant to him over the years."

"I appreciate that, Steve. You did the right thing. You say it's bad?"

"I don't think he'll be leaving the hospital this time." Fine's voice cracked on the last word.

"I'll tell the others. We'll come to Boston."

"Hurry, Jim."

Despite the mellowing effects the drinks provided, a somber atmosphere pervaded the plane's cabin as we sat around the conference table.

Kretchman ventured to break the uncomfortable silence. "Hell of a plane, Al. Are we flying on the taxpayer's dime?"

Granger chuckled. "In this day and age? It would be on MSNBC before we landed. No way. This jet is the firm's baby." He smiled. "I'm still a partner, just on a temporary leave of absence. My press secretary will announce I'm away attending to personal business."

Personal business. So much for the brief respite from depressing thoughts. Granger had just brought them back again.

"I still can't believe it," Kretchman said. "AIDS. I thought treatment these days worked pretty well. Remember Magic Johnson?"

"Antiviral therapy *can* be effective in controlling the HIV infection, Bob," I said, donning my physician's hat. "It can delay and even prevent the onset of full-blown AIDS. But Tom didn't get tested until it was too late."

"I wonder if he did drugs," Granger put in.

I stared at him. "Would that make it easier for you to accept, Al?"

He stared back for a moment then looked away. "No, I mean... oh, Christ! You're right. What difference does it make? Anyway, Tom's too smart to shoot himself up with dirty needles."

What about the stupidity of engaging in unprotected sex, I immediately thought but let it go. It *didn't* make any difference now. Our teammate was dying, and that was all that mattered.

After landing at Logan, we took a limo to the hospital. We checked in at the nurses' station on Tom's floor and were directed to his room. Steve met us outside of what I recognized as an isolation unit. Off an alcove adjacent to the room stood a side-entrance access door. Blinds inside a room window facing the alcove were closed.

"Glad you could make it," Steve said, and we all shook hands. A good-looking guy in high school, Steve had aged well. His short-cropped brown hair flecked with gray topped a maturely handsome face. He wore a light-blue crewneck sweater, jeans, and athletic shoes. "I told Tom you would be coming today for a visit. He pretended not to be happy about it, but I know he wants to see you. The nurse is busy with him now, but we won't have to wait long." He pointed to a rack on the back wall of the alcove. "You'll have to put on gowns and masks before going in."

Granger arched his eyebrows. "Yeah, the nurse at the desk told us. Is he that contagious?"

"It's for *his* protection, Al," I said. "Tom doesn't have much in the way of germ resistance."

"That's right. Give me your coats. I'll put them in the coffee room down the hall." Steve left with our coats and returned a few moments later. He handed out gowns and masks from the rack. Except for Granger, who wore a suit, we were dressed casually.

As we put on the protective gear, the blinds in the window opened. A masked and gowned nurse beckoned to us with a gloved hand. After we were all appropriately attired, Steve put his hand on the door's levered handle. "A little warning before we go in. Tom has changed a lot physically from the last time you saw him. He knows how he looks, of course, but shock on your faces would not be good. And don't pretend he looks great, either. Natural concern and sympathy, okay?"

"Sure," I said, and the others muttered their assents.

Granger still looked worried.

"Okay," Steve announced as he opened the door.

In med school, I had seen a number of dying patients, but they were strangers. Lying on the hospital bed was my friend. Though I prepared myself for a significant change in Webster's appearance, it still was jarring.

Gone was his thick blond hair, replaced by thin stringy strands matted across a scalp that reflected light from the overhead fluorescent fixture. Rheumy eyes looked at us, and sunken cheeks turned an attempt at a smile into a rictus-like grimace. Purplish lesions marked the skin of his face and once-muscular arms, now thin and wasted.

"Hey, masked men," he uttered in a raspy voice. "I don't have anything worth stealing, honest." His cackle sounded more like a throat clearing. "Besides, I recognize you, so you'll never get away with it."

I chuckled nervously in response. "Well, I guess we'll just have a friendly visit, then."

"Thanks for coming to see me. It's been a while." He raised an arm not encumbered with an IV and offered a hand.

"Now, Tom, you know the rule," the nurse chided.

"Okay, Cathy, I forgot. Stupid rule. And making everybody dress up like surgeons doesn't make much sense, either. Is there a bug to worry about I don't already have?"

"Hospital policy, Tom."

"Yeah, yeah. Sorry, guys. Not allowed to shake hands that aren't gloved up."

"No prob. We understand," Granger said. I detected relief in his voice. Standing next to me, he didn't move.

I blocked Kretchman, who stood behind me, so I stepped forward to the side of the bed. Kretchman followed and stopped at the foot, his shoulders hunched. Steve took up a position across from me by the head of the bed.

"Steve tells me you've had a rough time," I said.

"Well, yeah, you could say that. But it's almost over now."

"Tom," Steve rebuked, "we'll get you over this just like the other times."

Webster sighed. "Whatever you say, Steve, but I'm not expecting any miracles. And I want to get something off my chest while I still can." He looked at Granger, still standing by the door. "Al, come a little closer, okay? It's hard for me to raise my voice."

"Sure." Granger moved forward a few paces.

"Have a good visit with your buddies, Tom." The nurse slipped off her gloves. "I'll get your meds ready." She tossed the gloves into a medical waste container.

"Thanks, Cathy."

As she headed to the door, the rest of us waited for Webster to begin. A beeping sound interrupted the silence. I knew what it meant and looked at the IVAC pump controlling the flow through the IV tubing. The fluid bag was half-full, so that wasn't the problem. Had to be a blockage causing the warning beeps.

The nurse returned to the bedside next to me and tried to reset the pump. No luck.

"Can't you turn it off, Cathy?" Webster implored. "It's annoying."

"Let me check the IV site." She took two gloves from a wall dispenser and slipped them on.

"While Cathy is checking my lifeline," Webster said, "let me say my piece. At first, I didn't want you guys to see me like this. It's morbid, and I didn't want you to feel uncomfortable. But *I've* been uncomfortable for a long time, and I'm not talking about my disease."

I made eye contact with Steve. He shrugged and shook his head. The nurse began removing the bandage covering the IV site.

"We've never really talked about that night," Webster went on. "The four of us together. The accident. All these years, it's weighed on me. Lord knows, there are lots of things I regret in my life"—he gave us that peculiar smile again—"including why I'm lying in this bed. But that night has haunted me ever since." He looked at me. "Jim? Does it still bother you, or don't you ever think about it?"

I considered my response as I watched the nurse, with the bandage removed, palpate the skin around the IV site in the crook of his arm. "I *do* think about it, Tom. Every time I treat a baby in my practice, it comes back to me."

"What about you, Bob? Does the memory bring on any regrets?"

"It was so long ago, it's kinda fading, you know? But yeah, I wish it hadn't happened."

"Tom," Granger said in almost a whine, "it's in the distant past. Can't we let this die, finally?"

I gave Granger a sharp look.

He rolled his eyes, "I'm sorry, man. Poor choice of words. I mean, why dredge something up that's over and done with? How can that be of any benefit?"

"You were driving, Al," Webster responded. "I'd think you would have even more guilt than the rest of us."

The nurse was still intent on the IV site. "Tom," I said and gestured my head at the nurse.

He looked over at his arm. "Any luck, Cathy?"

"Working on it."

"She's good, Jim." He gave me that awful smile again. "Do you want to give it a try?"

He obviously misinterpreted my concern about Cathy. "It's not that. I'm sure she's better at it than I am. But maybe we should let her do her thing before we continue our visit, so you won't be distracted."

"Yeah, those damned beeps."

The nurse looked up at him. "The IV's shot, Tom. Sorry."

"Shit! Do I have to get another one put in? Can't I take pills instead?"

"The antibiotic only comes in IV form." She switched off the IVAC, and the beeping stopped. "Let me check with your doctor. Maybe we can discontinue it."

"That would be great."

Cathy slipped off her gloves again and took them to the waste container. "I'll be back to take the IV out after your visitors leave." She headed for the door.

After she left, I turned back to the bedside tableau.

Webster eyed Granger and said, "Tell me, Al, did we do the right thing?"

"Tom, like you said, it was an accident." The annoying whine was going full bore. "It could've happened to anybody. That's the way I see it. And we all made the decision to leave, not just me."

"Yeah, we all went along out of self-interest. But this is what I want to know. Do you think we did the right thing? Because I sure don't."

I turned at the sound of the door opening.

"The Favreau kid made it. We know that, right?" Granger stared down his questioner.

The nurse had come back. Webster hadn't noticed, apparently, and Kretchman and Granger were facing the opposite direction.

"Uh, Tom," I said.

Webster held up a don't-interrupt hand in my direction and said to Granger, "So you remember the kid's name. That's interesting. Yes, we know he survived, but no thanks to us. We should have made sure he'd be okay. *That* would have been the right thing to do. But we took a chance with someone else's life in order to save our bacon, and we lucked out. All's well that ends well? Is that what you're saying?"

Granger shifted his feet. "Yeah, I guess. Sure. Why not? The other thing was a done deal. Nothing we could do about that. And we would have had serious trouble if we did what you're insisting on now. Besides, I knew the kid would be fine."

"You did, huh?" Webster shook his head. "Anyway, we got away with it, able to move on with our lives. Hooray for us."

I made eye contact with the nurse and frowned. She must have gotten the message because she hustled out of the room. *How much had she heard?* I turned back to Webster. "Of course it wasn't the right thing to do, Tom. We were young, selfish, and scared. We fucked up, so we covered it up to stay out of trouble. I'll have to live with that on my conscience. Since I can't forgive myself, I can't forgive you, much as I'd like to."

"Too bad I'm a Methodist instead of a Catholic. Thanks for serving as my father confessor, though, Jim."

"Confession is good for the soul, they say," Kretchman offered.

"I hope so. Anyway, I feel better. But I'm kind of tired after all that, and I feel a nap coming on, so I won't keep you any longer. Thanks for coming, guys. It means a lot to me."

I took three gloves out of the dispenser. I slipped one on my right hand and gave the others to Kretchman and Granger. I held out my hand to the dying man. "You'll always be our teammate," I said.

He held my hand for a few seconds before releasing it. "Thanks, Jim."

Kretchman followed suit and grabbed Webster's hand. "Nurses are good, Tom, but don't let those doctors push you around," he said and winked at me.

"I'll try, Bob. Thanks."

Kretchman and I looked at Granger, who still held his glove. After a moment, he put it on. Stepping to the head of the bed, he reached down to give Webster's shoulder a slight squeeze. "Hang in there, buddy. The game's not over yet."

"I'll show them out, Tom," Steve said. "Be right back."

Focused on the memory of that fateful night and how much the nurse might have overheard, I had completely forgotten about Steve. He naturally didn't take part in the discussion, but I wondered, given his intimate history with Webster, if he already knew the story.

We took off the gloves, deposited them in the container, and left the room with Steve. After disposing of our gowns and masks, we waved at Webster through the window.

"I'll call you," Steve said to me. "It won't be long now. I sensed he had something bugging him he wanted to share with you all, but I didn't know what it was. I still don't, really. I'm glad you came to give him a chance to clear the air. When he said he felt better now, I know he meant it. Thanks."

We shook hands with Steve and left after exchanging cell phone numbers. In order to claim the trip as a business expense, Granger had arranged a meeting at a Boston law firm that worked with Litchfield, Boone & Prescott on cases involving Massachusetts jurisdictions. Then he flew back to Philadelphia later that day.

———— ◆◇◆ ————

Tim Howard took his tray to an empty table in the hospital cafeteria and sat. He had just finished helping a surgeon implant a cardiac pacemaker made by his company, and he had some time to kill before his next case across town.

As he took a bite of his roast beef sandwich, his fiancée entered the room. Cathy saw his wave and came to the table. "I was hoping to find you here," she said. "I went to the OR looking for you, and Dr. Tisdale said you'd already left."

"The case got moved up on the schedule, so we finished early. Got another pacemaker at Mercy in a couple of hours. Join me for lunch?"

"You bet. Let me grab a salad, and then I'll tell you something I heard today that will blow your mind."

CHAPTER 6

"**S**O WHAT DO YOU THINK?" Cathy asked. She emptied a packet of ranch dressing onto her salad.

Tim stared at his scrubs-clad lover as the story she'd just told him struggled to find purchase in his mind. "Do you know who these men are?"

She mixed the dressing and the veggies in the bowl with her fork. "Just first names, except for my patient and his boyfriend, but I can find out." Cathy smiled and her one dimple, actually a tiny scar from a childhood injury, curled up slightly. "I'll ask my patient this afternoon."

Tim looked down at his forgotten roast beef sandwich for a moment. "Think he'll tell you? You overheard their conversation, after all."

She speared a cherry tomato. "They knew I was there, Tim, and they didn't seem to care. I was just a fly on the wall to them. What're the odds a nurse in Boston would know what they were talking about? Something that happened some twenty years ago and hundreds of miles away? But if I hadn't remembered I hadn't redressed the IV site, I wouldn't have come back to hear the really good stuff, and it probably wouldn't have meant anything to me. Talk about serendipity!"

"You sure the one guy said 'Favreau'?"

"Definitely." She plucked the tomato off her fork with her teeth and gave him a smug smile.

"Could be a coincidence. Like you said, what're the odds?"

"How many times have you told me you'd like to know what happened that night?" She brushed a lock of blond hair off her forehead and leaned across the table. "Here's a good chance to find out. It might be a coincidence, but I don't think so. All we need are a few more details to rule it in or out."

"Did they say anything about killing someone?"

"No, not directly. The guy who said 'Favreau' was the driver of the car, and he said something about 'the other thing' that they couldn't do anything about. Could be referring to your mother."

"They acted upset about this accident?"

"Tom, my patient, was for sure. He said it had bothered him ever since, and that's why he wanted to talk about it. The others seemed to agree. Except for the one wearing a tie, the driver. He tried to downplay it."

Tim sat back in his chair and folded his arms across his chest. "So these five men—"

"Only four, I think. The boyfriend didn't say anything about it. I don't think he knew."

"Okay, four men were involved in a car accident some time ago. They abandoned a kid named Favreau to fend for himself and left the scene. And weren't caught. If only we knew when and where their accident occurred."

"Tim, don't you see? If *their* accident was *yours*, based on how old Tom is, they must have been in high school or early college at the most. Guys that age cruise around in cars together. It fits. And let's not forget the biggest clue in the story, the name of the child. Come on. They gotta be involved in what made you an orphan!" She forked some greens into her mouth.

Tim forced a smile. "Okay, Miss Marple, your deductions make a lot of sense."

"So what're you going to do about it?"

"Get me their names, find out where they come from if you can. Then we'll see."

———— ✦ ————

Wendell Logan directed his anger at the power button on the TV remote, and the screen went dark. Every time he saw that shit-eating grin, his blood pressure rose. *George W. Fucking Bush! You'd think I wouldn't have to be subjected to him anymore.* But no, right in the middle of a CNN broadcast, there he was, giving his "What, me worry?" smile as he stood alongside the other still-living presidents at some White House function.

Actually, Dubya was only the symbol for the true target of his hostility, Andrew Donaldson. Eighteen years later, he still seethed at the betrayal.

In 2000, Logan had orchestrated the whisper campaign against McCain in South Carolina. The Bush people, though they truthfully denied instigating it when it came out and expressed faux outrage at such a tactic, must have been thrilled. No way would the conservative citizens in that state vote for a candidate who had fathered a black baby with a prostitute. The rumor had been patently false, of course, but it worked. Bush won the primary and became the "inevitable" choice over McCain. And Donaldson, at least, must have known who had been behind the scandal rumor. Logan's reward had been a fucking "thank-you-for-your-support" form letter. No invitation to join the team, no hint his services or money might be requested later. Nothing else.

As the party jumped on the bandwagon after South Carolina and Bush was on his way to the nomination, Donaldson didn't return Logan's calls. "We can take it from here, thank you. We don't need you anymore" was the obvious conclusion. *I got Bush the nomination, and what did Donaldson do in gratitude? He turned his back on me.*

From that experience, yet another failed attempt to become a member of the inner circle, Logan decided on a bold new strategy. He wasn't going to give up now, not having expended all that time and effort in his quest. It bordered on obsession, a mission he could not refuse.

His days of sucking up to wannabe power brokers were over. Trying to get a presumed ally into the Oval Office would no longer be his play. He'd learned that lesson. Unless he was the driver of a campaign, someone could always screw him. So he determined that he would not just *help* get a president elected.

He would do it himself. No more middleman advisors calling the shots, getting their boy to follow *their* plans. *Hell, no!* Logan would see to it that the man who spoke at the podium bearing the presidential seal would be *his* man, would speak in *his* voice. The leader of the Free World would be his surrogate. The president, in essence, would *be* Logan.

It had gone far beyond just making sure his business interests were protected and advanced. Now that he knew he could actually accomplish it, being the power behind the presidential throne had an irresistible pull on him, an obsession he couldn't overcome even if he wanted to. It had never been done before, as far as he knew. What an incredible feat it would be.

The key to this grand scheme was to find his candidate before the pimps like Donaldson took over. Someone who had the ambition but not the support needed to realize it. Someone who relished the position, prestige, and the *illusion* of power but didn't care who actually pulled the strings.

After years of frustration in his search, he might have found, finally, the candidate he needed. It would be extremely tricky, Machiavellian-like, to bring the scheme to fruition. But if he succeeded, guys like Donaldson would look like rank amateurs. And he had found the vehicle with which to begin the journey: U.S. Representative Brent Marshall.

Logan rose from his chair and, dressed in pajamas and bathrobe, went back to the kitchen for a second cup of coffee. His housekeeper, a woman in her early sixties, stood at the range, frying bacon in a skillet. "Seen my wife yet, Martha?" he asked.

"No, sir."

Still in bed, as usual. His wife of ten years, a forty-year-old former Dallas Cowboys cheerleader and horror-film actress, was not an early riser.

As he poured a refill from the decanter, he thought of his first wife, dead now for twenty years. She had worked at his side from the beginning as he built his empire. She was his true partner in life, unlike the woman currently sleeping in the bedroom. He still missed Janet, especially on mornings like this, when they would have sat around the breakfast table planning their next moves.

Oh, well. He sighed and took his coffee out to the covered deck overlooking Lake Mead, which was just catching the rays of the early morning sun. The chill of the desert night still hovered; he cinched the belt of the robe firmly around his waist before sitting on a cushioned patio chair. He put his coffee mug on the table next to him and pulled a Cohiba from his robe pocket, along with a cigar cutter and a lighter. He amputated the cigar's tip and lit up. Logan leaned back in the chair and puffed away, the smoke wafting around his face before it drifted off into the Nevada air.

Life is good. He gazed at the hills on the far side of the lake and sipped his coffee. *But there's work to be done.* Leaning over the table, he lifted the receiver off a telephone console and punched in a number. He put the phone on speaker and replaced the handset.

After three rings, "Mornin', boss."

"Good morning to you, Mark. Any problems overnight?"

"Nobody called me."

"Good." Logan blew a smoke ring. "What's the latest on our project?"

"'Together for Tomorrow' is now officially a PAC. The registration process was completed yesterday."

Logan smiled. Step one completed. "And Bloomberg's up to speed on it?"

"Arnie will be calling Marshall's office today to get the ball rolling."

Arnold Bloomberg, a former Wall Street hedge fund manager, had been brought into Logan Enterprises after the 2008 crash, but off the books. Ostensibly, he was a financial consultant, tending to the investment goals of the Las Vegas well-to-do. In reality, he worked for Logan, managing offshore accounts and other tax dodges to hide as much income as possible from the eyes of the IRS. And now Bloomberg was the titular director of a newly established political action committee.

Democrat Marshall, who had served with Alan Granger in Congress, was now running against him. As with the Texas situation years earlier, Logan mused with satisfaction, the pundits weren't giving Marshall much of a chance to unseat the popular Pennsylvania governor. But Logan was about to change the dynamic of that race.

Money. No doubt about it, rare was the case in which a candidate's overwhelming advantage in campaign funds did not result in his election victory. Money talked, and money was what Logan had in abundance. Thanks to the Supreme Court decisions in the Citizens United and Speechnow.org lawsuits, Logan could legally finance an entire campaign on his own.

Or even more than one. If all went as planned, the funding of Marshall's gubernatorial run would just be the stepping-stone to the campaign that really mattered.

Of course, if the candidate was a complete bozo, he could still lose. It happened occasionally. But Brent Marshall was an intelligent man with a good political record. No one had discovered yet his fatal flaw, the secret that could derail him in a heartbeat. But Logan knew.

"Keep me informed, Mark."

"Of course."

Logan disconnected and sat back again in his chair, mulling over his strategy as he puffed on the cigar and pondered his deadline. The Pennsylvania election was nineteen months away. Plenty of time to work his money magic.

CHAPTER 7

CATHY DONOVAN PEERED THROUGH THE alcove window. Her patient, eyes closed, was apparently asleep. Steve dozed in the chair next to the outside window. After putting on a gown and mask, she entered the room.

Steve looked up. "Hey, Cathy."

"Hi, Steve. I was going to take the IV out, but I'll let him sleep for a while."

"The visit took a lot out of him."

"I talked to his doctor. Tom's temp has been down for two days, so he says we can discontinue the antibiotic."

Steve gazed out the window. "He was going to refuse another IV anyway, Cathy. He knows it was not going to change anything. Not really. What would be the point?"

Cathy nodded slowly as she gazed at her sleeping patient. "I understand. But it's what we do, you know? Someone comes in with a problem, we treat it the best we can. We have no choice."

"Yeah, I know that, and we appreciate the care you've given him. But he wants to go home. Can't hospice take over until...?" He wiped an eye with the back of his hand.

"I'll talk to Dr. Miller and the hospice nurse. If he doesn't need the IV anymore, I don't see why he can't go home."

"Thanks."

She checked the boxes of supplies on the window ledge. "You've been friends for a long time?"

Steve gave her a tight smile. "Since high school."

"Around here?"

"No, in Vermont. Burlington."

Bingo! "Never been there, but I hear it's a nice place to live."

"Yes, it is."

"His other friends that came today, are they from Burlington, too?"

"Originally. We went to the same high school. Graduated the same year, in fact. But we all moved away for our careers."

Cathy stopped there to avoid seeming too curious. Her theory so far was intact. Now all she needed were names. *Hopefully, Tom will supply those.* "Steve, you've been here for hours. Why don't you take a break and get some lunch? Meanwhile, I'll get Tom's IV out and see about getting him home."

"Sounds good." He stood and stretched. "Thanks."

After he left, Cathy put on gloves, grabbed a four-by-four gauze pad from a box on the ledge, and approached the bed.

"What?" Tom said, waking up.

Cathy held the bandage on his IV site with one hand and the catheter with the other. "Just in time, sleepyhead." She smiled. "You can hold this for me, okay?"

Tom applied pressure on the pad with his right hand as Cathy took the IV tubing to the waste container. She returned with a Band-Aid and replaced the bandage with it. After depositing the pad in the container, she changed her gloves. "Good news, Tom." She returned to the bedside. "You won't need another IV."

"That's a relief."

"Not only that, but I'm going to see about getting you out of the hospital, let your hospice nurse take over."

"You're a doll."

Cathy looked at the alcove window in response to a knock. "Lunch is here." She opened the door and took the tray from the foodservice employee. After she set it on the wheeled bed table, Tom pressed a control button on the bed rail to get into a sitting position.

"I actually have a little appetite today."

"Great." Cathy positioned the table in front of him. She removed the metal cover from the plate. "Your visitors must have had a good effect on you."

"In a way, yes."

"Who was that *huge* man? Kind of intimidating."

Tom emitted his throat-clearing chuckle. "Crushman. That's what we called him when we played football in high school. He was really good. Played in the NFL for a number of years." He cut into his Salisbury steak.

"I can believe that! So you played football in Burlington?"

Tom looked up. "Burlington? Why do you say that?"

Damn! "Didn't you mention growing up there?"

He frowned. "Hmm. I don't remember that." He fed a piece of meat into his mouth as he stared at her.

"I hear Burlington is a great place, with the university, the lake, and all. Never been there."

"Vermont?"

Cathy laughed. "Well, I don't mean Massachusetts. I've been to that Burlington."

Tom chewed the meat slowly, his eyes narrowed at her. He took a sip from his milk carton. "Yeah, that's what they say."

"So you didn't live there?"

"Boston is my town, Cathy." Tom scooped up some mashed potatoes.

I blew it! He knows. She smiled at him. "Enjoy your lunch. I'll contact Discharge Planning, see about getting them to stop by today."

"That would be good. Thanks."

Cathy left, cursing herself, and wondered if she could have handled it more adroitly. *But I did learn something. It might be enough.*

The day after I returned from Boston, I was sitting at the breakfast table reading the paper when my cell phone rang.

"Jim, this is Steve Fine."

Oh, shit! "Already?"

"What? Oh, no, Tom's still with us. In fact, he's back in his condo. But I need to give you a heads up. Remember his nurse?"

"Yeah?"

"She overheard your, uh, discussion about that accident."

The nurse! The image of her standing by the door, looking back at us, jumped into my mind. *But so what*, I immediately thought, even as my gut spasmed. "I remember she was there, Steve, but it couldn't have meant anything to her." *I hope.*

"I didn't think much about it either at the time, since I didn't know what you guys were talking about. But when she asked me those questions—"

"What questions?" My gut seized again.

"They seemed innocent, like how I knew you guys. So I'm afraid I told her we were in high school together in Burlington. Sorry, man, but I didn't know about that accident until Tom asked if I'd said anything to her. Then he told me the whole thing."

"You didn't give her our names, did you?" *Where is this going?*

"No, she didn't ask."

"Doesn't sound like much to me. It could've been idle curiosity."

"There's more, Jim. Later, after I left to grab some lunch, she tried to get your names from Tom."

Fuck! "Did he tell her?"

"No. Well, he let slip 'Crushman,' but then he got suspicious and clammed up."

Thank God for that, at least. "Well, no harm then. It has to be nothing. Why the hell would she be playing detective? It doesn't make sense."

"I have no idea. But Tom thought you should know. She has his name and mine and knows he and Bob were on the football team in Burlington."

"What's the nurse's name?"

"Cathy Donovan."

"Is that with a *C* or a *K*?"

"*C.*"

"Know anything about her?"

"Nope."

"Thanks for letting me know, Steve. I still don't think it amounts to anything, but I appreciate the heads up. Is Tom there with you now?"

"No, he's asleep upstairs."

"Say hi to him for me, and tell him thanks."

"I will."

"Bye, Steve."

The confession Tom Webster forced on us in the hospital had nagged at me. That terrible snowy night in 1995 had come back to me from time to time, as I told him. But since our visit, it seemed omnipresent. Webster's reminder of the tragedy was likely responsible, and it would undoubtedly fade away again.

But Fine's call made clear to me another factor contributing to my unease. Not only had the four of us confronted the incident directly, others were in on the secret now.

I had never told Michelle. Perhaps Kretchman had revealed the story to his wife. I never asked him if he did. Granger, I was sure, had kept Tammy in the dark. Fine, from his parting comments to us, indicated he didn't know what our conversation had been about. But his call told me he was now aware of that tragic history. And so was someone else.

As I mulled over this development, I gazed out the window. My two sons, John and Michael, played one-on-one basketball at the end of the driveway. They were both standouts on the high school tennis and basketball teams. I congratulated myself that I had passed on my athletic genes, though obviously improved upon, to my boys. And Michelle would be sure to remind me she played a role in that inheritance, too.

My sons. They were close to the same age I had been on that awful night. Back then, the other guys and I had worried about the repercussions with parents and future career plans. Now it was a different situation entirely.

If the story came out, there would be an investigation. A cold case, lying forgotten in some dusty file somewhere, would be reopened. And juicy publicity would inevitably accompany it, especially considering the players involved: a former NFL star, a respected physician, and last but certainly not least, the governor of Pennsylvania. It seemed the end of the world to us when we were teenagers if it got out. Now it really could be.

I envisioned the story going national, with reports on CNN and, because of Granger, discussions on the political talk shows. "How will this affect Governor Granger's political future?" The press would hound us and our families until something more exciting pushed the story off the front burner. But the damage would have been done.

Of the three of us—as sad as I was to admit it, I had already removed Webster from consideration—Granger would take the worst hit, of course. My practice would likely suffer; the group might even ask me to leave so as not to besmirch its reputation. And how would it affect my boys? Not only would their feelings about their old man inevitably change, they would have to live with the disgrace among their peers. And Michelle? She taught kids in school. *What would parents think about a woman influencing their children married to a man who almost let a kid die?*

I figured Kretchman would be relatively okay. Compared to all the athletes-acting-badly incidents, this long-ago event wouldn't even rate a position in the top fifty. His playing days were over, and it wasn't as if he had an ESPN job in jeopardy. But I'm sure he wouldn't appreciate the effect the publicity would have on his wife and daughter.

Having survived our initial fear of discovery, we had to live with the guilt for over two decades. But now fear had again entered the picture because of Fine's call. An inquisitive nurse could be a threat to our reputations and careers. The obvious question concerned her motivation. *Was she just making small talk? Or could she somehow have some knowledge of the accident?* The latter seemed implausible.

Unless she was from Burlington and heard the story. But no, she would have been about the same age as the Favreau baby at the time, so that didn't work.

I had to find out about this Cathy Donovan. As I looked at my boys having fun, it came to me. *Facebook!* She had a common name, but I knew what she looked like, kind of, if I mentally removed the mask she wore. And I knew her approximate age. Worth a try.

I rose from the table and went to my computer in the bedroom. After wading through a long list of Cathy Donovans, I found her. Maybe. A nurse who lived in a Boston suburb. Since she didn't restrict her info—that someone wouldn't do that amazed me—I had access to her educational history. She apparently had lived in Massachusetts since high school, at least. There were pictures for me to peruse, but they didn't help, except she looked like she could be the woman I sought. Much more attractive than the infection-control garb had allowed me to appreciate. So far, so good. No connection to Burlington or even Vermont.

Then I saw her "engaged" status. I went back to her photo gallery and found several snapshots of her fiancé, a man about the same age named Tim Howard. Good-looking young man with a pleasant smile.

Tim! The baby's name was Timothy Favreau. *It couldn't be, could it? An adopted name, perhaps?*

Worried now, I went to Tim Howard's page. Unlike Cathy Donovan, he closely guarded his privacy. I'd have to become his "friend" to get any information about him.

I sat back in the chair, my heart thumping in my chest. I was getting carried away, I reasoned. An imagined scenario had led me on this wild goose chase, and now I had found something to confirm my suspicion. Hardly the scientific method. One isolated datum could not prove a hypothesis. So this guy had the same first name as our victim. The odds he was *our* Tim had to be astronomical.

But maybe not, my paranoia told me. He was the right age, and Boston wasn't all that far from Burlington. *Shit!* I had to know more.

I went back to Cathy's list of friends and resumed my search for a connection, one I hoped not to find. After a half hour crosschecking friends and friends of friends, I found it. Barbara Howard. From her picture, she looked old enough to be Tim's mother. *Adopted mother?* She lived in Shelburne, Vermont, just seven miles down Route 7 from Burlington. And the clincher: *Children: Timothy.*

My wife was talking in the kitchen—on the phone, presumably—indicating she had returned from her hair appointment. I quickly logged out of Facebook. Not wanting Michelle to distract me as I pondered my next move, I stayed put, hoping she wouldn't come into the bedroom.

Assuming Tim Howard was Tim Favreau, and that might not be the case, could he find out who we were? *Of course, he could.* After less than an hour, look what I had managed to dig up. And he had two names with which to begin a search: Steve Fine and Tom Webster, both graduates of a high school in Burlington. He also had the first names of the rest of us, if the nurse could remember them. And only one high school in my hometown had a football team.

So if I were Tim, what would I do next? I stared at the computer, waiting for an inspiration. He could go the Facebook route, as I did. Granger and Kretchman had Facebook accounts for obvious reasons. I had one, too; it didn't matter that I hardly ever used it. Out of courtesy, I had agreed to be their "friend." But so had hundreds of others, including, I assumed, Webster. I doubted Fine would be included in that number. So he'd have to start by finding a suitable Tom Webster, again, a common name, and go from there. Not an easy task, but doable, I supposed.

Then I had another thought. I tiptoed out of the bedroom, still hearing Michelle's voice in the kitchen, and went up the foyer stairs to the second floor. In a bookcase in the game room sat my high school yearbook, *The Oread.* I turned to the football team picture, the typical three-deep lines of guys in uniform, the front row kneeling with the rest standing behind, and checked the names. As I remembered, we had two Bobs on the team. Bob Lacey wasn't as big as Kretchman. Granger was the only Alan. There was another James, though.

I put the yearbook back on its shelf and picked out a pool cue from the wall rack. Balls were scattered around the table, and I made random shots while thinking things through. Everything these days was online. Even yearbooks. By using Facebook and *The Oread,* an enterprising Tim Howard could find us all pretty easily.

But he'd have to be Tim Favreau to want to. I asked myself again, *What are the odds that he is that baby of long ago?*

Low enough to cause serious heartburn. No doubt about that. Though I'd be inflicting that on my buddies, they had to know. And besides, misery loves company.

———— ✦◇✦ ————

Tom Webster died a week later. Michelle and I drove up to Burlington for the funeral, picking up the Kretchmans along the way. Granger claimed pressing governor's business and didn't attend, which didn't surprise me.

Afterward, we visited with our families for a couple of days and then returned to resume our lives, now changed significantly. We had lost a friend, and in the process, we had gained our own potential calamity.

When I had called Granger and told him what Fine said, he took it hard, as I expected. He had the most to lose of any of us. People didn't usually vote for candidates guilty of child neglect, let alone killers, and he had an election looming. Not to mention how the senior partners of Litchfield, Boone & Prescott would take it. He kept asking me what we should do, and I kept telling him to wait and see. We didn't have any other options.

Kretchman wasn't pleased, naturally, but he took the news much better, confirming my prediction. Any publicity might even increase business for his restaurant. He had told Sheree all about it after they got home from Champ's that day, as I had suspected.

After making that last phone call, I decided it was time for Michelle to know as well. I got home before she did that day and made a pitcher of martinis. A little liquor to help the bad news go down. I was putting olives in two martini glasses on the counter when she came in from the garage.

"Martinis?" She gave me a puzzled look. "What's the occasion?"

"There's something I need to tell you." There was no smile on my face, so she knew I wasn't about to make a happy pronouncement.

"What's wrong?"

I held a glass to her. "Let's go into the sunroom."

Concern creased her forehead as she took the glass from my hand. "You're scaring me, Jim. Something with the boys?"

"No. C'mon." I led her to the sunken sunroom, gestured to an armchair, and sat in the loveseat a safe six feet away. I took a sip. She hadn't touched hers yet. "I did something a long time ago that I never told you about."

Her shoulders slumped as she looked down at her glass. *Does she think I'm going to admit to having an affair?*

"It was before I met you, Mish. I was seventeen."

She looked up at that and then did take a sip of her martini. "You got a girl pregnant."

I had to admire the way her mind worked at lightning speed.

That would explain the purpose of this confession and why I would tell her now. The bastard child, now an adult, had tracked me down. Jeez. *Would that be worse than the real reason that had brought me to this point?*

I shook my head. "No, nothing like that." I took another sip. "In 1995, Granger, Webster, Kretchman, and I were driving home from a ski outing at Bolton Valley..." I told her the entire story.

"So that's where we are now," I said, wrapping up the tale.

Michelle's glass was now empty. I took a big swig from my drink, which was no longer cold.

Michelle put her glass on the table and folded her hands in her lap. She gave me a look I couldn't translate—not anger, exactly. Certainly not shock. Just a level, neutral gaze. And that bothered me even more. "Why haven't you told me this before, Jim?"

"I just found out about it, honey."

"No, the accident."

"I should have, I know. I was ashamed, worried about what you'd think of me. I never thought it would come back decades later to bite me in the ass."

She looked out at the pool in the backyard. "I thought we told each other everything."

I had no response to that. She was right.

She turned back to me. "Do you think this nurse will cause trouble?"

Her question, involving the current problem rather than my long-ago deed, ironically made me feel better. "I don't know, Mish." I finished my drink. "But I wanted you to know ahead of time if she does."

"That would not be good."

"To put it mildly."

"Would this put you into any legal jeopardy?"

That question had concerned me, too, and I'd looked it up. The statute of limitations for the offense in the State of Vermont had expired years ago. "No. Thank goodness for that, anyway."

"I don't want the boys to find out if we can help it."

"That makes two of us." I went over to her. "But *you* know now.

What does that make you think of me?" As I waited for her answer, I hoped desperately her love for me would not change, that she would let us be the couple we'd always been.

She looked up at me, and I saw tears in her eyes. Not good. "It hurts that you didn't confide in me long before now. I'm sorry, but I can't help feeling a little betrayed."

I was afraid of that.

"But I love you, Jim, and I always will. The man you are today is not that high school kid. It was a tragedy, and you've had to live with what you did all these years. I've always been here for you, and that won't change now. We'll face this together, whatever happens."

Flooded with relief and admiration for my trouper of a wife, I grabbed her hands and brought her up to me. "Thank you, sweetheart. You don't know how much I dreaded having that conversation."

"No more secrets, okay?" She frowned but came closer, signaling that I had survived the ordeal.

I put my arms around her. "I promise."

Then we waited.

CHAPTER 8

March 2017

Brent Marshall, class of 2000, stood before the microphone at the top of the broad steps leading to Lehigh University's Fairchild-Martindale Library. He wore a dark blue windbreaker and jeans. Thick-soled hiking boots added an inch of height to his five-nine, medium-build frame. The sun hid behind a high overcast, but the air was still, making the temperature a relatively mild fifty-two degrees.

Standing with the congressman's staff a discreet fifteen yards to the rear, Arnold Bloomberg observed Marshall in action. Marshall reminded him of Howard Dean, the unsuccessful presidential candidate of thirteen years earlier, modest in stature but smart and with a coherent and compelling message.

"And so, my fellow Mountain Hawks," Marshall orated, winding up his ten-minute speech, "I need your help." He looked out at the throng of students gathered below his vantage point. He pointed at a young man holding a handmade sign proclaiming: THERE'S A NEW MARSHALL IN TOWN. "I like that. Mind if I steal that slogan?"

Laughter and applause erupted from the crowd.

"We can do this together," he went on. "Lehigh University is a special place. A place that fosters achievement. A place that teaches never to give up!" Cheers rang out. "Some of you weren't yet in high school five years ago, almost to this very day, when this university stunned the sports world."

Murmurs of understanding rose up as the students guessed what was coming next.

Marshall grinned at them. "No one gave us a chance that day. The fifteenth-seeded Mountain Hawks were facing the second-seeded Duke Blue Devils powerhouse. It was the first round in the NCAA basketball tournament, and Duke was already looking ahead to their next opponent. But we made it a bracket-busting day and sent them home!"

Marshall let the cheers continue for a few seconds before raising his hands. "And with your spirit, your can-do attitude, we'll shock the country again when we defeat the entrenched powerhouse in Harrisburg next November. Just like we're going to beat Notre Dame on Friday! Thank you for your support!" He waved at the cheering students and walked back toward his waiting staff as custodial employees dismantled the PA system and carted off the lectern.

Bloomberg stepped forward from the staffers as the congressman reached them. "Representative Marshall?"

"Yes?"

"Arnold Bloomberg. We talked on the phone." He offered his hand.

Marshall shook it. "Ah, the man out of nowhere who wants to support me. A pleasure to meet you."

"Good speech, well-received."

Marshall chuckled. "Well, they *are* a friendly audience. They get how Granger's policies are not on their side. Just have to encourage them to do something about it."

"About the campaign—"

"Excuse me for a minute." Marshall faced a man in a tan overcoat, his chief of staff, who appeared to Bloomberg to be in his mid-thirties. "Clark, I'll meet you guys at the car, okay? Mr. Bloomberg and I have some business to discuss."

Clark Munson checked his watch. "Our flight out of LVI is in two hours."

"Right. Plenty of time. I just need a few minutes." Marshall raised an eyebrow at Bloomberg, who nodded.

Munson glanced at Bloomberg. "Yes, sir." He and the other two staffers headed toward a blue minivan parked at curbside.

"Flying commercial?" Bloomberg asked.

"Yes."

Bloomberg reached into an inside pocket of his black trench coat and withdrew an envelope. "This should help with transportation expenses. It's a check from Together for Tomorrow made out to the Brent Marshall for Governor Committee, as we discussed over the phone."

Marshall looked at his people, their backs to him as they walked to the car, before taking the envelope and slipping it into a pocket of his windbreaker. "Thank you. You don't trust the U.S. Postal Service?" He smiled.

Bloomberg smiled in return. "I had business in the area," he lied. "Gave me the opportunity to see the candidate up close and personal. And I like what I've seen."

"Tell me, Mr. Bloomberg—"

"Arnie."

"Why, Arnie, are you supporting my campaign? It's barely started, after all."

"That's the point, Brent. We want your candidacy to continue, and we know it's tough financing a grassroots campaign." He scanned the area. The crowd of students had dispersed. "College kids are enthusiastic but not much for contributions."

"But you haven't really answered my question. Why me, and why Pennsylvania?"

"Does it matter?"

"Look, I'm grateful for the support. But yes, it does matter to me."

"Is that why you didn't want your staff in on our meeting?"

The congressman eyed his people standing by the car. "Well, I wanted a chance to feel you out. And in these times of campaign finance scrutiny..."

"You didn't want to be caught doing anything shady. I understand. But you can relax, Brent. Let me assure you, everything is on the up-and-up. Pennsylvania has no restrictions on PAC contributions. You can actually thank Governor Granger for keeping that freedom in place. Anyway, your man Munson knows that. I talked to him. Smart guy."

"Yes, I'm sure he's more knowledgeable about these things than I am. But running for statewide office is a different ball game. And I'm still waiting for answers to my questions."

"You said it. A statewide campaign ups the ante. And Pennsylvania is a big state, crucial in *national* elections. We want a governor in place who will espouse Democrat principles. We think you are that man."

"I appreciate that."

"But I'll be honest with you. You're our only option here. Nobody else has thrown his or her hat in the ring, and I haven't heard any rumors that another challenger might be forthcoming."

"Ha! Ain't that the truth? Yeah, no one wants to take on Granger. They're biding their time until his second term is underway. Former governor Ed Rendell tried to recruit an opponent, but no one bit."

"Except you."

"I don't like the direction my state is taking. Four more years of this administration might put us in a hole too deep to dig out of."

"We agree, and we admire the integrity and courage you've shown by taking the gamble. But aren't you concerned about your re-election to the House? Knowing you're running for governor might bring challengers for your seat out of the woodwork from both parties."

"Have you seen any yet?" Marshall smiled. "I'm in a safe district, Arnie. I won my last election by twenty points. My constituents want me representing them and will vote for me regardless. And as governor I'd be able to do more for them, theoretically, of course, than being just one of four hundred thirty-five representatives in Washington."

"So, even if you lose to Granger next year, you'll still have a job," Bloomberg remarked with a slight smirk.

Marshall chuckled. "Well, there is that, isn't there?"

"Are you flying back to DC?"

"No, Pittsburgh. Rendell arranged for me to meet some party bigwigs. Then it's back to Washington."

"These trips will be increasing as the campaign continues. You can't always be flying commercial or taking a bus or"—he gestured at the waiting car—"a minivan. Might consider chartering a plane."

Marshall eyed the other man. "Only if the budget allows."

"I think that can be arranged." Bloomberg stuck out his hand.

Marshall shook it. "Thank you again. I hope this will be the start of a successful campaign."

"I believe it will, Brent."

Marshall left to join his staff at the car as Bloomberg looked on, thinking about the congressman's last statement. If things went as planned, it *would* be a successful campaign. *But not in the way Marshall thinks.*

As Tim Howard drove to his apartment, he pondered the news Cathy had presented to him a few hours earlier. *What if she finds out the names? And if she does, what will I do with them?*

Ever since his parents told him about that night, the mystery had hung over him, a hole in his history demanding to be filled. The police investigation at the time had concluded another vehicle had most likely caused the accident, but that was the extent of it. And no one had come forward to confess.

But now that he might be able to discover those responsible for the tragedy, he wondered if he really wanted to. As Cathy said, those men were basically boys at the time. They couldn't have intentionally crashed into the car. Carelessness, probably, and bad-judgment negligence for sure. But no premeditation pertained. They had screwed up and then panicked. *Maybe I wouldn't have acted any differently.*

By the time he got home, he decided he didn't want to take the matter any further. If those visitors today were the ones involved, then the larger mystery had essentially been solved. He could finally close that door. Knowing the details wouldn't add anything of relevance, and pursuing it wouldn't accomplish anything of value.

Cathy was there when he arrived, a glass of wine in her hand and excitement in her eyes. Tim barely had time to take off his jacket before she began. "I found out some things about those men, Tim. Didn't get their names, but I learned they grew up in Burlington. They're the ones!" She grinned at him as if she'd discovered the location of a hidden treasure.

"Nice work, honey," Tim said flatly and went to the fridge for a beer.

"We can find out who they are, where they live now." She followed closely behind and almost bumped into him as he leaned over to grab a can of Bud Light.

Tim closed the refrigerator door, popped the top of the can, and took it to the dinette, Cathy still following. He dropped heavily onto a chair and took a big gulp of his beer as Cathy sat across from him. "I've been thinking about this," he said. "I don't see it helping me to know their identities. It was an accident that happened a long time ago. And they're still living with the guilt. They were kids who made a mistake, Cats. I'd just as soon let it go."

She stared at him, disbelief in her face. "But don't you think they should pay for what they did? They killed your mother, Tim! And they left you in the car—in winter. You could have died!"

"I *have* a mother. And I have wonderful parents who took me in when I *didn't* die, made me their son. So I came out of it just fine, maybe better than if the crash never happened. Who knows?"

"Aren't you the least bit curious how those boys turned out? I know one of them played professional football, so he did well. And the others? What if they all ended up having successful lives?"

Tim took another pull from his can and shook his head. "Cathy, give it a rest, okay? Even if they all became millionaires, so what? It's not like they profited from the accident."

"But getting away with it allowed those kids to pursue their dreams, a chance your mother didn't have because of them."

"Kids. That's what they were, Cats. It was snowing, and the road was slippery. Accidents do happen."

His fiancée went to the fridge to refill her glass. She returned to the table and sat. "Okay, you have a point. But I still can't get over how they just left you in the car."

Yes, I was in the car. He ran his hands up the sides of his head and clasped them together at the top. "I shouldn't have been in the car, Cathy. And my mother shouldn't have been driving anywhere that night. Dad told me I had a high fever from an ear infection, and that's probably why she was on the road—to take me to the hospital. So in a way, I was to blame for the whole thing. Maybe being left to sink or swim was some kind of payback for that."

Cathy rolled her eyes and shook her head. "Sure, you were responsible. Get real. You were a freakin' baby!"

"Look, honey." Tim put his hands on the table, palms down. "I've thought about it. I'm not going after them. There wouldn't be any point, except for revenge. Revenge for an accident caused by kids, who then ran off because they were scared? No, I'm not going to do it. That's not me." He looked around the kitchen, wanting to change the subject. "What're we doing for dinner tonight? You're not cooking something, are you?"

As Cathy stared at him, Tim hoped she wouldn't continue to press the issue. He'd made his decision. To his relief she smiled and said, "It's Friday, remember? Date night."

"I'll get changed. There's a new steak place over on Birchwood I want to try."

Tim left the kitchen, and Cathy remained seated at the table, nursing her chardonnay and thinking about what he had said. He might not care about looking into it further, but that didn't mean she couldn't. Not only had her curiosity been aroused, something else had occurred to her. Tim hadn't considered the possibility that knowing who those men were could benefit him. Not in a vague, questions-answered kind of way but something more tangible. *She* had thought of it, though. She took a sip of wine and smiled. *It can't hurt to try.*

CHAPTER 9

THE FOUR-YEAR-OLD BOY GIGGLED AS I poked around his belly, finishing my exam. After I lifted him off the table and set him on the floor, he ran over to his mother, who sat on a chair in the corner of the room. She hugged him and gave me a questioning look.

"Everything's normal," I said. "Justin is a perfectly healthy boy."

"But what about his size?" she asked, concern in her voice.

I went to the patient chart on the counter and perused the measurements my nurse had inserted on the graph. "His height and weight are fine, both in the same percentage. He's still in the lowest quartile, but just barely. He's moved up quite a bit from where he was a year ago. Nothing to worry about."

The mom rose from the chair, took her son's hand. "Thank you, Dr. Dawson." She escorted Justin from the exam room, and with that, I'd finished my well-child day at the clinic.

I took the chart to my office, where I sat at my desk. I wasn't on call, and it was only two thirty, an opportunity to get nine holes in at the club. The new wedge, which the Golf Channel infomercial had guaranteed would take at least five strokes off my score, had arrived by FedEx the day before. I was eager to try it out.

I wrote a note in Justin's chart, and as I tossed it into the outbox, my cell phone announced a call.

"Hey, Bob."

"Is this a bad time?" Kretchman asked.

"Nope. Just finishing up at the office. What's up?"

"It's happened."

My stomach did a flip-flop. "What?" I asked, hoping my suspicions weren't true.

"I got a call at the restaurant from Cathy Donovan."

Shit! "The nurse."

"You got it. I was the easiest one of us to track down, apparently. You were probably right about that damned Facebook."

"What did she want?" I held my breath.

"She told me she knew about the accident and who we all are."

Here we go. "And?"

"Blackmail, Jim. She called it 'compensation'—that her fiancé deserved to get justice, preferably of the monetary variety, for what we did to him. But failing a payout, she'd let the authorities know so we could get our just desserts."

I groaned. "How much is she asking?"

"A hundred grand."

"Oh, man!" The figure hit me hard, but then what did I expect? And it could've been worse. "Sounds like a Goldilocks amount."

"Come again?"

"Just right. High enough to make it worthwhile, but not enough to make us balk. Anyway, what did you tell her?"

"I didn't admit to anything and told her to take a hike. But she knows enough to give us trouble, like you predicted. She has our names, even my high school nickname. She knows we were buddies with Tom."

"Who she heard asking us if we'd done the right thing." I shook my head.

"Yeah, and Al mentioning the Favreau kid nailed it."

I replayed the hospital-room conversation in my mind for the umpteenth time. My fear had been well founded, obviously. *Now what?* "Tough to prove, though, Bob. The lawyers call that hearsay."

"Yeah, sure, but funny you should bring up lawyers. This nurse also mentioned a possible lawsuit. Juries, man. Can you imagine how the story would play out in a courtroom? A hundred Gs could just be a drop in the bucket."

He had a good point. When I had worried about the nurse and what she could do to us, my first thought was damage to our reputations. Then, when an even more ominous possibility occurred to me, criminal prosecution, a Google search of Vermont statute of limitations law put that worry to rest. A lawsuit, however, never occurred to me.

And it should have. Negligence and wrongful death claims against physicians were certainly not rare, but they weren't open-ended. Lawsuits also had time limits governing when actions could be brought. However, I knew the lawsuit clock didn't start until the offense had been discovered. We could be in real jeopardy there.

"What do you think we should do?" I asked. "Pay her off?"

"What choice do we have?"

"But the thing with blackmail, Bob, is that it doesn't have to stop when a payoff is made. What's to say they don't hit us again? And speaking of that, I wonder why *she* called, rather than the victim."

"He must be a pussy. Maybe he figured it would go over better coming from a woman. Wouldn't get our macho backs up as much."

"Yeah, maybe."

"But that's gotta be our play to prevent a double dip, Jim. We know who *they* are, too. We can make it clear that coming at us again would not be healthy for them."

This was spiraling out of control. *Now we were going to make threats like gangster goons?* "Christ, Bob, how can we do that? We're not mob enforcers. That's not us."

"Hey, I know that. But she doesn't. A bluff, okay? It's all we got to get us out of this pile of shit we're in. Let me be the heavy. She knows my football background. I haven't gotten any smaller since my playing days when I was a pretty intimidating dude, if I do say so myself."

Kretchman the leg-breaker. *What a fiasco.* I sighed. "Okay, I don't want to go down that road, but I don't see any other option. It might work."

"Want me to call Al?"

"No, I'll do it. If anyone can calm him down, it's me."

"The money won't be a problem for you, will it? Thirty-three thou and change?"

I could imagine Michelle's reaction when I hit her with this. Oh, she'd be pissed. Though we had a good income, she still cut coupons from the Sunday paper and only bought clothes when they went on sale. She was the penny-pincher in the family. To give away that kind of money would cause a Vesuvius-like eruption. Until she realized what the alternative would be—my secret exposed for the world to see. Including our sons. "I can do it. And it won't be any sweat for Al. You?"

"I'm good."

Thoughts of our bogus threat—at least, I assumed it was bogus—getting the money together and then delivering it, were running through my brain. Unavoidably, I was now thinking like a criminal trying not to get caught. And a possible trap suddenly occurred to me. "Bob, you said you didn't admit to anything over the phone?"

"I treated it like a nuisance threat. You know, like some bimbo claiming she had Tom Cruise's baby or something. She said we should all talk it over before blowing her off, that if she didn't hear from us tomorrow afternoon at four, she would 'take action.' That's the way she put it. No, I didn't admit to a thing."

"Good, because I just thought of something. She could have recorded the call."

"You think?"

"I don't know, but you have to be careful when you make that call."

"You mean talk around it? But what if she starts getting specific?"

"You'll have to ignore that and steer her into a conversation that won't have you owning up to anything."

"Jim, buddy, I don't know if I can do that. I might screw it up. You're the one used to diplomatic double-talk. I think you should be the go-between."

I had to admit he was right. The often tongue-tied Kretchman likely wouldn't be deft enough to handle the task. And Granger couldn't be trusted not to fly off the handle. His tough-talk confrontations at press conferences were famous. Probably why the Pennsylvania voters liked him.

"Jim?"

"I was just thinking. All right, I'll do it. I'll call Al with the happy news, and I'll get back to you after I talk with our blackmailer. Give me her number."

He did and then said, "Good luck."

"Thanks. We all need it." I disconnected and rocked back in my chair, hands clasped in my lap. My armpits were wet, my fingers cool. The classic cold sweat. Disaster loomed, a peril of our own making, and now we had to find a way out.

———◆◇◆———

At four p.m. the following day, I had one patient left on the office schedule, but the child was a new patient, meaning personal information questionnaires had to be filled out, so I had the time for the call. "Ms. Donovan," I began when she answered the phone, "this is a friend of the restaurant owner you called yesterday."

"Which one are you?" she asked in a surprisingly perky voice. "The doctor or the governor?"

"As I said, I'm his friend. Let's leave it at that, okay?"

"Sure, whatever. A tag team, huh?"

"Not exactly." The script I'd written lay on the desk in front of me. "He wanted to tell you to get lost, though he used stronger language when he told me about it. That was my first reaction, too, but then I did a cost-benefit calculation. None of us would want to be subjected to the publicity you threatened. So although your charge is completely baseless, you could hurt our reputations. Much as we think it's wrong, we've decided to agree to your proposal."

"Great. When?"

"Before we go on, Ms. Donovan, are you recording this call?"

Silence for a moment. Then, "No."

"Well, I am."

Dead air again. "I see. That's what all the beating around the bush was about. Okay, I've got no problem with that."

"It's a step we're taking to protect our interests. The negotiation should not be one-sided, don't you agree?"

"I guess." Softer, less confident now.

"Documentation of our conversation will preclude your taking the lawsuit route you mentioned."

"I wasn't really going to—"

"And we'd hate to come to an agreement with you, only for you to decide later it wasn't enough. So our offer, the figure you proposed, will be final. Do you understand what I'm saying?"

"You're treating me like a freakin' blackmailer! That's not what this is about."

"No? But regardless of your motivations, demanding payment to prevent potentially damaging action on your part is extortion by definition. We are willing to accede to your demand only because we decided it's an unavoidable cost of doing business, as it were. But it will be a one-time payment, not an installment on future demands."

"Fine. That should settle the debt."

The girl catches on quickly. She can do the circuitous talk, too. Good. Now for the big one. "Yes it will, and then you will hold us blameless for any further debt. Otherwise, we would find it necessary to hold any renegotiation in person. That could be quite unpleasant. I'm afraid my very large friend loses his temper easily. Am I making myself clear?" I cringed when I said that. Being a bully was certainly not my style, but the bluff had to sound good.

"Oh, wow! I don't believe this! You're threatening me?"

"Not at all. But you must calculate your own cost-benefit ratio, whether the unpleasantness you'd cause by reneging on the deal would be worth it. That's all I'm saying."

"Okay, enough of this bullshit. When and where do I get the money?"

"I assume you don't want it to be delivered in person."

No response for a few moments. Maybe she hadn't really thought this part through. Finally, "No way."

"All right. A bank check will be mailed to you at your address."

I heard a muffled exclamation of some sort before, "You know where I live?"

The concern in her voice made me smile. The bluff was working. "Of course."

"Well, make it soon," she said, bluster back in her tone. "I'll give you a week. Then I start calling people."

"I'll make sure the postal service is aware of the urgency. Goodbye, Ms. Donovan."

The sound of the front door opening startled her, almost making her drop the cell phone. Tim entered the living room.

"Something wrong, honey?" He took off his jacket and went to the closet.

"No, I just remembered I forgot to do something at work, but I called Trish, and she'll take care of it. Busy day?"

"The usual. Nothing exciting." He came up to her, a big smile in his face, and put his arms around her waist. "But I drove past the house on my way home. It's still for sale. I've been thinking, Cats, wanna make an offer? I think we can swing it."

She smiled back and offered her lips for a kiss. "I think we can, too, Tim. I'm about to get a big raise. Let's do it! The sooner we get out of this crummy apartment, the better!"

CHAPTER 10

July 2017
Harrisburg, Pennsylvania

ALAN GRANGER SAT AT HIS desk, tying up loose ends in preparation for his vacation. A TV on the credenza behind him was tuned to CNN, the volume low. His own voice coming out of the set made him turn around.

And there he was, giving his inaugural speech. A caption in the upper left corner of the screen read January 20, 2015. He turned up the volume. "—live in one of the most vibrant states in the country, able to meet any challenges that face us. You will not find a more productive workforce than what we have in Pennsylvania. Hard-working, patriotic citizens are the bedrock of our state, making it strong and vital. I will fight to keep it that way."

The scene shifted to shots of foreclosure signs on front lawns, going-out-of-business announcements on storefronts, and locked gates of manufacturing plants. As the images flashed on the screen, a rich, baritone voice intoned, "Pennsylvania has lost thousands of jobs to places like China and India in the last three years, and middle-class incomes have stagnated. We need strong leadership in Harrisburg, a governor who will fight for *all* Pennsylvanians, not just the wealthy elite who have become more affluent while the vast majority is struggling. Tell Governor Granger that you want *action* to strengthen our economy, not just empty platitudes.

"This message brought to you by the Together for Tomorrow Committee."

With the thirty-second ad over, the *Situation Room* program returned to report on the latest unrest in the Middle East.

What the fuck? Granger stared at the screen, not listening to the anchor's conversation with the CNN reporter in Syria. He turned back to his desk, the semi-trance ended. His sudden discomfort demanded an immediate inquiry. He picked up his iPhone.

Frank Bascomb, Granger's chief of staff, answered after two rings. "What's up, Governor?"

"I just saw a TV ad slamming me."

"Already? Jeez."

Granger sighed. "My sentiments exactly."

"Who's the challenger?"

"Don't know. The ad was paid for by a PAC called Together for Tomorrow."

"Never heard of it."

"Me, neither. Look into it, okay?"

"I'm on it."

"Thanks, Frank." Granger disconnected and sat back in his chair, the good mood he'd been in as he prepared to get away for a well-deserved vacation now evaporated. *Who the hell is coming after me out of the blue?*

⊶⊰⊷

The six of us sat in wooden rockers on a broad porch overlooking Lake George. The rustic house, clad in weathered Adirondack siding, sat along the access road leading to the Silver Bay Association complex.

The owner of the place, Bradley Stevens, a wealthy businessman and assistant director of the Association, lived in New York City. Brad and his wife, Linda, knew Michelle and me quite well from our summers working at Silver Bay while in college. A graduate of Syracuse University and subsequent booster of the football team, he had been a big Kretchman fan. So when I called him asking for inside dope on available rentals in the area, I dropped Kretchman's name, hoping it would give him a little extra incentive to help us. That's when I got the disturbing news: Brad had colon cancer.

"Oh, man, Brad! Sorry to hear that."

"Yeah, well, what can you do? Anyway, it's not too bad, but the oncologist recommended chemo to be on the safe side. He did say it was controversial for the stage of tumor I have. You're the doc. What do you think?"

"As a pediatrician, it would be quite rare for me to have a colon cancer patient, Brad. Never had one, in fact. So it's out of my comfort zone. But it sounds right. Why take a chance, you know?"

"That's what the second-opinion guy said, too. Bottom line, I'm starting the treatment next week at Sloan-Kettering. So we won't be coming up to Silver Bay this summer. Too bad. I'd love to see Kretchman again. How is he?"

"He's got a restaurant in Philly. He's doing well."

"That's good to hear."

"Maybe we can make this an annual thing, so next year, when you're completely recovered, we can all get together at the lake."

"That would be nice," he said without enthusiasm. Because he wondered if he'd be around a year from now, I assumed.

"Say," he continued in a livelier tone, "I've got an idea, Jim. Why don't you stay at our place? It's been empty since last fall. It could use some airing out."

I had seen his house once, when he'd hosted a party for the staff. It was a fabulous place. "We'd love to, Brad! It would be perfect for us." I didn't care about the rental price. *How high could it be?* "I'll send you a check today. How much?"

Stevens laughed. "I never rent the house out, Jim. You're like family to us, and I know you'll take care of the place. Use it for as long as you'd like."

Oh, wow! "That's extremely generous of you, Brad. I don't know what to say." *Wait until I tell Michelle!*

"There is one stipulation, though. A modest fee to make this an official *rental* agreement."

"Sure, anything. What?"

"A football with Syracuse University's logo on it, and Bob Kretchman's autograph."

I laughed. "You got it!"

We talked about where the hide-a-key for the house was located, things I'd need to know to avoid any problems, and one interesting tidbit I wouldn't share with Michelle until after we had seen the place again. And that was it. We had ourselves a house on Lake George for our vacation. I thanked him again for his generosity and ended the call wishing him good luck with the treatment and giving an optimistic opinion of his prognosis.

The property had a tennis court and a boathouse containing a vintage Chris-Craft inboard runabout. Three bedrooms, a large kitchen with updated appliances, and a roomy living room with a massive stone fireplace comprised the "camp." In this part of the country, a vacation home, no matter how large or well appointed, was referred to as a camp.

With the boys in tennis camp in the Poconos for the summer, Michelle and I were free for the getaway. We drove up with the Kretchmans in my Lexus. Granger and Tammy flew into Albany and drove the remaining eighty or so miles. They arrived about two hours after we did.

We were enjoying drinks in the late afternoon as we gazed out at the lake, which was about a mile wide at that point. A pleasant breeze kept us comfortable in shorts and T-shirts. One of the Lake George Steamboat Company's cruise ships went by, heading south to its berth at Lake George Village.

We'd have to make a food and booze run tomorrow to Ticonderoga, about twenty minutes to the north on Route 9N, but I'd picked up some supplies for our cookout this evening from the convenience store just down the road.

"I see you've appropriated the master suite," Granger said to me with that familiar smirk.

"First come, first serve, Al." I winked at him. "Besides, I'm the one who made the arrangements."

"Just joshing you, man. Our bedroom is fine. In fact, this whole place is great. Never been to Lake George. Very nice. I can see why you liked to work here."

"Yeah, lots of good memories for Michelle and me." I checked my watch. "Better get dinner started."

"What are we having?" Kretchman asked.

"Well, I've got a side of beef for you, Sasquatch, and the rest of us will have hamburgers."

"Good. Me hungry." Kretchman beat on his chest, King Kong-style, turned to his wife, and grinned.

She poked him in the belly. "Down, boy, and go easy on the chips and dip, okay?"

"Sheree, c'mon, I'm a big guy," he replied, still smiling. "I need a lot of calories to keep this body going."

"So you keep telling me. Didn't you just go up a waist size?"

Kretchman rolled his eyes.

"Sheree," Granger said, "give him a break. He needs to maintain his bulk to intimidate our blackmailer."

Leave it to Granger to spoil a fun time. I shot him a look but didn't make eye contact.

"Yeah, Jim," Tammy said, "have you heard anything more from that bitch?"

"Nada."

"No news is good news, right?" Kretchman asked.

We'd gotten the money together, and I mailed a bank check to the nurse three days after that phone call. I'd had no further contact from her. Our retaliation bluff and my recording of the call likely protected us from more extortion. Unfortunately, we couldn't know for sure.

"It's only been three months, Bob, but I hope we're good." Not wanting to continue this topic of conversation, I rose from my rocker and stepped off the porch to the patio where a gas grill waited to be ignited. I stood at the grill, tending to the burgers. The sun, about to dip below the mountains, cast a golden sheen on the lake, calm at this time of day.

Kretchman was down at the dock, checking out the boathouse. Granger was fetching me a beer from the kitchen, where the women sipped chardonnay while they put together a pasta salad.

With the passage of time, Michelle's animosity toward Tammy had mellowed to a polite acceptance. They would never be good friends, and I suspected Mish wouldn't care if the Grangers were no longer a part of our group. My attitude toward Granger had changed, too. Being a lawyer and a politician were likely responsible, but the fun-loving guy I once knew seemed to have developed a more calculating, what's-in-it-for-me persona. So what had always bugged my wife about Tammy I now saw in Granger. Sad. But we still had that bond of history to keep us connected.

Granger reappeared at my side and handed me a cold one.

"Thanks." I took a sip and held the sweating can to my forehead.

"Can't let the grillmaster get overheated." He took a pull from his can and gazed out at the lake. "Peaceful setting."

"Sure is." I flipped the patties. "Must be good to get away from the grind of politics for a while."

There was no mirth behind his chuckle. "You got that right. The election isn't for another seventeen months, and the negative ads have already begun."

"Who?"

"Some PAC called Together for Tomorrow. No candidate being pushed yet, but it's gotta be Brent Marshall."

"Don't know him."

"I served in the House with him. A bleeding-heart activist. He's made a few speeches around the state."

"Could he be a tough opponent?"

"Nah, I don't think so. My approval rating is high. That's why I was surprised at the early campaign against me. Last I heard, the Dems had no serious takers."

I glanced at him and saw the worry in his eyes. It reminded me of the look he'd get when it was third down, we were behind, time was running out, and the play called was for Webster to throw the ball to him in the end zone.

"Know anything about this PAC?" I asked.

"It's new, registered this year. Its only focus seems to be me at the moment." He gave another insincere laugh. "Like this PAC was started up to go after me. A former hedge fund manager, Arnold Bloomberg, runs it out of Las Vegas."

"Las Vegas? Why the hell would they be targeting a Pennsylvania election?"

"You got me, pard. Doesn't make much sense."

I opened the package of American cheese. "Lots of fat cats in Vegas. Could be the funding source. Remember that guy Adelson?"

"Yeah, I've thought about that. A billionaire with too much time on his hands flexes his financial muscle to influence an election, just to show he can. But why me? That's a mystery."

I placed cheese slices on the patties. "You're worried about this, aren't you?"

"Well, it surprises me, for sure. I assume these ads are backing a particular candidate. The only one I can think of is Marshall, and I can't figure how he would attract the support of some newly created PAC in Nevada. Unless there's a ringer out there I know nothing about."

I put the finished burgers on a plate. "Let's go eat. Take your mind off this puzzle." I called out to the dock. "Dinner is served, Bob." Kretchman followed us into the house.

The bedroom faced the lake, looking east. But thanks to a range of hills on the other side, by seven a.m. the room remained dark. I had been awake for a while. My problem sleeping in a strange place did not afflict Michelle. She was still out cold.

I slipped out of bed, grabbed my clothes from the back of a chair, and stepped into the adjoining bathroom. After draining my bladder and brushing my teeth, I went to the kitchen to make a pot of coffee. No sounds of activity emanated from any part of the house. Everyone was sleeping in.

I took my mug outside to the dock, where I dangled my legs over the end. Barely a ripple marred the lake's surface. About a hundred yards offshore, two men sat in an anchored boat, waiting for fish to attack their baited hooks. While die-hard crickets refused to surrender to the dawn, birds vocally celebrated the new day. Below my feet, a school of minnows darted through the crystal-clear water.

I turned to the sound and vibration of footfalls on the dock behind me.

Michelle, dressed in a purple kimono and bearing her own coffee mug, approached. "Hiya, mountain man." She sat down beside me.

I drew her to me for a kiss. "Morning, sweetheart."

She grabbed my free hand. "Thanks."

"For what? The kiss?"

"For this vacation, the nostalgia. I love this place. It will never change."

I took a sip of coffee. It was time for my surprise. "Do you like this camp?"

"It's wonderful."

I grinned at her.

"What?" She looked at me with her eyes squinted and her head cocked to the side. She knew me too well.

"I was just thinking. This place might be on the market in the near future."

Like Elaine in *Seinfeld*, she gave my shoulder a hard push. "Get out! Really?"

"Even if Brad conquers his cancer, he's getting on in years. When we talked, he told me he might consider selling. He has no other family. Linda is using a walker now, making getting around up here in the boonies problematic." My big grin returned. "What do you think? Would you like to own this house?"

"Honey, do you mean it? I would love to!"

We kissed again. "Something to think about. Let's see what happens with Brad."

The sun was peeking over the hills across the lake. A dove cooed in the distance behind us. I had just made the love of my life beam with joy. *Life is good.*

Michelle broke into my reverie. "What's wrong with Al? He wasn't his usual pontificating self last night."

"Politicians. Always worried about the next election. He told me some TV ads against him have started."

"That must be it. While you boys were outside yesterday, Tammy was bragging that Al might consider running for president."

President? "Jeez, Mish. President of the United States?" I chuckled. "Well, I never thought of him being a governor, either, so anything's possible, I guess. But I think he'd better win re-election first. Otherwise, he'd be pegged a loser."

"So, he must be really worried about that nurse. If she tells all, it would pretty much doom his chances."

"Yeah, it would." The stakes Granger had in the story never seeing the light of day assumed mammoth proportions. Re-election to governor was one thing. He could lose because of the scandal and then retire to a life as a consultant or lobbyist. As long as you weren't in the public eye, your personal baggage didn't count, only what expertise and contacts you could bring to the table. No big deal. Other politicians forced to leave office for one kind of moral infraction or another had no problems finding behind-the-scene jobs in the industry that was politics. *But if he wants to be president?* That certainly upped the ante considerably. *How far would someone like Granger go to protect his chances for that prize?*

And if Granger's secret got out through some ambitious reporter digging through his background, then so would mine. But I couldn't let that worrisome thought bloom into full flower. The beautiful morning wouldn't allow it. We were going to have a great vacation, no matter what, blackmailer or not. I was determined to make that happen. "C'mon," I said, standing. "Let's go cook up some breakfast for the troops."

CHAPTER 11

July 2017
Las Vegas

WENDELL LOGAN LIFTED HIS GLASS to the balding man in his early fifties. "Need a refill?"

"I'm good, thanks," Arnold Bloomberg replied.

Logan went to the bar in his office suite and added ice and bourbon to his tumbler. Retaking his seat, he said, "The ads are good, Arnie. Professional graphics, clear messages. Looks like you chose the right man for the job."

"Thanks. Hank Randall and I go back to when I was in New York."

"I want you to set up a meeting with Randall, you, and Marshall. I think it's time we got the congressman's name in the ads, have Granger hear the hoofbeats of a challenger coming after him."

"Any chance Granger's people will discover Marshall's problem before we can use it?"

"None. Only four people know about it, including the congressman himself. A leak won't happen."

Bloomberg pursed his lips. "Is that why I've been kept out of the loop?"

"Need to know, Arnie. It's not that I don't trust you. Experience and common sense say that the more people in on a secret, the greater the chance it will get out. You'll be filled in when the time comes, of course, because you will be the messenger."

"Okay, I can live with that."

"Good, because when it's revealed, it has to be a bombshell with no warning." Logan smiled. "If it's a surprise to you, too, no acting on your part will be required."

"More than what I've already been doing, you mean." Bloomberg returned the grin.

"Rightly so." Logan swirled the cubes in his glass. "But first we want Granger running scared. The ads should be stepped up over the next few weeks, and we should make sure we get a spot during the Eagles-Steelers game in November. By then, all of Pennsylvania should know that Granger's in a horse race. It will give the media a reason to start covering it in earnest. And start polling."

Bloomberg chuckled. "And we've got our own piece of the media." The Vista Group, owner of television and radio stations across the country, including Pennsylvania, and the owner of the *Pittsburgh Daily News*, was part of Logan's vast empire.

"Anything else?" Logan set his glass on the table, a signal the meeting was over.

"That should do it." Bloomberg put his own glass down and stood. "I'll set the meeting up with Hank and Marshall."

Logan rose from his chair and offered his hand. "You're doing a great job." He gripped Bloomberg's hand firmly.

"Thank you, sir."

"You're an important member of the team, Arnie. If all goes as planned, I've got another job you might find interesting." He gave Bloomberg a slight smirk.

"Oh, yeah? And what would that be?"

"How does Secretary of Commerce sound to you?"

<hr/>

I found the tennis net in Brad's toolshed, and we secured it to the posts. After clearing winter debris from the court, the Dawsons and the Grangers were ready to battle for bragging rights. Kretchman and Sheree, who didn't play tennis, had sauntered down the access road to check out the Silver Bay Association complex.

Michelle and I had played against the Grangers a few times over the years and were familiar with their game. Both played aggressively, as suited their natures. As a result, they made more than their share of unforced errors.

We, on the other hand, played a steady game, content to keep returning the balls hit in our court while waiting for the opportunity to put one away or for them to screw up, whichever came first. We easily won the set, Granger's frustration clearly showing as our game count mounted. When we met at the net for fist bumps, an unhappy Granger asked, "Best two out of three? Tammy is warmed up now, so we'll give you a better game."

"What do you mean, 'Tammy is warmed up now'? I didn't see many great shots coming from *you*." She shook her head and gave us a "what's with him?" look.

"Sure, we'll play another set," I said before the Bickersons could continue their finger-pointing, and headed to the side of the court where plastic chairs, towels, and bottled water waited.

Granger's phone, which he'd placed on one of the chairs, rang as he reached it. He picked it up. "What's up, Frank?" He moved to the far end of the court, out of earshot.

Tammy sat and removed her dark blue headband. "Hot today!" She shook the hem of her light green tennis skirt, presumably to create a breeze to cool off her nether region. Before the distracting image could fully form in my mind, she continued, "The racket kept slipping in my hands from the perspiration."

Women like Tammy didn't sweat, of course; they perspired. Like her husband, she had ventured an excuse for the defeat. What a perfectly matched couple.

Michelle sat next to her. "Maybe you need to get a better grip on it." She gave me a furtive wink.

I couldn't help smiling at the disguised put-down. *Oh, you're good.*

She showed Tammy her racket. "I don't have that problem."

Tammy pretended to test the grip's friction. "Yeah, I'll take it to the pro shop when I get back home." She looked at her husband engaged in an animated conversation near the back fence. "Frank Bascomb is always bugging Alan about one thing or another. I mean, really, a chief of staff should be able to handle things. That's his job."

She grunted in disgust, twisted off the top of a Deer Park, and took a sip of water.

Granger returned, shaking his head as he stared at his iPhone.

"Trouble, Al?" I asked.

Ignoring me for the moment, he continued to gaze at the screen. An indistinct voice came from the device before he shut off the phone and looked at me. "Another fucking negative ad," he explained. "My office sent me a video of it." He turned to his wife. "Tammy, Frank wants me in Harrisburg so we can develop a strategy to fight back."

She stared at him, disbelief in her face. "Alan, can't he start putting it together without you? We're on vacation!"

"I'm the governor, honey. The buck stops with me, okay? My job. Sorry, but I have to be there."

"But we just got here!"

Granger looked away for a moment then fixed his wife with a steady gaze. I knew from experience he was fighting to keep his cool. "I know, sweetheart. I wish I didn't have to, and I'll make it up to you. But Frank's right. We have to get on this before it gets some traction."

"Alan—"

"Tammy, unless you'd rather I didn't win re-election, we're going back to Harrisburg."

"Is it that bad?" Her tone had gone from petulance to worry.

"Not yet. That's the point." He turned to me. "Sorry, Jim, but we have to cut our visit short."

"I understand." Glancing at Michelle, I caught the faintest of smiles.

"Now I've gotta change the damned flight reservation." He started to finger his phone again as he walked off the court.

"Looks like I better pack." Tammy sighed. She picked up her husband's racket and her own and followed Granger to the house.

Michelle watched them go. "Now we can have some real fun."

"Mish—"

She held a hand up. "Sorry, dear. I'll be good and show the requisite sympathy for their plight, I promise."

I smiled as I put our rackets into my tennis bag. "Don't bust a gut pretending, okay?" I pulled Michelle up from the chair and kissed her. "Besides, wouldn't you like to spend a night in the Lincoln Bedroom? Be invited to all those gala parties at the White House? Rub elbows with ambassadors and rock stars?"

She cupped her chin with a hand and squinted. "I'd need a new wardrobe, of course." Her tongue touched her upper lip as she arched her eyebrows.

I laughed and gave her ass a pat. "You got it, babe. Now let's go be appropriately upset at the breakup of our vacation party." I slung the bag over a shoulder and grabbed Michelle's hand, and we walked to the house.

Arnold Bloomberg drove his rental to Dulles International following the sit-down at Marshall's office. The meeting had gone well. Hank Randall had outlined his ad strategy, and the congressman suggested the key points he wanted included in the campaign. The two seemed to hit it off, even taking into account Randall's obvious motivation to please the client.

Randall had no idea of the ultimate strategy, but Bloomberg was not concerned the ad man would have a problem switching gears when the time came. If anything, Randall was a practical man like himself and did not let personal beliefs get in the way of business.

As he navigated through heavy Beltway traffic, Bloomberg thought back to his time on the high school debate team, when he had to prepare to argue the affirmative and negative sides of a proposition. One's individual views were irrelevant. It was a purely intellectual exercise. You took a side and went with it. Winning was all that counted.

Winning in this case, though, would be quite different. It would be like one side of a debate, clearly headed to victory, suddenly conceding the opponent's argument. Marshall's side was set. Granger was an unknown variable at this point. Logan had done his research and thought he had the man pegged, but was there a factor he didn't know about, something that could wreck the whole deal?

Taking the airport exit, he concluded it wasn't really his problem. A cabinet post certainly intrigued him, but it had to be a far-fetched idea. He would do his part to bring the scheme to fruition. In the end, however, it was Logan's gamble, not his.

CHAPTER 12

September 2017
Chicago

L UKE ELLIOT LOOKED THROUGH THE scope of the M110
SASS from the lake-facing tenth floor of the Chicago Hilton.
He'd pulled the room's desk in front of the open window and
used it as a platform for the weapon's bipod mount. Though the rifle
held a ten-round magazine, just in case, he didn't think more than one
shot would be necessary.

Beyond Grant Park, across South Michigan Avenue from the hotel,
sailboats on Lake Michigan took early advantage of the beautiful fall
day. To the north, Navy Pier, still relatively free of tourists at this hour
of the morning, jutted out into the lake. Bordering the park to the
south stood the Adler Planetarium, Shedd Aquarium, and the Field
Museum. A little farther south rose the massive oval structure that
was Soldier Field, where his Bears played their home games.

Now a resident of Santa Fe, New Mexico, Elliot had a fond place in
his heart for the Windy City, where the road to his current profession
started. Whenever his business took him to Chicago, it was more than
just a job for him. Unfortunately, this visit would be a short one.

Surveying the area and its landmarks made him feel like a tourist
himself. *Time to get back to why I'm here.* He focused the scope on a
path running through Grant Park that his target would take for his
morning jog. Tony Rizzo, a man in his early sixties, prided himself on
his fitness, and that would be his undoing.

He had factored into the shooting solution a steady, light breeze coming off the lake. The range to target would be less than one hundred yards. Piece of cake. He had managed much more difficult shots during his tour in Afghanistan. Thanks to the U.S. Army, he had added another lethal skill to his repertoire.

His brother, Mark, making big bucks as a billionaire's gofer in Las Vegas and unaware at that time of what Luke really did for a living, had called him crazy for wanting to enlist. Patriotism had been the reason given to Mark, but the real motive was self-preservation.

Back then, the man targeted for assassination today had been his boss. Elliot's putative job title was "account executive" for the mobster's enterprises. In reality, it meant account executioner—a "button man" in the parlance of those old gangster movies—a young man on the make, hoping to move up in the organization.

There was good money to be made in his occupation, if one had no compunctions about killing, a mindset that had served him well subsequently in combat. Besides, those he killed in battle were enemies of the United States. Enough said. But the civilians his boss had tasked him with eliminating were just Rizzo's enemies, real or imagined. Of course, they were all scum, nothing but criminals and killers themselves. Good riddance. Elliot had convinced himself he held the higher moral ground.

But there were other men on the make in the organization, too. When one of them tried to curry favor with Rizzo by making it look like Elliot had helped himself to a target's assets instead of passing them on to the boss, Elliot's days were numbered. The penalty for stealing from thieves was severe. An example would be made. So he'd escaped into the willing arms of Uncle Sam.

Sniper school provided an unexpected benefit of his enlistment. Right up his alley. And now, four years after he left the service, he would use what he learned there to bring down, ironically, the man indirectly responsible for it. Rizzo had taken him under his wing and given him the job in his organization. But for Rizzo to turn on him the way he did... well, Elliot had no regrets about his current contract.

He leaned back from the scope, rubbed his eyes, and checked his watch. He had at least ten minutes before he'd have to monitor the kill zone continuously.

As much as he loved Chicago, he looked forward to returning to New Mexico's high country, where Emily was likely at this very moment transferring her vision of the striking landscape to canvas. Sweet Emily, his lover for the past two years, who thought he was a licensed gun dealer.

And he was. But she had no idea of his lucrative side business. *Have gun, will travel.* Elliot smiled at the phrase, the title of that old TV series. He'd been introduced to it recently when, unable to sleep one night, he checked out channels he normally didn't watch. He happened upon one that specialized in movie and TV westerns. And there he saw a San Francisco dandy who attended the opera suddenly become a dressed-all-in-black gunfighter in response to a request for his services. *That's me, except for the dandy part, of course*, Elliot thought with fascination as he watched the show. Like Paladin, the character played by Richard Boone, Elliot took contracts to solve problems with controlled violence then returned to his "normal" life. And like Paladin, Elliot only took contracts he could rationalize as justified.

The similarities were obvious, though the times had changed, of course. Telegrams asking for Paladin's help had become e-mail contacts via shootingsolutions@gmail.com. If the inquiry interested him, he would call the potential client by prepaid cell phone for the real details of what had been, if the inquirer were smart, a disguised description of the problem. Once he had accepted the contract, and only after his offshore bank account had received payment, preparations would begin. When he had determined the date for the contract fulfillment, he would notify the client to allow for the establishment of an alibi.

The client never knew who he was, never saw his face. Even if the client came under suspicion and then cracked under pressure, a search for his or her hired gun would dead-end at the e-mail address. Finding the owner of the address through a court order was a possibility, but that would reveal a false identity. To this point, as far as he knew, he had remained anonymous.

Elliot put his eye to the scope again and slowly panned the view north along the path, spotting a woman wheeling a stroller and an old couple walking a poodle. Then he saw the gray-haired man dressed in sweats and wearing a Chicago Cubs ball cap, leading his two men in a moderate jog. Rizzo insisted his bodyguards be capable of keeping up with his morning exercise.

In fifteen seconds, the mobster arrived at the kill zone and stopped. Elliot knew Rizzo's routine from his days working for him, and one previous day of observation had told him this habit hadn't changed. Rizzo must have recognized some sort of mileage marker at that location. Rizzo stood, hands on hips, waiting for his trailing men to reach him. Elliot pulled the trigger of the sound-suppressed rifle.

A red spray erupted from the target's head before the crack of the 7.62 mm round broke the sound barrier. Rizzo crumpled to the ground, and Elliot backed away from the window, taking the weapon with him. Quickly removing the suppressor and the bipod mount from the gun and ejecting the magazine, he put those accessories, along with the rifle itself, into their designated slots in a foam-lined aluminum case on the bed. He closed its lid and locked it with a key then put the case into an already-packed, wheeled duffel bag. After closing it, he secured the zipper with a small combination lock attached to the zipper's terminus. He moved the desk and chair back to their normal locations and took one last look around the place, including the bathroom. Satisfied, he pulled the duffel behind him as he headed to the elevator.

In order to remain successful, an assassin could not draw attention to himself and must certainly not look like someone to be wary of. Elliot was no exception to that tradecraft axiom. He had unremarkable facial features, neither handsome nor ugly, and a height of just under six feet. After he and Emily had become lovers, his ego demanded he raise the issue of what she saw in him. "After all," he'd said, "I would describe myself as nondescript." Sweet Emily chuckled at the oxymoronic statement and replied, "It's not what you show to the world that matters, my love, but who you really are as a person. I see you as strong and principled, a man of his word, and goal-oriented. A man who would never leave a task undone." She smirked. "And that lovely cock of yours certainly helps."

Elliot smiled as he waited for the elevator, remembering that day.

Except for the last one, of course, the traits she mentioned were what made him good at his job.

Dressed in a corduroy sport coat, white button-down shirt, and jeans, Elliot left the elevator and walked unhurriedly through the lobby, wheeling his duffel. Just another forgettable traveler in his mid-thirties on his way to who knew where. Having already checked out, he left the hotel through the South Michigan Avenue entrance. As he waited for a taxi, he heard the siren of an approaching ambulance, and a Chicago PD cruiser raced into Grant Park. Three hours later, Elliot looked out the window of the American Airlines 737 as it flew over the Mississippi River on the first leg of the flight back to Santa Fe.

CHAPTER 13

February 2018
Harrisburg, Pennsylvania

THE FAMILY DINING ROOM OF the governor's residence was set up to accommodate those attending the meeting with continental breakfast fare. Coffee and orange juice dispensers, along with a variety of pastries, sat on a side table against one wall. The attendees had supplied themselves with refreshments and were taking their seats when Governor Granger entered the room. Light from the two hundred-year-old leaded crystal chandelier reflected off the polished surface of the long wooden table beneath it.

"Thank you for making it through the snow, people." He took his place at the head of the table. "Frank," he said to his chief of staff, "let's get started."

"Yes, sir." Bascomb turned to the middle-aged man on his left. "Cal, what's the latest?"

Calvin Stryker, chairman of the Committee to Re-Elect the Governor, looked down at the spreadsheets in front of him before responding. "Governor, the trend in contributions is down over the last two months. This isn't unexpected just before and after the holidays, though. The Blackbaud Index shows a similar decline in charitable giving across the board during this period. February usually has an uptick, but we don't have those numbers yet, of course."

"So no real problem, then?" Granger asked.

The political strategist took a sip of coffee as he perused his notes again. "Well, we've upped the ad campaign to counter the deluge of negative spots coming out of the Marshall camp at a time when contributions are down."

"Meaning?" Granger fixed Stryker with a cold stare.

"Bear in mind, I expect the trend to reverse. But at the current rate of expenditures, unless we get a significant influx of cash, we'll be out of money by June."

"Shit!" Granger banged his hand on the table. "Calvin, have we done enough to put the bite on our major donors? What about Keystone HealthNet and, uh, Erie Oil? And let's not forget about U.S. Steel. Aren't they on board?"

"We've contacted our corporate supporters, naturally. Many of them are holding back for now. Their reasons for doing so are all over the map but none ostensibly related to any change in loyalty. They're still with you in principle. That's the feedback I've gotten."

"But?"

"I think Marshall's strategy of connecting their support of you with government favors is making them a little gun-shy."

"Give me a fucking break!"

"It's true, Al," the red-haired, burly lieutenant governor, Barry Harrington, spoke up. "I've talked with Ben Patton. He's getting pressure to start a corruption investigation. Marshall's supporters are feeding reports they've picked up from their districts to Ed Foley, and—"

"Who's that?"

"The ranking member of the Senate Ethics Committee. He's got a list of targets and word is the insurance commissioner is number one on that roster."

"Chairman Patton will stifle that." Bascomb shook his head. "It'll never get out of committee."

"You're probably right, Frank," Harrington replied. "But the publicity will."

"The governor's hands are clean, Barry," Bascomb said. "Nothing to worry about."

Harrington shrugged. "Fact of life, Frank. It's bound to focus attention, unwarranted though it may be, on the man in charge."

Granger drummed his fingers on the table. "Damn that Marshall.

How the hell is he doing all this? *He* doesn't seem to have any money problems."

"'Together for Tomorrow' obviously has a source of funding that so far exceeds that of CREEG."

Granger slapped his hand on the table again. "Jeez, Calvin. I hate that name. Wasn't Nixon's PAC called CREEP? That turned out to be appropriate! Ours sounds like Queeg. You know, that fucked-up Bogart character in *The Caine Mutiny*? Can't you come up with something else?"

Stryker gave Amy Mills, Director of Public Relations, a questioning look.

"We could reverse it, maybe. Governor's Re-Election Committee," she said then frowned. "No, that would spell GREEC, and we don't want to be linked to that bankrupt country."

Granger sighed as he ran fingers through his hair. "Well, work on it, okay? But that's just window dressing. What're we going to do against Marshall?" He stared at Stryker. "While we still have funds, that is."

The strategist let a smile break his face for the first time since the meeting started. "The he's-too-liberal-for-Pennsylvania strategy is getting some traction. We started out focusing on Marshall's spending votes in Congress, but we've just begun targeting the social issues. Evangelicals and Catholics are polling solid for you. We'll hit the right-to-life organizations. Throw in the anti-immigration folks, and I think we'll be okay."

"Yeah, but we'll give up a good chunk of the female and Hispanic vote, and lose the gay community completely in the process."

Stryker shrugged. "Pennsylvania isn't California. A good part of it is like the Midwest. It's a numbers game, Governor. And we'll have most of the military and veterans come November, too. I'm sure the corporate donations will start coming in when those guys realize what the stakes are."

"Scare 'em, Calvin. We need that money."

Same day
Melrose, Massachusetts

Tim Howard stood on the front porch of the brick two-story and looked down the quiet street. Yesterday's six-inch snowfall covered what was left from the storm of a week earlier with a pristine layer of white glistening in the morning sun.

Plows had not yet cleared the street, so no piled-up snow blocked the car from the driveway. Across the street, two boys threw snowballs at each other in a front yard. A man shoveling his driveway next door looked up at his new neighbor and returned Tim's wave.

"Tim," Cathy said, her breath visible as vapor streams, "can we go in, please? It's freezing out here!"

"Just getting a feel for the neighborhood, honey." He took a key from his coat and held it up as he smiled at his fiancée.

Cathy grinned back at him and grabbed his other arm, bouncing excitedly up and down on boot-clad toes.

Tim unlocked the door and turned the knob. The door swung open, exposing a hardwood floor in the foyer and stairs leading to the second level. An ornate chandelier hung from a vaulted ceiling. "Ready?" he asked, blocking the doorway.

Cathy gently tried to push him forward. "I'm more than ready! C'mon, Tim. Quit fooling around. Move it!"

"Not so fast." He faced her, sporting a huge grin. "Our first house, right?"

"Yeah?"

"I think I should carry you over the threshold."

She laughed. "Okay, big boy, do your thing." She put her hand around his neck, and he lifted her in his arms.

After stepping through the doorway, he set her down and kissed her. "Welcome to your new home."

"*Our* new home." Cathy looked around. "Let's check out the kitchen." She started to move off, but Tim caught her arm.

"Honey, wait a sec. I've got something to say." He put his arms around her waist, drawing her to him.

Cathy looked up at him, eyes shining with excitement. "Okay."

"We kinda did this backwards, sweetheart. We got the house. Now I think we need to put the same last name on the address. Would a June wedding give you enough time?"

"Oh, Tim." She stood on her tiptoes for a kiss. "I'll check with Mom. She'll be thrilled. When we bought the house... well, she wondered if we'd ever set a date. June would be great! We'll work it out." She grinned. "Of course, you know what that will mean."

"What?"

"You'll have to carry me over the threshold again. The first time didn't really count." She pushed his chest. "Now can we please look over our place?"

Same day
Las Vegas

Mark Elliot poured coffee for his boss and himself and brought the cups to the dinette in the small kitchen of Logan's office suite. After taking a seat across from Logan, he consulted a legal pad on the table. "The latest polls show Marshall is closing in on Granger. The *Daily News* has him within the margin of error."

"Our paper," Logan responded.

"True. The editorials have helped, I'm sure, and the polling firm you hired leans Democratic. But the trend is the same across the state."

"So the strategy is working." Logan sipped his coffee.

"Seems to be." Elliot eyed his notepad. "Marshall has established satellite offices in Scranton, Allentown, Harrisburg, Altoona, and Pittsburgh."

Logan smiled. "All it takes is money."

Elliot sat back in his chair and folded his arms across his chest. "Arnie Bloomberg has some doubts."

"Oh?"

"Not about making Marshall a strong candidate. You've proved you can do that. And I know what we've got on him will work. But Arnie's worried about the wild card. Granger. Whether he'll do what you've counted on. Frankly, sir, that concerns me, too."

Logan rose from his chair and went to the coffee machine for a refill. After returning to the table, he said, "You're right about the unknown factor, but I've done my research on this man. He'll go along with the program."

"If you say so, boss."

"But rest assured I'll get some insurance when we have the face-to-face." Logan smiled. "Everyone has something to hide, Mark. And ambitious politicians are especially motivated to keep their secrets hidden. Some can get away with exposure, but that's rare. Stories about Kennedy's philandering didn't hurt him, but they were just rumors. Clinton's popularity saved his presidency—but just barely—and that was only over a blowjob." Logan chuckled and shook his head.

"What we know about Marshall is much worse, so that part of the plan is solid. But that brings me back to Granger. Do you have some dirt on him you can leverage?"

"Not yet." Logan gave a knowing smile. "But I will because he's going to tell me what it is."

⸻ ⬦ ⸻

The next day
Villanova, Pennsylvania

I had been up most of the night with a sick three-year-old and got back from the hospital this morning with just enough time to shower and get ready for the office. Thankfully, it was my well-child day, and my hospital rounds after I saw my last office patient revealed that the kid I'd admitted appeared to have turned the corner.

A late-winter blizzard had punched through Pennsylvania on its way to the northeast two days earlier. Michelle's school was still closed, so she had no fourth-graders to teach today. An enticing aroma met me when I entered the kitchen from the garage. I spotted the Crock-Pot on the counter.

"Mmm. Something smells good." I stepped up behind Michelle, who was unloading the dishwasher, to kiss her neck. "And so do you."

"Thank you." She was putting glasses away in the cabinet. "How are the roads?"

"Wet but clear now. School should be open tomorrow."

"It will. Laura called me thirty minutes ago."

I went to the slow cooker and lifted the lid. A savory scent of garlic, sage, and thyme drifted to my nose. "Pork roast?"

"Yup. Should be ready in an hour. Can you stay awake that long?"

I laughed. "Sure, even after a drink. Join me?" I took a tumbler from her hand.

"Chardonnay, please." She handed me a wineglass.

I filled it from a bottle in the fridge and set it on the counter next to her. Then I poured myself bourbon over ice. I took it to the sunroom, plopped into a stuffed wingback chair, and gazed out at the sea of white in the backyard, the blue pool water providing the only contrast. I'd stopped covering the pool and putting it into hibernation at the end of the swim season, and kept the water circulating. It was in our DNA, it seemed, to like water views even if that water was a pond or, smaller yet, a swimming pool.

Michelle came over, bringing the *Philadelphia Inquirer* with her. She dropped it in my lap and sat on the couch across the room from me. "Al's getting a run for his money. This Marshall guy is rising in the polls. Maybe we should invite him to dinner soon." She grinned at me. "You know, just to hedge our White House bets?"

"Ha! You could have something there. Where's the article?"

She picked up the novel she'd been reading. "Front page, second section."

I found it, scanned it briefly, then turned to the op-ed page. Nothing there about the gubernatorial race. I took out the sports section and dropped the rest of the paper on the floor. As I perused the basketball scores, thoughts of Granger and his campaign entered the back of my mind.

I didn't like the direction Granger's ads were taking. He had always been a Republican and, I had thought, a moderate one, a country-club type rather than a right-wing ideologue. But his ads were hitting hot-button social issues now rather than the fiscal responsibility line that had served as his prime message.

I tossed the sports pages onto the rest of the paper and sipped my drink, brooding a little. I thought back to Tom Webster and Granger's obvious difficulty accepting his homosexuality. *Is it worse than that? Intolerance, perhaps, of equal rights for gays?* Add to that a strong anti-abortion stance, an immigration policy that focused on arrest and deportation rather than reform, and a *laissez-faire* attitude toward the healthcare industry, and I wondered if I really knew my lifelong friend. *Or is this just political expediency, a pandering for votes with no central core of such beliefs?* That was my guess, but it still troubled me.

I took a drink, savoring the smoky flavor of Maker's Mark, then said, "Mish?"

She looked up from her book. "Yeah?"

"Marshall has made the contest interesting. I like what he has to say. So, do we vote for someone we've been close to for years or a man whose policies we agree with?"

Michelle chuckled. "Good thing it's a secret ballot."

"I hear you. Can't say I disagree, though sleeping in the Lincoln Bedroom is an attractive inducement." I shot her a smirk.

"Uh, Jim"—she simpered in kind—"like I hinted at before, maybe there could be a President *Marshall*. So what do you think? Would my lasagna be suitable enough for when he comes to dinner?"

"Sure. He's only a congressman."

I managed to catch the paperback she hurled at me.

CHAPTER 14

June 2018
Villanova, Pennsylvania

"I CAN'T MAKE IT TO THE lake this summer, Jim," Granger said over the phone as I sat with Michelle at a poolside table in the backyard. "Huh. Actually, I didn't really make it last year, either, did I? That one day hardly counts. Anyway, I've got a tight race here and can't afford to take that time off."

"I understand, Al." The news really didn't disappoint me. "Who would've guessed Marshall would do so well?"

"Money talks, and he apparently has plenty of it."

"Your job approval is still good." I tried to inject some optimism into this downer of a conversation.

"That's true, and it should be the difference in the end. But these snipes from the media about cronyism and even possible corruption have hurt."

I had been following the investigative series in the *Philadelphia Inquirer.* "Just speculation, though. Rumors. No hard facts that I can see."

Granger sighed. "Yeah, I know. Still, it's going to be a tough four months. I appreciate your support."

If he only knew. "Well, good luck, man. Tell you what. After you win in November, let's get together for a golf outing. Someplace warm with palm trees and a beach involved?"

He chuckled. "You got it, buddy. Have a great time at Silver Bay."

"Thanks. Take care, Al." I disconnected and looked across the patio table at Michelle. "The Grangers will not be joining us at the lake."

She didn't look up from her magazine. "So I gathered. What a shame. I was looking forward to beating their butts on the tennis court again."

I smiled, sat back in my chair, and gazed out at the pool. Our boys were headed for tennis camp in the Poconos Association, so Michelle and I would be empty nesters for a good part of the summer.

Brad Stevens' latest checkup revealed no evidence of recurrent disease. But his wife, Linda, broke her hip just before Christmas, and that was the last straw. He put the lake house on the market, and we now owned it, much to Michelle's delight. Her wish all those years ago of having a summer place on Lake George had come true.

After our two-week vacation next month with the Kretchmans, Michelle, on summer break from school, would stay, and I would drive up on long weekends off. For the first time, the thought of retirement, at least twenty years in the future, appealed to me.

Granger's political problem did not interest me much. He'd do just fine if forced to return to the private sector. And four years from now, who knew? Maybe he could still manage a run for the presidency. I wouldn't put it past him.

The blackmail incident, well, that was over a year ago, and I had pretty much put it behind me. The memory of the cause of that extortion, though diminishing as a source of angst with the passage of time, remained with me. I resigned myself to the fact it always would.

I glanced at Michelle, chin cradled in her hand, apparently engrossed in a magazine article. Like me, she wore a swimsuit. Unlike me, she was not wearing a T-shirt, so nothing obstructed my view of her figure. A lovely day in June, my beautiful wife enjoying it with me. Life was, indeed, good.

I stood and slipped off my shirt. "I'm taking a dip. Join me?"

She looked up and removed her sunglasses. "Sure."

Grabbing her hand, I pulled her up from the chair and led her to the pool steps.

June 2018
Harrisburg, Pennsylvania

Alan Granger had just returned to his office following a groundbreaking ceremony for a new Sheriff's Department building in Carlisle. Although a good law-and-order photo op, more importantly, it was the last item on his schedule for the day.

He was tired. Tired of smiling and shaking hands with strangers, trying to woo voters; tired of the constant struggle to pry money from donors; tired of reassuring Republicans and pretending empathy for Democrat concerns in the legislature. Some days he wondered if it was all worth it. But then he thought of the grand prize that could lie ahead, and he reached down into his reserves for the strength to labor on.

In just a few minutes, he'd head to the Governor's Mansion, where a crisp martini, maybe two, would help soothe the pressures of the day. He stepped through the reception area toward his inner office and saw Maggie at her desk. An attractive brunette fifteen years his senior, she held the phone to her ear.

She looked up and beckoned to him as she said, "I'll see if he's available, Mr. Logan. Please hold." She pushed a button on the console and grinned at her boss. "That's Wendell Logan!"

"Who?"

"The Las Vegas billionaire!"

He arched his eyebrows as recognition kicked in. "Oh?"

"He wants to talk to you. I suggested Frank, but he insisted on speaking only to you. About the campaign," she whispered, smiling broadly and rubbing her thumb against the fingers of her right hand in that universally recognized pantomime.

"Huh. That's interesting. Did his number register on the caller ID?"

"The area code is right."

"I'll take it in my office." He went into his office, closing the door behind him. The strange development had pushed the thought of a relaxing drink from his mind. He sat in his desk chair, took a deep breath, and picked up the handset. "This is Alan Granger, Mr. Logan. What can I do for you?"

"It's what I can do for you, Governor. Thank you for taking my call. Let me get right to the point. I have a proposition I think you will find quite appealing." A firm, deep voice, reminiscent of Richard Nixon.

"I'm always willing to listen to new ideas. You have the floor, sir."

"I know that you are having some difficulty raising campaign funds, and—"

"Why would you think that?" Granger interrupted.

"Governor, I assume you know who I am. So you know I have considerable resources, and they include the area of information gathering. My enterprises depend on it. But let's get to my proposal. I am prepared to supply whatever funds you need to win your election."

Granger's eyes grew wide, and his pulse kicked up several notches. *Is this for real?* "In return for what, Mr. Logan? I think that would answer the obvious question of why."

Logan laughed. "Very perceptive. I expected nothing less. My offer is on the table, but I think we should discuss the substantive aspects of such an arrangement face to face. I can have my plane in Harrisburg any day convenient for you. I'll fly you to Las Vegas and put you up in a suite at the Phoenix. Bring your wife; make a mini-vacation out of it." He chuckled again. "No reason you can't enjoy yourself just because a decision which could affect your future is to be made."

"Forgive me, Mr. Logan, but this is all rather sudden, and I need some time—"

"Time is precious, Governor. Every day brings you closer to November. Look, it's a no-lose proposition. If, after you've heard what I have to say, you decide in the negative, you'll still have been wined and dined in my luxurious hotel, in *the* most exciting city in the world."

What the hell does he want? Granger couldn't get his mind around why this tycoon would approach him. But he was compelled to find out.

"Your offer is hard to resist, I must admit, Mr. Logan. I *would* like to hear more about this deal. Let me check my schedule—and with my wife. But I think she'd like a trip to Las Vegas. Is this the number at which you can be reached?"

"Yes."

"I'll get back to you tomorrow."

"That's fine. And Governor, it would serve both our interests if this is kept on the QT."

"Certainly. If I do come for a visit, my secretary and chief of staff would have to know, of course."

"Of course."

"I'll call you tomorrow, then."

"Looking forward to our meeting, Governor." Logan disconnected.

Granger replaced the handset in its cradle, his fatigue of just a few minutes earlier now replaced by ebullience. Logan had essentially offered unlimited funding for his campaign, at just the time he needed money desperately. Almost too good to be true. He wondered if Logan's motivation was what he had discussed with Dawson the summer before at the lake. An ego thing, being a power broker.

Or is it more mercenary than that? Granger, hands folded in his lap, rocked back and forth in his chair. *What can a state governor do for a billionaire?* Easing government regulations, most likely. No problem there. That was already part of his philosophy, tree-huggers and too-big-to-fail crybabies be damned. Perhaps Logan didn't want to take the chance a new governor would hurt his financial interests. *In Pennsylvania, just one state out of fifty?*

A startling thought broke through his musings. *Could Logan's goal coincide with my own? Does he want to see me become president? Holy shit!*

Other super-rich folks had tried using their financial clout to affect presidential races in the past. The Koch brothers and Sheldon Adelson immediately came to mind. As the logic of the hypothesis grew more compelling, so did his excitement. *Alan Granger. President of the United States!*

He pulled out his cell phone and punched in a number. "Honey," he said when Tammy answered, "get the martinis ready. I'll be home shortly and will be bringing some amazing news with me."

The next day
Melrose, Massachusetts

Tim pulled into his driveway and saw his wife's car through the open door of her side of the garage. He hit the remote. While waiting for his door to rise, he glanced at the front porch. A package of some sort lay on the welcome mat.

After parking, he went back out to investigate. The item in question was the new phone book. He picked it up and carried it back through the garage to the kitchen, where Cathy was peering into the refrigerator. She turned to face him.

"Look, Mrs. Howard." He held up the directory. "The new phone book."

"Our listing! Come on, let's see."

He tore off the plastic wrap and set the book on the counter. He quickly shuffled through pages until he found it. "There it is. Howard, Catherine and Timothy."

"Our marriage is now officially recognized by the phone company. Cool."

"Yeah. I was afraid I had notified Sprint too late to get in this year's edition." He got a beer from the fridge, popped the top, and took a sip. "Next step will be joint checking and savings accounts. We should get to our banks in the next couple of days."

"Oh… yeah. Good idea," Cathy said, her voice flat.

"Something wrong with that?"

"Uh, no. It's just that… I'm used to having my own account."

"Cath, we're married now. What's mine is yours and vice versa, right?"

She gave him a tight smile. "Of course. You're right."

"Sharing expenses, separate accounts. Those days are over, honey."

"It's about time!" She forced another smile. "Now we can pay my Macy's credit card bills from *our* account."

Tim laughed. "Oh, jeez, I didn't think of that." He leaned over and kissed her. "I'm going to change. What's the plan for dinner?"

"You're doing chicken on the grill, and I've got potato salad I just made chilling in the fridge."

"Works for me."

CHAPTER 15

One week later
Las Vegas

THE FIFTEEN-HUNDRED-SQUARE-FOOT SUITE AT THE Phoenix was impressive even for the jaded Grangers. Laid out in the shape of a staple, the entrance at one end opened into a short foyer containing a closet and guest half-bath. A serving counter with barstools separated a small galley kitchen from the dining area. The other end of the staple housed the bedroom with its attached marble-and-tile bathroom, complete with a jetted tub, twin sinks, and a roomy walk-in shower with multiple spray-heads. Between the ends, a sunken living room with two separate sitting areas filled the space. A floor-to-ceiling window comprised the exterior wall. Sixty-inch flat-screen TVs hung from each side wall.

After they took the tour of their lodgings, Granger led Tammy to the window. "Look at that, Tammy. All that glitter, and it can't match nature's color display." The multitude of lights on the other hotels and casinos could not yet blaze their invitations into the sky, as a brilliant orange-red sunset put the manmade spectacles to shame.

"Beautiful." She leaned into him. "What a view. I wonder what this place costs a night."

Granger laughed. "I'm sure there's a rate attached to it, but I'd guess it usually doesn't apply. High-rollers get comped to suites like this when they come to town."

"And people like us."

"Right. People doing business with the owner."

She moved away from him slightly and faced him. "Is that what we're doing? Going into business with this man?"

"We'll see, honey. Have to hear what he's going to say first. Meanwhile we can enjoy—"

A two-tone bell ring interrupted him. He looked through the peephole and saw a man in a suit. Granger opened the door.

"Governor, I'm Mark Elliot," said the tall man who reminded Granger of George Clooney, "Mr. Logan's executive assistant." He carried a cloth sack in his left hand and offered his right.

Granger shook it. "Come in."

Elliot came into the foyer. Tammy stepped up to join them, and Granger introduced her.

"Nice to meet you both. I hope your accommodations are satisfactory."

"Very nice," Tammy said.

Elliot put the sack on the counter, its contents clinking as he did so. "Some chips to use at the gaming tables, if you're so inclined. Compliments of the house."

"Thank you," Granger said.

Elliot pulled a leather, wallet-like case from an inside jacket pocket and flipped it open. On each side, plastic cards nestled in transparent pockets. He pointed to one bearing a gold seal in which the letters *WL* were printed in black. "This card will be honored at all of our shops and restaurants. No signature will be required, and any applicable gratuity will be included. It's coded for the room, but you will not receive a bill." He smiled. "If you misplace it, please let us know right away."

Granger smiled back. "I understand."

"The card will also grant you entrance to the Limelight Room, where we have Michael Bublé as the headliner this week."

"Oh," Tammy said, "I like him."

"The other card is for the penthouse elevator, located next to the bank of main elevators off the lobby." He handed the case to Granger. "Mr. Logan would like to meet with you this evening in the penthouse at eight. It will give you time to catch the Limelight Room entertainment later."

"Can my wife accompany me to the meeting?"

"I'm sorry, Governor. Mr. Logan wants it to be a private conversation. But he invites both of you to be his guests for breakfast in his suite tomorrow morning. Las Vegas is a town that never sleeps, and I'm sure you two will want to sample its nightlife. Shall we say breakfast at nine-thirty?"

"That would be fine."

"Enjoy your stay, Governor. Mrs. Granger." He turned quickly and left.

"We're really getting the *carte blanche* treatment," Tammy said. "Just like he promised."

"Well, he can afford it. I think I know what he wants, so this could be just the beginning, sweetheart."

"Better than this?" She gestured with a sweeping motion, indicating the lavish suite. "I can't imagine."

"That's because you've never been on Air Force One."

As soon as Granger stepped off the penthouse elevator, a very large man—bigger than Kretchman, he quickly assessed—greeted him. Sporting a crew cut and dressed in a black suit that had to be custom-tailored, the man carried what looked like one of those metal detectors used by TSA officials at the airport.

"Excuse me, Governor." The giant held up his hand. "Routine security." He ran the wand up and down Granger's body. Apparently satisfied, he stepped aside. "Mr. Logan is expecting you. It's the door at the end of the hall. Go right in."

"Thanks." Granger walked on plush mauve carpet to the door, turned the knob, and stepped into the suite.

A man with short-cropped, jet-black hair and wearing a navy blue pinstripe rose from an armchair and approached his guest. "Welcome to my home away from home, Governor. I'm Wendell Logan." He held out his hand.

Granger shook it, experiencing the firm grip of the man he knew to be in his mid-seventies, hair color notwithstanding. The tycoon was in very good shape for his age.

Logan led him into the living room. "Can I get you something to drink?"

Eyeing the tumbler of amber liquid sitting on a lamp table next to Logan's chair, Granger said, "Whatever you're having will be fine."

"Mark," Logan called out, "fix the governor a Wild Turkey, please."

The George Clooney lookalike emerged from another room and went to a bar set against the far wall.

"Have a seat, Governor." Logan gestured at a chair matching his own and separated from it by five or six feet. It, too, had an end table perched next to it.

The two men sat. Elliot handed Granger the drink.

"You've met Mark Elliot, of course," Logan said.

Granger smiled. "Yes."

The assistant sat in a chair set apart and at a right angle from the cozy arrangement of the other two and crossed his legs.

"I hope you don't mind if Mark is present during our discussion, Governor. He's my right-hand man and needs to be aware of all my operations. He has my full confidence."

"No problem."

"Good. I don't want to keep you from your lovely wife any longer than necessary, so I'll get right to the point: the answer to your question last week of why I've offered to fund your campaign." Logan sipped his drink then set the glass on the table. "Now that we've met, I'd prefer continuing on a first-name basis. May I call you Alan?"

"Certainly."

"And I'm Wendell. I'll be honest, Alan. From a business standpoint, I don't really care who the governor of Pennsylvania is. I've got interests in your state, but mostly media operations. Not materially affected by regulations your legislature might impose."

Granger focused on the glass he held in his lap as he swirled the cubes. He looked up with eyebrows raised. "Then why this meeting?"

"Your re-election is important to your political future, and *that* is what I'm interested in."

Here it comes. "I'm listening."

"You're an intelligent man. Surely it has occurred to you that a man who controls an international corporation would have business concerns that go beyond the boundaries of the Keystone State."

Yes! "I did wonder about that, Wendell." Granger took a sip.

"Naturally. Tell me, Alan, have you ever considered holding a higher political office?" Logan peered at him over the rim of his glass.

"A United States senator could be considered a step up, at least at the national level."

Logan leaned forward, arms on his knees. "Don't be coy with me. You don't need to win re-election to run for the Senate. Senator McGinn is retiring in two years. I'm sure your party would consider you a good candidate to fill his position if you were available. I'm talking about the presidency, as if you didn't know." He sat back, his dark eyes boring into Granger, demanding a reaction.

Though Logan had just confirmed Granger's hunch, he tried not to let his excitement show. "In 2024?"

The billionaire laughed, defusing the tense moment. "So you *have* thought about it! No, not in six years. I'm still in good health, but by then I'll be in my eighties. I can't afford to waste that much time. It's the next presidential election I'm shooting for. And to be a part of that, you have to be in your second term as governor, not someone who got defeated trying to be the chief executive of just one state."

"A replay of Bush Forty-three?"

Logan smiled. "Yes, a similar situation. Are you interested in the proposal?"

The possibility that excited Granger when the mogul had called him eight days earlier was now a real scenario. That he could actually achieve his inchoate dream exhilarated him.

But don't act like a kid in a candy factory. Stay calm, reasoned. "I'm a politician, Wendell. Politicians at any level are, by nature, ambitious." He grinned at his host. "The old saying that every U.S. senator looking in a mirror sees a potential president applies to governors, too. Actually, especially governors, who have a much better track record in this regard than senators. The highest office in the land would be the ultimate prize, one obviously worth aspiring to."

"And one I can help you achieve."

Granger squinted his eyes. "Okay, you've explained your motivation for supporting my campaign. You want me to use my re-election as a springboard to take a shot at the presidency, and you'll support that effort financially. But there remains an unanswered question. And if I get a bullshit response from you, we're done here. Why?"

Logan slapped his knee and laughed. "Ha! I like your style!" He turned to Elliot. "Didn't I tell you?"

Logan's assistant smiled slightly.

"No bullshit from me," Logan continued. "Not *my* style. Here's the long and the short of it. I want my man in the White House, simple as that. A president who will protect my interests. Based on my research, you could be that man. I won't care what else you do as president, how you run your administration, but when it comes to what's good for my enterprises, you will support it, including having nominations for members of your cabinet meet with my approval. That is the quid pro quo."

Just what I expected. Granger sat back, calmly crossed his legs. "I admire your optimism, but there's still that pesky re-election I'd have to win first. As you say, a necessary first step in your goal."

Logan stared at his guest for a few seconds before responding. "I can guarantee you will win."

"Guarantee? That's quite a claim." Granger shook his head. "You have money, sure—a lot of it—but so does my opponent. I could still lose."

Logan sat back in his chair, looking smug. "That would be possible if Marshall remained a viable candidate, true. But I have it on excellent authority that Representative Marshall will be dropping out of the race very soon."

Granger's jaw dropped slightly. *Marshall quitting? Why?* "How do you know this?"

"I know a lot of things, Alan." Logan waved a dismissive hand in the air. "It will happen, and let's leave it at that. I'm sure Marshall will provide an explanation for his withdrawal when he makes the announcement."

Granger couldn't respond for a few moments as the startling news sunk in. "This is certainly unexpected, to put it mildly. I don't know what to say."

"Say you agree to my proposal. Mark and your man, Bascomb, will work out the details. But with Marshall out of the picture, my contribution won't have to be as large as it otherwise would have been. It's after your re-election, when we begin planning for 2020, that my financial support will be crucial. Do you see any problems with the deal?"

"It's a lot to think about." *Is it ever!*

"Of course. But keep this in mind while deciding: you have nothing to lose. If, after you are re-elected, you then change your mind about running for the White House, that is the risk *I* take. Think about it tonight and give me your answer in the morning."

"Wendell, I'd be lying if I said I wasn't excited about the proposal. As you say, I don't see a downside for me. But I *will* consider it tonight."

"All right, then." Logan rubbed his hands together. "There is just one more issue remaining before you leave."

Uh-oh. Like Detective Columbo in that TV series back in the day, it appeared Logan had a parting zinger. Granger chuckled to disguise his sudden unease. "I knew it was too good to be true."

Logan gave a smile probably meant to be reassuring but which Granger took as predatory. "Alan, I do need to protect my investment. That's why I do extensive research before beginning a new venture. I don't like surprises, and when I find out an associate has held back important information from me... well, we part ways immediately. With Marshall no longer a factor, you will have a clear path to victory. But a presidential run is a quantum leap from a governor's race. You'll be on the national stage like never before, subject to intense scrutiny. Investigative reporters working for newspapers I don't control will put your life under a microscope. Count on it. So tell me. Do you have any skeletons in your closet?"

"Enjoy the show, Governor. I'll see you in the morning." Logan closed the door and came back into the room, taking off his suit jacket. He draped it over the back of a chair. "Remember what I said about everybody having something to hide?" he said to Elliot, who stood behind the bar.

"That's some story. I'm surprised he told it to you." Elliot poured himself a scotch.

"He had to though, didn't he? I implied the deal would be off if he held back on me and I found out about it. And with a blackmailer out there, the secret could come out at any time." Logan sat on a barstool and loosened his tie. "Hand me a beer, will you?"

Elliot came up with a bottle of Heineken from the mini-fridge and gave it to his boss.

"So what do you think, Mark?"

"Could've been worse. No suggestion of a wandering eye. His marriage seems strong, so no bimbo eruptions on the horizon are likely, and he doesn't do drugs." He winked. "Unlike someone else we know. Granger seems to be a straight shooter, no vices. Bottom line, he's got just that one thing against him, when he was in high school."

Logan took a long pull from the beer bottle. "Yeah, just that one thing. That other people know about. And one of them has already blackmailed him over it."

"The others, Granger's buddies, they were accomplices, so we're good there. The nurse is not about to own up to being a blackmailer, and there's a recording of it, according to Granger."

"But she's got a personal connection to the incident. If she... what's her name again?"

Elliot pulled out a notepad from his suit jacket. "Donovan. Cathy Donovan."

"If this Donovan sees Granger running for president... I don't know, Mark. She might decide to get righteous and spill the beans, a possible prosecution for extortion be damned. She or her boyfriend, who was the kid actually involved in the accident, could gum up the works."

"Thinking about withdrawing your offer?"

Logan got off the stool and started pacing. "He's perfect in every other way. Obviously malleable, since he had no objections to my prerequisites. His basic principles are in line with ours anyway, so he can rationalize my calling the shots as irrelevant. And now we've got something on him to ensure he toes the line in case power goes to his head and he thinks he can renege."

"Want me to put Charley Blaisdell on it? He can get more dope on the couple."

Logan's calculations had already put him past an investigation and into a more active intervention. With what he was contemplating, he didn't want a licensed PI in the loop. "No, let's keep it between us for now. We know who they are, where they live."

"So we're still good?"

"Let's see what Granger says in the morning. Too late to start all over again. It's Granger or nobody. If he decides to come onboard, I'm willing to take the chance. And then it will be time for Bloomberg to drop the bomb on Marshall."

As Logan lay in bed, he went over what he had to do to ensure the wild card in Boston wouldn't torpedo his plan. He'd lied to Mark about being willing to take the gamble the blackmailer wouldn't surface again. He'd invested too much time, effort, and money to take such a chance. He had to *guarantee* it wouldn't happen. And there was only one way to accomplish that.

As he'd built his empire, he'd come across a few nefarious characters. No, that was too euphemistic. They were criminals, violent men whose only qualms against murder involved the likelihood of being caught.

He'd used such a man in the past to eliminate a rival. But the competitor employed illegal tactics against him, so Logan felt no guilt over his demise.

He had to deal with the problem of the Boston couple. They were extortionists, after all. Which made them criminals, too. Chances were they hadn't told anybody else about what they knew, because then the question would arise of what they were going to do about it. But he'd have to find that out. And the wives of Granger's buddies could be trouble in the event of a nasty divorce. He'd have to monitor that as well.

Any deaths required would be for the greater good. His own

interests were at stake, true, but unfettered industry was good for the country. Moguls like Vanderbilt, Rockefeller, and Morgan were out for themselves, of course, but their ruthless drives to accumulate immense wealth were responsible for making the United States the envy of the world. The words of the Gordon Gekko character in the movie *Wall Street* came to mind: "Greed is good."

Calvin Coolidge had it right. He smiled. *The business of America is business. And my business will involve a partnership with America's chief executive. That gives me the right to ensure* it *isn't disrupted.*

Satisfied he had no moral dilemma, he banished those thoughts from his consciousness and drifted peacefully into sleep.

CHAPTER 16

The next day

THE FLIGHT ATTENDANT, WEARING A navy blue skirt and a matching blazer with the *WL* logo on the breast pocket, handed the Grangers glasses of chardonnay. "If you need anything," she said with a smile, "I'll be back there." She gestured toward the rear of the Gulfstream.

"Thank you." *Logan sure doesn't skimp on the amenities. But then he wouldn't have to, would he?* The thought of having that much money... well, Granger couldn't get his mind around it.

The attendant left them alone in their side-by-side soft leather seats. They were the plane's only passengers.

"No second thoughts, Alan?" Tammy asked.

Granger peered through the window at the isolated cloud puffs passing beneath them. "I don't see a downside, honey."

"But if Marshall drops out, you won't really need Logan."

"Yes, that's true. Not for *this* election. But if I'm going to try for the presidency, I'll have a ready-made financial base."

"You have other donors. Once you're in your second term and establish... what do they call it? An exploratory committee? The money will come in."

Granger turned away from the window. "Maybe so. But Logan would make funding a certainty."

She frowned.

"What's wrong, Tammy?"

"I don't trust that man. With his money he could... well, do anything. It wouldn't surprise me if he paid Marshall to quit. If you do something he doesn't like, who knows what would happen? What if he changes his mind and decides to support another candidate? Then what would you do? You're putting all your eggs in one basket."

Granger took a sip of wine. "You have a good point. I've thought of that. But he wants what I want for the country. He chose me because we think alike, and he knows I have no problems with his agenda. And as he said, he's the one taking the risk. I could change *my* mind. Worst-case scenario, he reneges on the deal for whatever reason, cuts off the cash. By then I'll be on my way, and other donors will want to jump on board the train. But if not, what have I really lost? A dream that was improbable to begin with? I go back to the firm and make a fortune instead?" He grinned. "Gee, what a terrible alternative."

She sipped from her glass, still frowning. "Okay. You're probably right. It's just that Logan gives me the creeps. So smooth, so sure of himself."

Granger chuckled. "Like me, you mean?"

She punched him in the shoulder, causing him to spill a bit of wine on his lap. "You know what I mean. And there's something else. He knows about your... secret."

"Honey"—he blotted the spill with his napkin—"Logan's not about to reveal that. And it didn't appear to bother him much. My take was he didn't think it was a problem. He's committing a lot of money, and the deal is still going forward, right?"

"It seems so."

"Relax. We're good."

An hour later, with the Rockies behind them, the clouds had disappeared, and the geometric farm patterns of America's heartland filled the view from Granger's window.

"Alan?"

"Yes?"

"Logan knows the names of that nurse and her boyfriend, right?"

"Yeah, why?"

"Just wondering."

Same day
Santa Fe, New Mexico

After making love with Emily Covington, Luke Elliot lay on his left side, supporting his head with his hand, and smiled at her. "Now that's how I like to start the day."

She smiled back at him. "Mmm. Me too." She stretched her arms, clasped her hands behind her head, and looked at the ceiling.

Elliot ran a fingertip from the hollow of her throat down between her breasts, ending at her navel. He kissed that spot, gently pushing it inward. Emily wiggled her hips in response.

He gazed across her through the bedroom window and saw Tetilla Peak highlighted by the rays of the morning sun. Smiling, he turned to look at the same image hanging on the wall above his dresser, the mountain captured on canvas by his lover's talented brush strokes. "Will you be painting today?" he asked.

"Maybe later. I have a customer coming into the gallery this morning. And George is on vacation, so I have to mind the store."

"I'll make the coffee." He climbed out of bed, picked up his boxer shorts from the floor, and slipped them on. When she started to get up, he held up his hand. "Stay there, darlin'. I'll bring you your coffee. And how about I rustle us up some breakfast? Bacon and eggs sound good?"

"Come here." She crooked a finger at him.

"What?" Elliot put his hands on his side of the bed and leaned over, bringing his face near hers.

"Are you being this sweet because you'll be going out of town again?"

He stepped back, slapped his hands on his chest, and gave her a look of mock dismay. "Baby, you hurt me. I need a reason to be nice to you?"

"Ha! You're avoiding the question."

"No, Miss Prosecutor, I currently have no plans to leave hearth and home."

"You don't take these trips because you need breaks from me, do you?" She pouted. "You never ask me to go with you."

"Emily, honey, I've got a business to run. Like you do. But mine requires that I keep up with the latest in firearms, pick up specialized guns I need for the shop. These trips aren't vacations." *They sure aren't.* He flashed a smile. "Besides, with me here, you don't get much painting done."

She rolled over, got up on her elbows, and nestled her chin in her hands. "I wonder why."

"Let me get that coffee going." He started for the bedroom door then came back to the bed. "I love you, sweetheart." He bent to kiss her. "Whenever I'm away, I can't wait to see you again." He cupped a breast, giving it a slight squeeze. "And to feel you." He winked and stood up. "Now for that breakfast."

"I'll help you." She groped over the edge of the bed for her nightie.

As he waited for the English muffins to pop up in the toaster, Elliot thought about what he had told Emily. It wasn't a complete lie, since he hadn't committed yet, but he could be leaving again soon. The latest e-mail and follow-up phone calls proposed an assignment he was leaning toward accepting. It would be tricky, though. He'd have to make it look like an accident because of the circumstances. "Muffins are ready," he announced to Emily standing at the range.

"So are the eggs. Let's eat."

———— ❖ ————

The next day
Washington, DC

The Sound Bites delicatessen was a popular lunch place for the staffs of the nearby K Street lobbying firms and attorney offices. When Arnold Bloomberg, who had asked for the meeting, came through the front door at eleven forty-five, the mixed aromas of spiced meats, onions, and olive oil met him.

He spotted Brent Marshall sitting in the last booth along the right-hand wall of the deli's shotgun layout. He walked up to the booth and slid in across from the congressman. A thick Reuben, its contents threatening to spill out of the sandwich's cut halves, sat on a plate in front of Marshall.

"Thanks for coming on short notice," Bloomberg said.

"Always can find time for my supporters." Marshall smiled. "You better get your order in. This place will get crazy soon."

Bloomberg didn't return the smile. "Maybe later. I want to get this out of the way first."

"What? Is there a problem?" Marshall now looked worried.

Bloomberg folded his hands together on the table edge. "Huge problem, Brent. When I learned of it, well… shock would pretty much describe my reaction."

"Learned what?" Marshall's eyebrows arched over his wide eyes.

"I'm amazed they kept this quiet at all, let alone for as long as they did." Bloomberg fixed Marshall with an unblinking gaze. "Your adventure at a Las Vegas hotel a few years ago."

"Oh." Marshall looked down at his sandwich, shook his head, and sighed. "The Phoenix."

"Yes."

The congressman slumped back on the vinyl bench seat. "They said they would take care of it, that the publicity would hurt the image of their new hotel. What's done is done, they said. No point in making it public."

"You remember the night manager, Sam Ballantine?"

Marshall looked at the empty booth behind him before replying. "Ballantine. Oh, yeah. I remember him, all right. He's the one who told me the woman was well known around the Strip. A hooker with no family. She could just disappear and no one would miss her."

"And you were okay with that?"

"Arnie, I panicked. I'd been drinking and got carried away. I knew she was a prostitute. But like a classy call girl, I thought. You know, so you can pretend she's a date? I met her in the hotel casino at a blackjack table. After a few drinks, we ended up in my room. We were laughing, having a good time. So when she brought out the cocaine, it just seemed to go along with the party atmosphere. What the hell? I snorted some. It was the first and only time in my life." He paused, apparently waiting for Bloomberg's reaction.

Bloomberg didn't change his deadpan expression. "Go on."

"So she takes off her blouse—I already knew she wasn't wearing a bra—and sits on the edge of the bed. While I'm staring at her tits, she reaches into her purse and pulls out a syringe. 'Same stuff,' she said. But she liked it that way because it gave her a bigger rush. Before I knew what was happening, she was injecting the shit in her arm."

"And then she OD'd," Bloomberg said in a matter-of-fact tone.

"Oh, man." Marshall massaged his forehead. "I can't get that scene out of my mind. She gets this big smile on her face and flops back on the bed. I'm trying to get out of my pants as quick as I can, and then I see she's passed out. Or so I thought."

"When you realized she wasn't just sleeping, you called 9-1-1?"

"No." Marshall shook his head slowly. "I called the front desk, asked for the manager. Told him the situation. I assumed he'd make the call. It was his hotel. But I did do CPR."

"Good. At least you tried."

"Ballantine came to the room. 'Help is on the way,' he said. Ten minutes later, this other guy shows up. Don't know his name, but I remember he looked a little like George Clooney. By this time, it was obvious she wasn't going to make it." Marshall used a napkin to wipe his hands then balled it up tightly in his fist. "These guys took charge, said they would handle everything."

"But you knew that wasn't right."

"Arnie, they were giving me a way out. I had a dead hooker in my room, alcohol and cocaine in my system. One night of bad judgment could destroy my career. They said they would clean up the mess and I shouldn't worry about it. So I went along. They sent me down to the coffee shop to sober up."

Bloomberg stared at the congressman for a moment, saw the fear in his eyes, then pursed his lips. "I understand."

"But how did you hear about it? Did Ballantine blab?"

"No, he was a company man. Still is, in fact. But he had a wife. Her, he told. And now his wife is the ex-Mrs. Ballantine and currently involved with the biggest contributor to Together for Tomorrow. Got the picture?"

"Jesus."

"Well, Jesus would forgive you, but this guy won't. Family values are his thing. He liked your working class hero campaign, but the incident with the hooker and the drugs crossed his line. He informed me that either we stop supporting you, or he'll look elsewhere for a cause to back."

Marshall picked up one end of the pickle on his plate and stared at it as if scrutinizing it for impurities, then let it fall back next to the Reuben. "Nothing you can do?"

"Look, Brent, I'm on your side. I'm the one who suggested we get behind your campaign in the beginning. But I'm not the boss. I have a job only as long as the PAC is viable. If we lose this guy's contributions, we might as well fold up shop. Sorry, man, but I have no choice. Have to cut you loose."

Marshall stared at his plate again. "No hard feelings, Arnie. I appreciate what you've done." He looked up and smiled. "And you've made me a candidate who could win. I'll just have to carry on without you now."

Bloomberg shook his head. "Won't work, Brent. If you want to keep this buried, you have to drop out. That's the deal. Daddy Warbucks doesn't give a shit if you're a congressman, but if you stay in the governor's race, he'll make what happened in Vegas public. Seems he has a daughter and granddaughter who live in Wilkes-Barre, and he couldn't abide having them living in a state run by a man who—this is how he put it—'has such a depraved character.'"

"I see. So it's up to me, then. Whether or not to take the chance some big shot's story will be believed." Marshall gave him an inquiring look, as if he wanted confirmation his campaign could still be salvaged.

"And put your House seat in jeopardy, too?"

"My constituents won't take the word of some Sin City Donald Trump."

"Well, that's your call. But consider this before you make a decision." He squinted. "Photos of the scene were taken."

"What?"

"You didn't know that, right?"

"Hell, no!"

"Must have been when you were down in the coffee shop. Don't know what the motivation was, but Ballantine's wife got hold of them."

Marshall closed his eyes and groaned.

"Sure," Bloomberg went on, "you can claim they're bogus, but can you imagine what the media would do with this? I've seen them. Not pretty. And it would be a cinch to discover you were with the whore in the casino—they have cameras all over the place—and that you were staying in that hotel room. It's over, Brent. Take your lumps and go back to being the best damned Representative for your district you can be. You've convinced me you're basically a decent sort and just made a terrible mistake. No one will find out about that indiscretion from employees of the Phoenix or me. And the fat cat donor doesn't want to get involved in the tawdry publicity if he can help it."

Marshall didn't answer but stared into space, jaw clenched. Finally, as he gazed at nothing in particular, he said, "What's the reason?"

"Huh?"

Marshall turned back to him. "I can't just quit. I need a reason. What should I say?"

Bloomberg shrugged. "Personal matter. Could be anything. You don't have to specify. Happens all the time. But spending more time with your family won't cut it, since you're not married. And you're going to keep your job. Medical stuff usually works, and there's the doctor-patient confidentiality thing. Possible heart problem, cancer scare, whatever. Be as vague as you can. Go to the hospital for tests. Then announce before the congressional election that you've been given a clean bill of health. And when the reporters ask, you can tell them you haven't ruled out another run for governor in four years."

Marshall stared at him for a few seconds before climbing out of the booth. "Sounds like you've got everything figured out."

Bloomberg ascribed to the old saw George Burns made famous in his stand-up routine: "Sincerity is everything. If you can fake that, you've got it made."

"Brent, I started this because I believed in you. Still do. I feel terrible about this."

"Yeah, well, thanks for the memories. It was fun for a while."

"You forgot your sandwich."

"I've lost my appetite. A double Scotch is more my speed right now. Good-bye, Arnie."

"Take care, Brent," Bloomberg said to the back of the departing congressman. He looked across the table at the Reuben, still untouched, and slid the plate in front of him. Smiling, he lifted one half of the monster sandwich and took a bite.

CHAPTER 17

Two days later
Philadelphia

AT ELEVEN THIRTY A.M., BRENT Marshall appeared from the Fifth Street side of Independence Hall, accompanied by his chief of staff. A crowd of newspaper and television reporters and curious onlookers had gathered in response to the news barely two hours earlier that Congressman Marshall would make an important announcement at this time. After conferring with Clark Munson for a moment, Marshall stepped to the microphone. "Thank you for coming. I have a brief statement to make, after which I will not take any questions."

The reporter for WCAU glanced at his cameraman, who met his surprised expression with a shrug and continued filming.

"It has been my honor to be the Democratic Party's candidate for governor of Pennsylvania. In my travels across the state, I have been moved by the overwhelming numbers of my fellow citizens who want to bring change to Harrisburg, and I have been encouraged and humbled by their support of me in this effort." He gestured behind him. "Independence Hall stands as a symbol of the freedom on which this great nation has been built. It is here, in Philadelphia, in this iconic building, where the principles of our liberty were established. So I decided here would be an appropriate place to announce my candidacy to be your governor. It is fitting, then, that I return to this site to announce that I am ending that campaign."

Marshall let the expected outburst from the audience continue for several seconds before raising his hand. "A circumstance beyond my control has brought me to this painful decision. It is a personal matter, and I will not elaborate on it. Suffice it to say that this development would not allow me even to continue an active campaign, let alone give my all as governor, should the voters elect me to that office, and Pennsylvanians deserve no less from their chief executive. So with deep regret, I must bring to a close my efforts to become the governor of this wonderful state. Thank you."

Marshall turned away from the microphone and, joined by his chief of staff, walked quickly to their waiting car on Fifth Street as shouting reporters hurried after them.

───────◆◇◆───────

That same day
Melrose, Massachusetts

Cathy and Tim Howard sat at a table with an officer of Tim's bank, completing the paperwork for their joint account. Cathy noted Tim's shocked look when she presented the cashier's check, her contribution to the cause. But Tim held his tongue, not voicing his reaction until they were in his car headed home. "Jeez, Cathy, I didn't know you were rich." He glanced at her, shaking his head in puzzlement. "Over a hundred grand? I had no idea."

"And here I thought that's why you married me." She smiled at him, her false front a tactic to delay however briefly the inevitable, because Tim had a right to know. It might as well be now. "About the money... well, it's complicated." She stared through the windshield at nothing in particular, gathering her thoughts.

"Hey, if you don't want to talk about it, no big deal." He chuckled and gave her a nudge in the shoulder. "As long as you didn't steal it, because it's *our* money now. But you're right. I would have married you a long time ago if I knew." He laughed once more, seemingly unconcerned.

But she knew him. It would bug him even if he didn't bring it up again. But he would eventually.

When she used to complain about the apartment—its small size, its inadequate water heater, the deplorable state of the linoleum in the kitchen, whatever—he would nod, agree, and that would be that. Until the last time she vented about an issue with the place. He told her he was tired of her nagging all the time. He apologized later, and that had undoubtedly increased his nascent interest in the house they ended up buying. But that was his way.

When his father died unexpectedly, Tim had been the calm comforter of his adopted mother right up through the funeral. One week later, Cathy had come home to find Tim crying as he looked at a scrapbook containing pictures of his father and him when Tim was a boy.

Presenting a calm front when confronted with problems, not showing his emotions, and then reveal his true feelings later; that was what Tim did. And that made him hard to read sometimes. She dreaded what she was about to do. "Tim," she began, "I did something I probably shouldn't have, but I thought it was right at the time. I still do, in fact."

He frowned at her. "Are we in some legal trouble here?"

"No, I don't think so. Well, maybe… I'm not really sure."

"Oh, man. What did you do?" He tightened his grip on the steering wheel.

"Remember when I said those boys who killed your mother and abandoned you in the car should pay for what they did?"

"Yeah… Oh, no. Tell me you didn't do that." He looked over at her, eyes wide.

"I made them pay, Tim."

He shook his head and groaned. "Goddamn it, Cathy, that's blackmail! Christ!"

No calm, tacit acceptance this time, obviously. The incubation period for dealing with the issue had only involved nanoseconds. Cathy leaned closer to the door to put more distance between them. "I prefer to call it compensation." She folded her arms across her chest.

"How many times?"

"What?"

"How many times did you hit them up for money?"

"Just once, more than a year ago. It's over and done with." She touched his arm. "You're mad at me."

Tim shook his head again. "Well, yeah! I told you to forget about the whole thing and then you… you did that."

"Tim, they felt guilty. That's why they were willing to pay. Look at it this way. Maybe it helped their consciences to compensate their victim for what they did to him." *Maybe that'll fly.*

"Buy some peace of mind, huh?"

"Something like that. A win-win for all of us."

Her husband blew a gush of air through his lips as he slowed the car for a traffic light. "I still can't believe you would do that!" He glanced at her and returned his gaze to the windshield. "Well, too late now, isn't it? Can't undo it. Shit!"

"Tim, I'm sorry for going behind your back. But they had to pay for what they did."

"Maybe we can give the money back." The light turned green, and Tim drove forward.

"Don't even think about it!"

"Why not?"

"You deserve that money."

"Blood money, you mean." Tim turned the car onto their street.

"What do you call it when someone gets a settlement in a personal injury lawsuit? Blood money? No, it's compensation for damages. And that's what we got. Besides, they could afford it. I told you about the pro football player. Another is a doctor, and get this. The one who drove the car that night is the governor of Pennsylvania!"

They had just pulled into their driveway, and Tim brought the car to an abrupt stop, causing them both to lurch forward in their seat belts. "The governor of Pennsylvania? Oh, shit!"

"What's the matter?" Cathy stared at him, mouth agape.

Tim put the car in park and faced her. It was not anger now but worry—no, fear—in his face. "He's a politician, Cats, and a big one. I was talking with Dr. Tisdale the other day between cases. He's into politics, and he was giving his opinion on possible Republican candidates for president next time around. Governor Granger was on his list."

"So?"

"Don't you see? He has a secret that could ruin a try at the presidency if it got out. And he knows you know about it!"

She reacted to his intense stare with one of her own. "You mean... No, he couldn't possibly—"

"Don't be naïve, Cathy. He's a powerful man. Powerful men can eliminate people who get in their way."

"You're scaring me!"

Tim pressed the remote to open the garage door. "We could be in big trouble, Cats." He drove into the garage and shut off the motor.

"You really think he might come after us?" *He wouldn't, would he?*

Tim groaned. "I don't know, honey. I'm trying to think. You've put us in the big leagues, now. We need some kind of leverage."

"Like what?"

"Who did you make the, uh, blackmail arrangements with?"

"The doctor, I think. He never did identify himself."

"But you got his number?"

"Yeah, from the caller ID."

"He could have been using a throwaway cell phone."

"Jeez, Tim. You're sounding like a mystery writer or something. But it doesn't matter. I know his office phone number."

"Good. Okay, call him. No, I'll call him and say... say what?" He looked at her for help.

"The doctor implied they would come after us if we reneged on the deal. And I believed him. But I didn't think about them changing *their* minds. I hate to say this, but you're starting to convince me."

"We need something that would make it hard for them to move against us. Something that would hurt them if they did." He drummed his fingers on the steering wheel as he looked straight ahead. Then, "I got it! I'll tell him our lawyer has a sealed letter that tells the whole story. That it will be opened if either of us is killed."

"Tim!"

"Sorry, honey. I hope I'm overreacting, but we need to take precautions."

"The only lawyer we have is the one who did the house closing. Who should we get for this?"

Tim opened his door. "I assume you don't want any of this to get out if we can help it, right?"

"Right."

"Well I don't trust lawyers. I don't want one to have that kind of dope on us."

"But you said—"

"Cathy, these guys won't know if we did the letter thing or not. They can't take the chance. It's like putting a security system sign on your front lawn even if there's no system. But it's even better than that. A thief can run if he takes a chance and then gets the alarm. Granger can't take that risk. We'll be okay as soon as I make that call, I promise. Now promise me you won't ever do anything like this again."

"I promise, cross my heart." She made the finger sign on her left breast. "But something like this will never come up—"

"Cathy, I'm serious, okay? A partner should always know what the other partner is doing that could affect them. If you'd leveled with me about this scheme of yours before you went ahead, we wouldn't be in this trouble now."

"What can I say? When you're right, you're right." *And he is, damn it.* "Can you forgive me? I was only trying to get what you deserved."

"That's what I'm afraid I *will* get." He ran his fingers through his hair. "Yes, of course I forgive you. I'm just glad I found out about this before it was too late."

———— ✦ ————

The next day
Villanova, Pennsylvania

"Dr. Dawson, I've got a Tim Howard on the line. He says it's personal and urgent."

What the hell? My stomach suddenly lurched south. "Uh, okay, I'll take it." I tried to keep my voice even.

"Line one."

I picked up the phone. "Dr. Dawson," I announced.

"Sorry to bother you at the office, but I tried your cell phone and only got voicemail. This is Tim Howard. I assume you know who I am." The voice sounded much calmer than I felt.

I tried to match it. "The former Tim Favreau?"

"That's right. Look, Doctor, I just learned today of my wife's, er, arrangement with you and the others last year."

He didn't know about it. That's interesting. "So you and Cathy are married now."

"As I told her today, I thought it was a stupid thing to do, but what's done is done, and I don't want any reprisals."

"That was the deal, Tim. Silence on your part in exchange for the payment. You're not thinking of reneging, are you? Because if so—"

"Doctor, we're not going to reveal your secret. But it occurred to me that at least one of you guys might have a good reason to make *sure* we don't tell. If you know what I mean."

What's this? "No, I don't. What are you saying?"

"Tell Governor Granger that a sealed letter detailing the incident in Vermont and also the payment you made to keep it quiet is in the hands of our attorney. To be opened in the event Cathy or I end up dead."

Jesus. "You're kidding me, right?"

"I don't sound serious enough to you?"

"Hey, Tim, forget about it, okay? What's done *is* done. As far as I'm concerned, it's ancient history." I took a deep breath. I had the victim of that terrible night on the phone. Whether he was recording this call or not made no difference to me now. I had to get this off my chest, as Tom Webster had done last year. "And let me add this. Self-serving though it may be, it's also the truth. An accident killed your mother. The snow squall came out of nowhere, and we didn't see her car until we were on top of it. Our sin was leaving you to fend for yourself until we could safely call 9-1-1. I was against that, but I went along to save my skin. That's the whole story. My only excuse is that I was an idiot teenager."

Silence for a few seconds. "Yeah, that's what I figured, Doc. When Cathy told me she learned who you all were, I wanted to let it go. I understood the shit you guys found yourselves in and wondered if I might have done the same thing. Cathy, unfortunately, thought otherwise."

"If you're okay with it, then what's the problem? We just want to put this behind us and move on. In fact, we were concerned about you coming after *us*. You certainly don't have to worry about the reverse."

"I think you believe that, and I hope you're right. But I'm not taking any chances. A deterrent works only if the opposition knows about it, so make sure you tell Granger what I said."

"I will."

"Have a nice day." He hung up, and I exhaled slowly. So the blackmailers were worried about what *we* might do to *them*.

Did I play the role of the heavy too well in my conversation with the nurse last year? I couldn't help smiling. For the past year, we feared they would renege on the deal. Now they were the ones running scared. Good for us.

But the "us" included Granger, and Tim's concern about his motivation was logical. *Al couldn't be that ruthless, though, could he?*

I shook my head at the absurdity of such a thought. Of course, he couldn't. But I grabbed my cell phone to call him, anyway. I had told Tim I would, and why take chances?

Granger laughed when I told him what Tim Howard had said. "Really? I'm the one he wanted to make sure you called? I thought Kretchman was supposed to be our enforcer." He laughed again.

"He seems to think you're the one with the most motivation to guarantee their silence."

"You were always good with euphemisms, Jim. You mean 'whack' as in 'kill,' right? Just call me Michael Corleone. Ha! I'm about to unleash my Murder Incorporated killer when I get stymied by the old letter to the lawyer ploy. Rats!" He chuckled.

"Yeah, well, I told him he was worried about nothing. Anyway, I did my duty. So now you know you can't whack them and get away with it."

"Thanks, buddy. You informed me in the nick of time. I told Carmine to keep his cell phone on, so I can now cancel the hit."

I'd had enough of playing the straight man in Granger's comedy routine. "Bye, Al." I disconnected. Granger's sarcastic response *was* funny; I had to admit. And reassuring. No way could he do what the Howard kid feared.

The receptionist buzzed me. "Dr. Dawson, the ER on line two."

My night on call had started early, apparently. "Okay." I sighed and picked up the phone.

CHAPTER 18

June 2018
Boston

As Cathy Howard drove to work the morning after her husband's call to Dr. Dawson, she thought of Tim's wild supposition and concluded he was being too alarmist. *To kill someone over that secret? Too extreme to be plausible. Okay, Granger and the others ponied up the money to keep us quiet, so they were willing to go that far. That makes sense. But resorting to murder?*

Granger *might* become an actual candidate for president. But just because some political-junkie doctor thought it possible didn't make it so. Having witnessed the clown-show debates during the Republican primaries of the last two election cycles, she knew getting nominated was a messy process. Too many variables in play. Anything could happen.

She shook her head at the odds. The governor would have to announce he was running then battle other wannabes for the nomination. Even if he did emerge as his party's candidate, eliminating people who had dirt on him seemed too much of a stretch.

Still, she just couldn't ignore Tim's caution. What he proposed wasn't impossible, after all, just... well, damned unlikely. Better safe than sorry, though. And Tim's solution should eliminate any possibility his dire scenario would come to pass.

Eliminate. There was that word again. She shivered as she turned into the parking garage. She swiped her employee ID card in the slot at the gate then drove up the ramp.

At the third level, an enclosed pedestrian bridge connected the garage to the hospital. Vacant parking spaces there almost never existed, she'd discovered long ago, and she'd stopped looking. Besides, there was less of a chance her new car would get dinged on the sparsely used sixth level. She pulled into a space on the left side and parked.

Cathy grabbed her handbag from the passenger seat and climbed out of the Camry. After closing the door, she hit the lock button on the key fob and then put her keys into her bag. She had just turned to walk up the gentle incline to the elevator when a man wearing a baseball cap walked rapidly toward her, holding his right arm strangely by his side.

"Hi," he said, causing her to stop.

Who's this?

When only ten feet separated them, she heard a shout behind her: "Cathy, wait up!" *Julie.*

Startled by the sudden intrusions, she was about to turn toward her colleague when the man's right hand came up, holding a gun pointed directly at her.

Oh my God! Tim's crazy idea flashed through her mind as her knees went wobbly. *It can't be!* Frantic, Cathy threw her handbag at the man and ran to Julie, expecting a bullet in her back at any moment. Waving her arms, she yelled, "He's got a gun!" When she reached the astonished nurse, she grabbed her arm and pulled her behind a parked SUV.

"What the hell?" Julie crouched next to her.

"That man. He has a gun." Cathy's breaths were shallow and rapid.

"The guy I thought you were talking to?"

"Yes!"

Julie rose to peek through the Escalade's windows, but Cathy grabbed her arm. "Stay down! Don't let him see you."

"He already knows we're here, Cathy. I want to see if he's coming." She looked up the ramp.

Cathy peeked, too. The man looked their way. Her handbag lay in front of him. *My phone!* "Julie, call 9-1-1," she pleaded as he took a step toward them.

As Julie dug into her purse for her phone, a car drove past them and parked in a slot on the right side between the women and the gunman. A large black man in a suit and carrying a briefcase climbed out of his Jaguar. The gunman held his weapon at his right side, out of sight of the new arrival who said something to him Cathy couldn't hear. Then the gunman ran up the ramp, disappearing around the corner. *Thank God!* "He took off." She turned to Julie, who had her phone to her ear.

The black man picked up her handbag and headed to the elevator. She wanted to call out to him but didn't dare, not knowing if the gunman was still lurking around the corner. Her co-worker said things into the phone, but the words didn't find purchase in her brain screaming Tim's ominous hypothesis to her.

Cathy stood by while the detective questioned her co-worker.

"So you didn't get a good look at the man?" the detective asked Julie.

"No, sir. Like I said, I saw someone in front of Cathy. I thought they were talking or something. Then she threw her handbag at him and came running toward me, saying he had a gun, and we ducked behind a car. Then another car came, and he took off."

"Okay, Ms. Springer, you can go. Thanks."

Julie gave Cathy a sympathetic look. "I'll tell Sally you'll be a little late." She headed to the garage elevator.

The cop turned his attention back to Cathy. "Besides the ball cap, what else was the man wearing?"

"Jeans, I think, and a dark T-shirt."

"Would you recognize him if you saw him again?"

"To be honest, Detective, that gun got all my attention. He could have been anybody, for all I know."

"He was white, though, and not a kid?"

"That much I'm sure of. I'd guess he was in his early thirties, but he could be a few years either way."

"You said the gun had a long—"

"Detective Raines?" A uniformed officer approached, carrying Cathy's handbag "The security guy doesn't remember seeing a man in a baseball cap come through the bridge." The officer turned to Cathy. "Is this yours?"

"Yes, thank you." She took it from him.

"A lawyer who came to see a client picked it up and gave it to the security guy, who knew him. So I was able to track him down. He couldn't give me much of a description of our perp, though."

"Okay."

Another police officer emerged from the elevator and walked toward them. "The cashier remembers a man wearing a ball cap going through the exit. But she was taking care of a customer and didn't get any kind of look at him. No drivers fitting the description went through during that time frame that she remembers."

"Thanks…" Raines noted the officer's nametag. "Hixon. So our man was on foot."

"Looks that way. Want us to check all the parked cars?" The officer's tone indicated displeasure at that prospect.

"No. This guy's long gone. You and your partner can take off."

Hixon and the other officer went to their cruiser.

The detective glanced at her hand holding her purse. "You're married?"

"Yes."

"Mrs. Howard," Raines began. The patrol car passed them on its way out. "You said the gun had a long barrel."

"Well, it looked long to me. You know, like maybe it was one of those huge guns Dirty Harry used?"

"A revolver, as opposed to an automatic?"

Cathy shook her head. "Sorry, Detective, but I have no idea. I'm not familiar with guns. And I was pretty shaken up at the time. Any gun would have looked big to me."

"Sure. He didn't say anything, like 'Give me your purse,' or something like that?"

"All he said was 'Hi.' Do you think he was a robber?"

"Do you?"

Do I? Cathy pressed her lips together and looked away for a moment before replying. "Who else could it be?"

The detective arched his eyebrows. "You tell me. Do you know of anyone who might wish you harm enough to ambush you like that?"

"No, of course not! I don't have enemies. Well, not that kind, anyway. I suppose some people might not like me for one reason or another. Only natural. But no men I know of." Her smile hinted at the unstated meaning. *What am I doing? Cool it, girl. Just answer his questions.*

She waited for the next question but received only a silent stare instead. Then she got it. "Uh, Detective, I'm happily married and don't fool around. And I don't have any angry ex-husbands or boyfriends. This... whatever it is, doesn't have anything to do with that."

"So, no problems in your marriage?"

"Like, would Tim want to kill me?" She laughed. "We lived together for two years before getting married earlier this year. Absolutely no problems in our marriage." *Not until yesterday, anyway.*

"What about money issues? Any big debts?"

"A mortgage and a car payment, that's all. We both make decent salaries. No gambling, no loan sharks." She laughed again, knowing it looked inappropriate but unable to control her nervous response. "Covering the waterfront, are we?"

Raines smiled. "Routine questions, Mizz... er, Mrs. Howard. We have to consider the usual motives. But most of the time, the simplest solution is the right one."

"A mugger?" *Was he?*

"Chances are you were just in the wrong place at the wrong time and were almost the victim of a random crime."

"That must be it."

"Thank you for your cooperation, Mrs. Howard."

"I appreciate your thoroughness." She held out her hand.

He shook it and then fished out a business card from a pocket of his sport coat. "Call me"—he handed her the card—"if you can think of anything else about this man."

"Thank you." She smiled and walked toward the elevator.

"Oh, Mrs. Howard," Raines called out.

She stopped and turned. "Yes?"

"Do you always park on this level of the garage?"

"Pretty much."

"You might think about changing that routine."

"Already have, Detective."

———— ✦ ————

Cathy called Tim as soon as she entered the pedestrian bridge but only got his voicemail. *Damn it! He must be in the OR.* She left a message to call her before he left the hospital across town. He knew to call the nurses' station to get her, since she couldn't use her personal phone while working.

Two hours later, she had just gotten one of her patients settled after he had returned from a CT scan, when her pager buzzed. *Tim?* When she hurried to the nurses' station, the unit secretary confirmed her hope. "Your husband called. He's on fourteen."

"Thanks." Cathy went to a vacant carrel used to dictate medical records, picked up the phone, and pushed the extension button. "Tim!" she said.

"What's up, Cats?"

"A man pointed a gun at me in the parking garage this morning!"

"What?" he shouted. "Are you all right?"

"Yeah. He ran when he saw Julie. The police came."

"Wow, honey! Was it a holdup?"

"That's what the detective thought. I think. But he asked me a bunch of questions about possible enemies, and about us and our marriage."

"Jeez. You didn't say anything about... you know."

"Absolutely not. I'd been thinking about what you said, so when I saw that gun... well, I thought you might have been right, after all. But like the detective said, it was probably just a robbery attempt." She lowered her voice. "You don't think it's connected to Granger, do you?"

"It better not be! That fucking doctor said he'd put the word out."

"Maybe he didn't get around to it in time."

"Well, I'm calling him again, find out if he talked to the governor like he said he would."

"Okay, but what else should we do now? The thought of going into the garage again after work scares me."

"Sure, honey. Look, I'm not on call and I have only one more case today. I'll meet you at the hospital end of the garage bridge when you get off work. I'll take you to your car and then follow you home. By then I'll have talked to Dawson again, hopefully, and will have a better idea of what's going on. Chances are it was just a robbery."

"I'm so sorry, Tim. If I hadn't... done that, we wouldn't be in this mess."

"Relax, Cats. We'll be okay. Even if those guys were responsible for what happened today, there must have been a screw-up somewhere along the line. They aren't crazy."

"Maybe we should really do that letter thing."

"Cathy, think about it. How would that help us? It's supposed to be a deterrent, only to be used if, well, you know. Then it's too late for us, of course. And they couldn't possibly know there isn't any letter. So either Granger doesn't care about the letter, which doesn't make sense, or he's still in the dark about it. Or the man today was just a creep out to mug you, and that's the most likely."

Over the connection, Cathy heard a beeper going off.

"Gotta go, Cats. I'll see you this afternoon. Don't worry."

"I'll try not to."

"This is getting annoying, Jimbo," Granger said when I called him from the office to relate the latest from Boston. "What do I have to do to convince these paranoid blackmailers I'm not out to get them? It's ridiculous!"

"A gunman did confront the nurse today, Al. I can understand the paranoia."

"Coincidence. A mugger in a big-city parking garage. Not exactly unheard of. Or, she pissed off somebody else. Who knows? It wasn't my doing, Jim. End of story. Besides, you and Crush wouldn't let me get away with murder, now would you? Sure, we're good friends, old teammates, but I can't imagine you wouldn't rat me out to the cops."

I chuckled. "You've got a point there."

"I'm a little offended you'd even think it's possible, buddy. Okay, I panicked twenty years ago. But it was an accident. I didn't kill that woman intentionally. And I'll clue you in on a secret if you promise not to tell."

"What's that?"

"I haven't murdered anyone in my entire life. Now what do you think of that? Pretty amazing, huh?"

"Al, I'm the go-between here. It's not what I think that matters."

"No?"

"I believe you, man."

"Thank God for that, anyway. And I still don't get why he's singled me out as the bad guy. Why not you or Bob?"

"You still thinking of running for president?"

Silence for a moment. "Maybe."

"So you've got more at stake now, Al, and that's why Tim is worried about you. He's heard the rumors."

"Look, give me his number. Let's cut out this middleman shit. I'll set that asshole straight."

Granger's emphatic denial was believable. He'd convinced me. Whatever else I thought of his egocentric maneuvers, I couldn't seriously entertain he'd arrange a contract killing. But then an idea invaded my thoughts to shake up that conclusion.

"Jim? Still there?"

"I was just thinking. Who have you told about that... incident?"

Dead air again. Then, "Tammy knows, obviously." He snickered. "What, you think she could be standing by her man a little too aggressively?"

"How about your staff, your political people?"

"Ah, I see where you're headed. My people *are* loyal, thank goodness. But for any of them to take such drastic action on my behalf, without my knowledge, would be beyond belief."

"Not out of the question, though."

Granger sighed. "But they'd have to know about the secret, Jim. And they don't!"

"Okay."

"So we're good here?"

"Yup."

"Fine. Now give me that number so I can reassure that Massachusetts scaredy-cat."

———— ◦◦◦ ————

After the call ended, Granger stared at the phone number Dawson had given him. He would call Tim Howard and put an end to this foolishness.

But will I be telling him the complete truth? When Dawson asked him whom he had told about the secret, that evening in Logan's suite at the Phoenix came to him in a rush. Billionaire Logan, who meant to install his man in the White House and had the power to overcome any obstacles on the way to that goal. And he knew about the blackmail. Somehow, Logan had orchestrated the end of Marshall's campaign. *Perhaps Tammy was right; Logan paid my opponent off. But what if Marshall hadn't gone along, had even threatened to expose the bribe? Would he be alive today? Jesus!*

The temperature in the room seemed to drop a few degrees as Granger sat back in his desk chair, analyzing the shocking hypothetical, searching as a lawyer would for arguments against it. His own life experience did not prepare him to accept the scenario as realistic. Courtroom battles to sway juries, political campaigns to win over voters, including downright shady tactics to do so—he knew those strategies. But considering human lives expendable because they stood in the way of an important goal—that wasn't part of his world.

Whoa there! Tim Howard's paranoia must be contagious! Granger shook his head, upset he allowed himself to get so carried away. *First the blackmailer, then my buddy Jim, and now I've been caught up in this fantasy.*

"Now don't think of a red-faced monkey," his father used to say and then laughed, making the point that an image in the mind couldn't be ignored once considered. And he had to confront the image of Logan, Zeus-like, directing human behavior from his throne high atop the Phoenix, his Mt. Olympus, in order to banish it from his thoughts. Before calling the Howard kid, he had to put his own mind at ease.

He picked up his phone.

CHAPTER 19

Las Vegas

"WHAT CAN I DO FOR you, Governor?" Mark Elliot said to Granger over the phone.

"I need to speak with Mr. Logan about a matter that's come up. He's not returning my calls."

"He's been under the weather lately." *And not interested in being pestered by a worrywart candidate.* "Anything I can help you with?"

"I'm not sure. Uh, well, you already know about those Boston blackmailers, so I guess you can pass this along to your boss."

"They haven't hit you up again, have they?" Elliot's interest picked up a notch.

"Not exactly, but they contacted me through an intermediary—my friend, Dr. Dawson. You remember, he was involved with me in the extortion."

"What did they want?"

"They have the idea I'd like to see them dead."

Why now? Puzzled, Elliot chuckled. "And you don't?"

"Well, that *would* be convenient, but seriously, they seem to think I want to have them *killed.*"

What's he talking about? "Because?"

"They've concluded that being a presidential candidate would give me the motivation to ensure that story never saw the light of day."

That makes sense, but only if they knew about the plan. "I see. Let me assure you, nothing about that campaign has been leaked by us."

"Not on my end, either. The political shows have speculated about it, but that's beside the point. It would become public knowledge eventually."

Elliot checked his watch. He had a meeting with the hotel staff shortly, and this call seemed to be going nowhere. "I'm afraid I don't understand, Governor. How does Mr. Logan figure in this?"

"That's what I'd like to know. I haven't done anything to threaten them in any way. Yet they're scared enough to take a precaution—a letter to an attorney laying out the whole story, to be opened if any harm comes their way."

"That's understandable from a blackmailer's standpoint, I suppose. It *is* a risky enterprise."

"Let's cut to the chase, Mark. I'm not the only one with a stake in my becoming president. Wendell approached *me*, remember?"

Ah, so that's where he's going. "Come now, Alan. Are you suggesting we might threaten these people?"

"Well, I—"

"Look, I'm sorry they're pestering you, but it's really their problem, isn't it? Let 'em be afraid of you. So what? Stop taking their calls."

"That's what I thought at first, too. Even joked about it with Jim Dawson when he told me. But the situation has changed, making that letter a big problem for me, and for your boss. Someone threatened the nurse today with a gun."

Elliot sat up straighter in his chair. "Tell me about it."

Granger did.

"So it could have been a stickup attempt," Elliot said, positing what he hoped was the case.

"Yes. But the reason I called is to apprise you of that letter. I know about it, and now so do you."

Elliot laughed. "Because you think we might have sent an assassin to Boston?"

"I'm not accusing anyone. I'm sure it was just a coincidence. I just want to make sure we're on the same page here, that's all. You *will* tell Mr. Logan about this, right?"

"I tell him everything, Alan."

"Good. I feel better now that you know what I do."

"You did the right thing. Partners should confide in each other."

"I agree." Granger paused a beat. "Thanks for putting up with my concern."

"Always ready to listen, whatever the issue, Governor. We're in this together, after all." *We're in this together*, Elliot mused after hanging up. And Granger had just called into question what "this" might entail. He rose from his chair, stepped to the window, and gazed idly out at the glitzy panorama that was Las Vegas. Elliot knew Logan was obsessed with being the power behind the throne of the presidency. Donaldson's betrayal in 2000 had cut Logan deeply, thwarting an ambition that, for whatever reason, had been paramount for the mogul.

Logan had setbacks over the years, but he always managed to advance his interests. One step back, two or three steps forward. Since he had taken control of his dream, he could be so determined to reverse that defeat of almost twenty years earlier that he would stop at nothing to achieve it.

In college, Elliot had become acquainted with the writings of F. Scott Fitzgerald, including his lines about the very rich, that they were "different from you and me." In their approach to people, their innate feeling of superiority, they looked at the world and its rules differently than did the average Joe.

And Logan was more than very rich. Elliot had witnessed firsthand Fitzgerald's observation in practice during his tenure working for the billionaire, who had no compunction about bending the law to best rivals. And now with this political obsession of his...

Yes, Elliot concluded, his boss *was* capable of doing what worried Granger; he might have already done such things in the past. He recalled Logan saying he'd like to wring Donaldson's neck. A natural hyperbolic response, Elliot had thought at the time. But he also remembered the cold glare of determination when he said it, the vision memorable enough to see in his mind's eye after all this time.

Then, a few years later, there was the fortuitous death of Constantine Poulos, Logan's competition for the property on which the Phoenix now stood. The Greek tycoon had been found in an alley, shot through the heart, his watch and wallet gone. A random street crime was the police verdict. *But was it?*

Elliot picked up the phone and dialed an extension. "Ed, this is Mark. I have to put the staff meeting back half an hour."

"Okay, I'll tell 'em."

Elliot disconnected and went to the private stairwell that led up one flight to the top floor.

The bodyguard, who was sitting at his desk watching ESPN on a small TV, stood when Elliot emerged from the stairwell. "Morning, Mr. Elliot."

He smiled at the former NBA power forward. "Hey, Alex. I hear the Lakers are trying to get their hands on Bondu."

"Yeah, well, they need *somebody* to beef up their inside game."

Elliot gestured at the end of the hall. "Anybody in there with him?"

"Only Mrs. Withers. Been pretty quiet today."

Elliot walked down the hall and pressed the door buzzer. Moments later, a short and slim middle-aged black woman opened the door. "Mr. Elliot." She smiled broadly.

"Good morning, Mrs. Withers." He flashed a smile of his own. "How's he doing?"

She shook her head and clucked. "I tell you, that man should have stayed home. He thinks the place will fall apart unless he shows up for work."

"I need to see him for a few minutes. Is he up to it?"

"Oh, sure. He's been on the phone all morning in his office." She stepped aside, allowing Elliot to enter. "I just made him a pot of tea. Can I get you a cup?"

"No, thanks. I won't be long."

"Maybe you can convince him to go home and rest."

"I'll try." He winked and walked through the living area, past the small kitchen, and knocked on his boss's office door.

"What is it, Agnes?"

Elliot opened the door. "Just me, boss. Got a minute?"

"Sure, Mark. Come on in."

After closing the door behind him, Elliot stepped to the desk. "Casual Wednesday?" He smirked.

Logan looked down at his cardigan sweater and shrugged. "What?

Are you the fashion police now?" He grabbed a tissue from a box on the desk and wiped his nose.

"Agnes is worried about you."

"Yeah, she's a fussbudget. Just a cold that's going on forever, it seems. No big deal." He tossed the Kleenex into a wastebasket and pointed to a visitor's chair. "What's on your mind?"

Elliot sat and crossed his legs. "I just got a call from Governor Granger, because he got a call from his doctor buddy, Dawson. And *he* was contacted by Tim Howard."

"The blackmailer."

"Yes."

"So what's this all about?" Logan grabbed another tissue and coughed into it.

"Howard's wife was confronted by a man with a gun in a parking garage today." Elliot, looking for a sign of recognition, saw something subtle flicker in Logan's eyes.

"Good. She deserved it, I'm sure. But how does that affect Granger, and now me?"

"Howard thought Granger might have been responsible. And then Granger wondered if *we* were behind it."

Logan frowned at him for a few seconds. "That's quite a conspiracy theory, Mark. A crook trying for a score in a hospital parking garage is supposed to be somebody we hired... to do what? Kill her?" He laughed.

I didn't say anything about the hospital! Elliot stared past his boss at the window, the revelation sinking in.

"Mark?"

"Uh, yes, I know. It sounds crazy. But this Howard guy is convinced enough of a planned attack that he's taken precautions."

"You don't say."

Elliot noted a slight eye squint. *That got his attention.* "He wrote a letter outlining the story of the accident, the four teenagers involved, and then the blackmail payoff. The letter is in the hands of his lawyer. You know the cliché—to be opened if they die, whatever the apparent reason."

Logan coughed again for several seconds, turning his head to the window behind him. "I see. So Granger better hope no harm comes to those people."

"That was the general idea, and why he called. You see, he knew about the letter already, but you didn't."

"Ah. Since we didn't know about Howard's fail-safe plan, it wouldn't protect him from us. Is that it?"

"That's Granger's concern." *And now mine!*

"And now that I know, not only do I have to be a good boy, I have to share the fear of anybody whacking them." He smiled and sat back in his chair, arms folded across his chest. "That makes sense. Except for one thing, Mark. Howard only knows about Granger. The governor and his buddies are at risk of exposure, not us."

"But if something does happen, Granger's campaign would be over. A murder suspect won't be able to run for president, let alone win. And then he'd have nothing to lose by fingering you as the bad guy. 'That evil silent partner of mine did it, not me.'"

"With no proof?"

"Does it matter? Forget about any political action after that. No candidate would want to be associated with you."

"This is my last hurrah in politics, anyway. It's now or never. But all this is just wild speculation without basis in fact." He picked up his teacup, rose from his chair, and went to a side table. "Care for some tea? Earl Grey."

Elliot stood. "No, thanks. I've got a staff meeting in a few minutes."

Logan poured tea into his cup from a carafe. "This debate has been amusing. But it's just a hypothetical exercise. Fascinating, for sure, but of no consequence." He sipped from his cup. "Tell Granger you've delivered the message and that his worry is groundless. Which, of course, it is."

"Yes, sir." As he descended the stairs to his office, Elliot shook his head. *The son of a bitch did it! Now what?*

———— ✦ ————

Logan stood at the window, looking down at the Strip without really paying it any attention. Mark's information had shaken up the plan considerably. *Good thing the hit never went down. Sure dodged that bullet.* "Huh," he grunted at the unintentionally appropriate metaphor.

The Boston couple thought they had a Mexican standoff now, but from his perspective, they actually had the edge. They could divulge the story at any time, and then they'd be safe because killing them after that would serve no purpose. And they had effectively prevented a preemptive action against them. The only thing holding them back from exposing the story, he reasoned, was the fear of prosecution for extortion. But considering the bombshell the story would be, especially if it broke with Granger the Republican candidate for president, they might figure their sudden celebrity status would outweigh any downside.

He envisioned the Howards appearing on talk shows, only after selling the tale to a tabloid, of course. And sympathy for the Howard kid who lost his mother and almost died himself could result in the law giving them a pass.

He could abandon the project and let Granger take the hit if the secret went public. *No! I've come too far to stop now. There must be a way.*

Another coughing fit disrupted his calculations. *Damn this cold!* He went for a tea refill. Okay, the Howards had protected themselves. He had to admire their foresight. *How can I get around that?*

A glimmer of light slowly emerged through the fog of uncertainty as he examined the factors. *What if they did break the story? What's the proof of their claim? Those teenagers, now prominent men, who were there when it happened!* They, and only they, could provide the proof. Everything else was just supposition or hearsay, nothing to back it up. A conspiracy theory invented by wannabe celebrities for self-gain.

One of those men was already dead. Three were left, and Granger didn't count. Logan smiled.

CHAPTER 20

July 2018
Silver Bay, Lake George, N.Y.

"I'VE GOT SOME BATTER LEFT," I said. "Anyone want more pancakes?"

Michelle, Bob, and Sheree sat at the oak dinette scarfing down the high-carb, high-fat breakfast prepared by yours truly. But it was vacation time, I reasoned, when normal dietary restraints weren't allowed to intrude. And with the invigorating mountain air and our calorie-consuming activities, our bodies needed proper fortification. Anyway, that was my rationalization, and Michelle and Sheree voiced no objections. Bob, of course, never would.

"I'll have a couple more," the big man said as if reading my mind. "Any more bacon?"

"Coming right up, Crush." I poured the batter, enough for two large flapjacks, and took the rest of the bacon to the table.

Michelle looked out the window. "Starting to burn off. Should be another nice day." Patches of blue had appeared in the overcast sky over the mountains across the lake.

"Does Lake George have its own creature?" Sheree asked. "You know, like Lake Champlain's 'Champ'?"

"Well, kinda." I grabbed a piece of bacon and returned to the range. "Michelle, remember that story Brad told the staff around the campfire? About the lake monster?"

"George!" She laughed. "That's what the locals called it, Sheree. Original, right? Like Champ's name."

"Really?" Sheree's pancake-laden fork stopped abruptly on its way to its intended target. "What happened to it? Is it still around?"

Michelle laughed again. "It never existed. Turns out it was a hoax perpetrated by some rich dude to play a joke on his fishing buddy at the turn of the last century. Decades later, he owned up to it."

"Well, I saw something weird last night." Sheree finally forked the syrupy morsel into her mouth.

"What, honey?" her husband asked.

"I couldn't sleep. Must have been all that coffee during our Scattergories game. And you were snoring up a storm, Bob. Anyway, I went out to the porch to catch some fresh air, and I saw something in the water by the boathouse. It was just floating along, easy as you please. I don't know why, but the first thing I thought of was Champ. It had what looked like a neck and a head sticking out of an upper body just above the water. Didn't see a tail, though."

"Holy paleontology, Batman!" I chuckled.

"You can laugh, Jim, but I tell you, it got me thinking about Champ because one of those pictures I saw of the Loch Ness monster looked like what was in the water last night."

"Probably just a log, sweetie," Bob opined.

"Going in a straight line along the shore?" She rolled her eyes. "I ran down to the dock to get a better look, but all I got to show for it was a stubbed toe." She held up a flip-flop-clad foot to show us the bruise. "By the time I got there, it had disappeared around the bend."

"I think we should alert the media," Michelle piped in with a smile. "What's the most influential newspaper around here? The *Lake George News*? The *Glens Falls Gazette*?"

"Oh, you guys." Sheree shook her head.

I flipped the pancakes. "Something to tell the grandchildren. 'The night I saw the monster of Lake George.' Have I ever told you about the time I saw a UFO?"

Michelle groaned. "Not that again. I was there, and I never saw it."

"Well, if you remember, sweets"—I smirked—"you weren't exactly in position to see what I did."

"And you were so bored making love to me, you were looking around for other excitement?"

"No, honey. As I told you, I was just making sure no one was sneaking up on us in the dark." I turned to Sheree and winked. "As you can see, we've had this conversation before." Chuckling, I brought the skillet to the table and delivered the last of the pancakes to Kretchman. I reached for the last piece of bacon, but he got there ahead of me. "So what's on the agenda for today? Can we get Bob and Sheree on the tennis court?"

"I was thinking about taking a cruise in the boat." Kretchman looked at his wife and grinned. "Maybe we can find some evidence of George."

She rolled her eyes.

"Okay," I said. "The key's on the hook by the door. Just make sure you use the blower for four minutes before switching on the ignition. It's an inboard engine; gas fumes can build up."

"Hey, Jim, I can't do tennis worth a lick, but I do know boats. My old man had one of those Chris-Crafts, remember?"

I did. Summer nights of beer and bonfires on the islands of upper Lake Champlain. "Yeah, those were fun times."

"I see another trip down high school memory lane coming," Michelle said. Of the four of us, she was the only one not to grow up in Burlington. As such, she had to endure our stories whenever we got together. At least when Tammy was present, she had an outsider ally. "While you're talking about the good old days, I'm getting ready for tennis. Can't wait to humble Jimbo on the court."

"That'll be the day," I said in my best John Wayne. I looked at the dirty dishes on the table. "Loser cleans up the kitchen?"

"You're on."

"Let's go!"

Michelle scrambled for a shot I made deep into the corner and could only manage a weak lob to me at the net. I was about to smash the ball into the opposite corner when a thunderous explosion ripped the air.

The boat! I dropped my racket and ran off the court. With mounting dread, I rounded the side of the house and looked toward the waterfront where the boathouse used to be. I scanned the floating debris as I rushed to the water's edge, hoping to see my friends swimming among the wreckage. "Bob, Sheree," I called out, but I knew in my heart there would be no answer.

I jumped off the wall into the water, barely missing a section of the boat, which dashed my last hope that Bob and Sheree were now cruising down the lake, the explosion caused by something else. Shoving chunks of wood out of the way, I tried to see what lay beneath the water's surface, but the blast had disturbed the silt on the bottom, making visibility impossible. I felt with my feet, still wearing my tennis shoes, as I waded out, hoping to discover... shit, I didn't know what I hoped for, except for some sign they could still be rescued.

"Jim!"

I turned to see Michelle standing on the wall, a look of horror in her face. "The boat?"

I opened my mouth to respond, but nothing came out. My expression must have answered for me because she slumped to the ground.

I sat on the porch with Michelle, numbly watching sheriff's deputies and firefighters poring over the wreckage both in and out of the water. Most of the large chunks of wood had already made their way ashore in the mild waves. Other fragments littered the lawn, where two blanket-covered mounds lay side by side on the grass. What was left of Bob and Sheree. My good friends. Dead.

"I told him to use the blower!" I pleaded to Michelle, not for the first time since it happened. She didn't respond, just stared straight ahead with wet eyes.

My shock had given way to anger, directed at myself for letting it happen and at my dear friend for being so careless as to remove himself permanently from my life. I had entered the stages of grief, so well known to me from my experience in dealing with patient tragedies in my practice. And now I had to deal with the process directly. And suddenly. At least with Tom Webster, there had been time to prepare.

Another officer appeared at the side of the house. Wearing a tan uniform as the other deputies did, and hatless, he glanced at us then headed to the lakefront. After a conversation with a deputy and one of the fire crew, he walked back to us. "Dr. Dawson?"

"Yes."

"I'm Sheriff Broussard." The tall, rawboned man came up the steps and nodded to Michelle. "Ma'am." He leaned against the railing in front of us and ran a hand over thin, sandy-colored hair. "I understand this is your camp?"

"Yes," I said again.

"Both of you and the victims are from the Philadelphia area?"

"That's right." It suddenly occurred to me Bob and Sheree's families had to be notified. *Damn it!*

"Had they used the boat before?"

"No, but Bob was familiar with it. He had one like it growing up."

"Not a new boat?"

"Pretty old, actually, but it was in good shape. I had it checked out by a mechanic just after we arrived."

The lawman took a pad and pen from his shirt pocket. "Who was that?"

"Gary Tuttle, Silver Bay Marine. I've used him before."

Broussard wrote down the name. "He's good. And your friend knew about the blower?"

"As I said, he was familiar with that type of boat. And I reminded him about the blower, anyway."

The sheriff glanced behind him at the activity by the lake and then turned back to me. "Did he or his wife have any enemies?"

The question caught me by complete surprise. "Enemies?"

"What kind of business was your friend in?"

"He owns—owned—a restaurant. What's this about enemies?"

"Did he have any problems with organized crime?"

I didn't need to see his raised eyebrows to tell me this wasn't a routine question. "Organized crime! What, like the Mafia? That's ridiculous!"

The sheriff shifted his weight against the railing. "Maybe so. But I have to ask myself. Why does a boat explode, not that common an occurrence around these parts, killing a man who supposedly knew what he was doing? A man from the big city who owned a restaurant?"

"His name was Kretchman, not Corleone!" *What's with this guy?*

"Yeah, *The Godfather* was a good movie. Must have seen it a dozen times. Michael Corleone came close to being blown up in his car, as I recall."

"C'mon, Sheriff, there's no way—"

"And that brings up another thing. It was Michael's Italian wife who started his car when it exploded. It was your boat. Do *you* have somebody out to get you?"

I stood, took a step toward him, and leaned into his space. "Sheriff, two of our best friends have just died. We have to notify their families. This talk about murder is not only insane, it's inappropriate. And it's pissing me off!"

Broussard put a hand on my chest and gently pushed me back. "Easy, Doc. Just doing my job. I have to consider the possibilities when something like this happens. I don't mean to upset you any more than you already are."

I backed away and tried to calm down. Michelle met my glance with a shake of her head. Turning back to Broussard, I said, "I'm sorry, Sheriff. You've got a job to do. I know that. It's hard for me to come to grips with this."

"I understand." He stood upright, away from the railing. "We'll keep looking, but with the water and all, even if there was some kind of bomb, I don't expect we'll find any evidence of it. For now, it'll go down as an accident."

"What do we do about..." I gestured at the bodies on my lawn. "Their families will want to know when I call them."

"Of course." He took a card from his pocket and handed it to me. "The county coroner will take custody of the remains. I'll coordinate with him and can be reached at that number."

"Can we leave?" Michelle spoke for the first time since the sheriff had arrived. "We can't stay here after..." She wiped her eyes with the palm of her hand.

"I don't see why not. Leave me a number so I can reach you if something comes up."

I gave him my cell number, which he wrote in his pad.

"Sorry, folks." The sheriff gave us a sympathetic look and rejoined his people.

"We've got calls to make, Mish." I sat down next to her.

"I know."

"I don't have the numbers for Bob's folks. Or the Stallings, either. I'll have to call Dad, see if he knows."

"Oh, God! Angela!"

Bob and Sheree's daughter. "Don't know how to reach her." I sighed. "She's on college break, working a summer job somewhere in Syracuse, Bob said. Hopefully, his folks will have her number." I sat there, putting off the inevitable chore for a while longer.

"Jim?"

"Yeah?"

"What the sheriff said. You don't think there's anything to that, do you?"

Two young men dressed in scrubs, one carrying a stretcher, approached the bodies. I turned away from the sight to face Michelle's red eyes. "About it being an assassination? That's crazy, honey."

"I couldn't help thinking about that Boston couple. *They* were afraid of being killed."

"Yeah, by Granger." I shook my head. "Even crazier."

"But the woman, the nurse, *was* assaulted. And you were concerned enough about that to wonder if someone on Alan's team might have gotten carried away."

"Okay, but he said no one on his staff knew about the secret." The EMTs maneuvered one of the mounds onto the stretcher. *Bob or Sheree? Jesus.* I got up. "Better call Dad, get this over with." I went into the house for my phone, thinking about what Michelle had said. She had seen a possible connection between the Howard incident and what had happened to our friends.

Not even a coincidence let alone a connection. But I couldn't ignore the fact that Bob and Sheree did share something with the blackmailers—knowledge of what happened on that Vermont road almost twenty-five years ago. And the other fact, that Granger had the most to gain if those who knew the secret didn't live to tell about it, reared up again in my mind. But he couldn't possibly be involved in the deaths. *My God, they were his friends, too!*

I spotted my cell on the dinette still littered with the aftermath of breakfast. And then it hit me. *That talk about a lake monster this morning. Sheree saw something last night by the boathouse! Could that have been a hit man?*

And if Granger wasn't behind it, who was? Someone we didn't know about? The follow-up question chilled me even more. *Are Michelle and I next?*

CHAPTER 21

Dad ONLY KNEW THE NUMBER for the Kretchmans, but the Burlington phone book gave him the Stallings listing. After assuring him Michelle and I were all right, I hung up.

Bob and Sheree murdered. Once raised, I couldn't banish the possibility from my head. The shroud of sorrow that draped over me, heavy enough by itself, had accumulated weight. Though relieving my sense of guilt—their deaths could not then be my fault—the element of threat that replaced it increased the gut-wrenching burden. But no way would I share that with grieving parents.

First up were the Kretchmans, whom I'd known quite well growing up but hadn't seen in years. Bob's father answered the phone.

I held my cell in a tight grip. "Mr. Kretchman, this is Jim Dawson."

"Hi, Jim. Gee, I haven't heard from you in a long time. Isn't Bobby vacationing with you guys?"

My pause was too long.

"Oh, no! Is he all right?"

"Is your wife there with you?"

"What happened?" he shouted.

Here it goes. "I have terrible news, sir. Bob and Sheree were killed today in a boating accident."

"No!" he wailed, and I heard his handset hitting a hard surface. Then an anxious female voice in the background: "Bob, what's wrong?" followed by a mournful groan. "Bobby's dead."

I waited, listening to the keening of mother and father. I heard my name, and a few moments later, Mrs. Kretchman picked up the phone. I stumbled my way through the awful details, including the sheriff's contact number. "I wish I knew what to say." I choked up as she sobbed. "Michelle and I... we loved Bob and Sheree."

"I know, James. Oh, dear God," she cried. "Bobby and Sheree... gone."

"It's hard for me to accept, too," I floundered.

"Angie!" she shouted. "Does she know?"

"I was hoping you had her number."

"Oh, Angie." She started crying again. "Yes... we'll tell her."

I had to make my getaway from this painful conversation. "Call me in a day or two if you can, okay?"

"Okay," she said with a sob and hung up.

I composed myself for a minute or so before the next call. I'd only met the Stallings once, at Bob and Sheree's wedding, and I hoped that would make it easier.

Perhaps the close mother-daughter bond explained it, but Mr. Stallings had to be the strong one in that case, taking over from his distraught wife who answered the phone. I did my duty again. It *was* a bit easier the second time around, thank goodness.

The devastating loss of a child was something I had encountered a number of times in my pediatric practice. Even when that child had entered middle age, it couldn't be any easier for a parent to accept. Outliving one's offspring shouldn't happen; it upset the natural order of things. I prayed I never had to experience that trauma.

Emotionally shaken, personally and by proxy, I went to the liquor cabinet to make stiff drinks for Michelle and me.

We couldn't remain paralyzed by shock and grief. With the hard part—breaking the news—over, other arrangements required our attention. Mine, anyway. Michelle needed more time.

That included letting Granger know.

After Michelle finished half her drink, she said she wanted to lie down for a while, and went into the bedroom. I made a fresh drink and called him.

"Oh, man!" he said for the third or fourth time. "Crush and Sheree. I can't believe it!"

"I know."

"As bad as I feel, Jim, you must be taking this much worse."

"Yeah, I was right there when it happened."

"Well, sure. But something wrong with your boat got them killed. Jesus. That's gotta be tough to take."

That figures. His first reaction is to blame me. A personal injury lawyer's mindset: a tragic event is always the result of someone's negligence. "I had the boat checked out by a mechanic, Al. It was in good condition. And Bob was familiar with the Chris-Craft. His old man had one like it, remember?"

"Oh, yeah, that's right. Why the explosion then?"

"Michelle and I are concerned it might not have been an accident."

"You're kidding! Somebody out to get them? Why, for heaven's sake?"

"That's what we're trying to figure out."

"Do the cops have any evidence to suggest it was intentional?"

"Not that I'm aware of."

"Then what makes you think it was? Mechanics miss stuff all the time. I had to take the Mercedes to the shop three times before—"

"Al, hear me out, okay?"

He gave a long sigh of annoyance. "Okay."

"Two people who knew about our Vermont secret are dead."

"Christ, Jim! Back to that again? What's with you and this conspiracy shit?"

"I don't think we can afford *not* to consider the possibility of murder."

"Aw, jeez," he groaned.

"Because, as you pointed out, it was my boat. Chances were I would have been at the controls with all four of us on board. Then I wouldn't be calling you now. No one would be left of those in the car that night, except you."

"And I'd be free to advance my political plans without fear of disclosure. Is that it?" A pissed-off tone came across loud and clear.

"Running for president," I trudged ahead, "is a pretty huge deal. Drastic decisions might be made to facilitate it."

"Killing my fellow conspirators, eliminating all the witnesses? You've gone off the deep end, pal!"

My previous phone conversation with Granger came to me. "Al, remember when you said that killing the blackmailers wouldn't be feasible because Bob and I would rat you out? If we weren't around, we couldn't do that, could we?"

After a short pause, he said, "Brilliant, Doc. But you're forgetting one thing. Those blackmailers are still alive, and I can't touch them now. Duh, the safeguarded letter that tells all? I'm sure they wouldn't mind feeding me to the cops if you all ended up dead."

I was about to counter with the theory that the killer didn't know about the Howards when a startling thought hit me. *Tim Howard isn't a witness! He was a baby at the time. He's just a man with an incredible story.*

"Got you there, didn't I?" Granger said.

"The Howards have no proof, Al. All they would have would be an accusation. Who would believe it without corroboration?"

"What about that recording you made when you called the nurse? The cops find it, and the story suddenly makes sense, right?"

He would have a point there if the tape still existed. I had forgotten to remove the mini-cassette from the portable recorder on my desk that day when I left the office. My enterprising secretary, wanting to get caught up on dictations, took it and put it in her own machine to transcribe my letters to referring physicians. A malfunction of her device destroyed the tape. I was now glad I decided not to reveal that to my fellow conspirators. Let Granger think I still had it, just in case. "I've got that hidden where no one will find it, Al. But I can dig it up if I have to."

"Okay, Jim. This has gone far enough. I have a meeting in five minutes. It's bad enough to learn Crush and Sheree have been killed, without your suggestion I had something to do with it. You can think I'd kill my friends if you want. I can't stop you. But don't expect me to sit here and take it when you're essentially accusing me of murder! Have a nice day!"

"Wait, Al! Don't hang up. Of course, I don't think you would do such a thing. Neither does Michelle. Let's get that straight. But maybe someone on your side would. That's all I'm saying."

"We've already been through that. The mysterious staffer who's so devoted he would kill for me. Ridiculous. But to humor you, I took care of that."

"What does that mean?"

"It means… I, uh, went over everyone on my team and couldn't find a candidate. I told you before, none of my people knows the secret or the Howards. Very few even know about you. Look, I've gotta go."

"One more thing to think about before you do. With Bob and Tom gone, you and I are the only ones left who were there that night."

Another sigh. "So?"

"Somebody could want payback for what we did."

"Not the Howard kid."

"No, I don't think so. I've talked with him. You have, too, right?"

"He wasn't pissed, only worried. Just wanted to be left alone."

"Exactly. You know he's not out for revenge. But there might be another player we know nothing about. Bottom line, you should watch your back."

Granger grunted. "Okay, Jim, I'll do that. Is your mission accomplished now?"

"I guess."

"Good. Later."

Granger sat back in his chair, the tragic news allowed to sink in now without the distraction of having to engage in conversation. To think he'd never see his old teammate again… *Oh, man.*

As grief threatened to disrupt his self-control, his desk phone rang. "We're all here, Governor."

"Give me five minutes, Frank. Something's come up."

"Anything I can do?"

"No. See you in five." Granger hung up and sighed, thinking of what Dawson had pointed out. Kretchman was not the first of the group to die. And now two were gone. *But Tom really did it to himself. That was different. He wasn't the same guy I knew all those years.*

He had to admit, Dawson's revenge idea did give him a chill. But if not the Howard kid—he agreed with that—then who? *Some psycho Howard told about his history who wants to wreak righteous vengeance on the sinners? Nah, that's too much of a stretch.*

Then he thought about his slip of the tongue. *Jim didn't make anything of that, fortunately.* And he *had* taken care of that implausible theory. He hadn't really lied to Dawson. No one in his staff knew about the accident. And the two outsiders who did know and had the means to ensure it was kept quiet had been put on notice. Any plan to silence the Howards had to stop. It was a warning Granger didn't really think was needed, anyway.

Dawson brought up a hypothesis he couldn't ignore, though. His friend *was* the only one left besides Granger who had first-hand knowledge of that snowy night. The only other one who could testify the incident actually happened. And the implication, unlikely as it was, put Logan back on the suspect list.

Damn it! He'd have to call Las Vegas again. And this time he wouldn't settle for Logan's flunky. He would confront the big man himself, settle this thing once and for all.

It took another day to get an insurance adjuster out to assess the damage and to arrange for a dock repair and the dismantling of what was left of the boathouse. The only tradesman I knew in the area was Gary Tuttle, the boat mechanic. I called him, and he referred me to a carpenter he knew. Meanwhile, I kept the car locked in the garage, and we pretty much stayed indoors. Two deputies in scuba-diving gear explored the lakebed in a hundred-yard radius from the blast site. If they found anything of interest, they didn't tell me about it.

The next morning, we closed up the house for the winter—we wouldn't be returning this year, for sure—and hit the road. Neither of us spoke during the drive south on Route 9N along the western shore of the lake then up and over Tongue Mountain.

When I turned onto the Northway, that segment of I-87 that runs through the Adirondack Mountains to the Canadian border, Michelle broke the silence. "Jim?"

"Yeah?"

"I'm worried."

I squeezed the steering wheel. Her statement jibed with what I had just been thinking. "Me too," I admitted, though I couldn't pin down the why. It didn't compute.

"To think Sheree and Bob could have been murdered... It's unbelievable."

"I know." I glanced at her. Concern creased her face. "And maybe that's why it isn't true. Look, I've gone through everything. Al couldn't be behind this. He can be a complete jerk, but planning murders to protect his political ass? I don't see it. I know him, know when he's trying to game me. If he were lying when I talked to him, I would have known. And he's the only suspect." *That we know about.*

"So you're saying it must be a coincidence. The nurse's gunman, the boat. Not connected."

"Honey, I can't possibly know for sure. But yeah, it probably is just a coincidence. A random mugger, an accidental explosion." But I had to address Sheriff Broussard's hypothesis. "Or Bob was involved in something like the sheriff suggested. Maybe some kind of protection racket. Knowing Bob, he'd tell some crook trying that to take a hike." Even as I said that, I knew the explanation to be implausible. Bob's refusal to be extorted would get his restaurant blown up maybe, not a boat in the Adirondacks. *Could he have been involved with loan sharks?* No, that wouldn't work, either. Killing the borrower ended the payments. Beating him up, okay. But that wouldn't happen hundreds of miles away in upstate New York. And in either case, a killer out to get Bob couldn't count on his being the one to start up my boat.

"You don't really think that, do you? Bob mixed up with the Mafia?"

I shook my head. "No, I don't. Was just thinking out loud."

"And *you* certainly aren't involved with criminals."

"Not that I know of." I forced a smile. Michael Corleone, my ass. *Bump me off, gangland style?* Ridiculous. The sheriff's suggestion, though logical, I supposed, was obviously way off base.

But perhaps not entirely. The Chris-Craft *was* my boat. I would likely be the captain, with the four of us taking the boat for a cruise, as I had told Granger. Four targets nailed in one fell swoop. If the deaths of my friends were assassinations, that could have been the killer's plan. To get us all.

And assuming that, it had to involve the secret the four of us shared. The unavoidable question was why. *Goddamn it! What the hell is going on?*

"What's going on, Jim?" Michelle asked, using her uncanny ability to tap into my thoughts. "Are we in trouble?"

I banged the steering wheel. "I wish to hell I knew. I was looking at the situation from only one angle and only because the Howard kid called me. In a perverted way, his fear made sense, though I didn't really believe it had any basis."

"Until what happened to his wife."

"Yes. And then Al convinced me it was stupid to accuse him, had to be a coincidence. Okay, he denies personal involvement and claims no one on his staff knows jack shit about the Howards. Fine. End of story. No connection between a parking garage incident and our secret. Until what happened two days ago, it never occurred to me the same potential threat to the Howards could apply to Bob and Sheree."

"And us. We could have been on the boat."

"Yes, us. All the people who knew about that accident." All *the people.* "And that brought up another possibility, one I raised with Al. He and Tammy are included in that group. The politics angle could be all wrong. Maybe everyone who knows the secret is at risk, including them."

"But why? That doesn't make any sense." She shook her head. "This is getting crazy."

She was right. Trying to think outside the box presented even more logic flaws. A piece of the puzzle always seemed to be missing. But we could be trying to solve a puzzle that might not exist.

"Honey," I said, "I think we're getting carried away. We've taken Howard's paranoia and run with it. But we have nothing to go on except conspiracy theories."

"So convince me I'm scared for no reason." She slipped off her sandals and put her feet on the dashboard.

I glanced at her red-painted toenails and smiled inwardly. Like every other part of her body, even her feet were attractive. The distraction calmed my swirling thoughts and helped me address her request with a level head. "Okay, some guy with a gun approached the nurse. That's fact one. We have no confirmation of that, but let's assume it happened."

"Right."

"Fact two: the boat exploded with Bob and Sheree in it."

Michelle took her feet off the dash and looked out the side window. "Go on," she said softly.

"That's it, honey. All the rest is stuff we've made up. The most likely thing is the two events are not related. A street crime and an accident." *But Sheree saw something that night.*

She turned to me, frowning. "The sheriff was suspicious, and he didn't know about the Boston thing."

"That's his job, Mish." I sighed, a reaction to my frustration rather than a dismissal of her argument. I really wanted to assure myself we weren't in danger, but so far, it was a losing effort. "Can we go over the what-ifs objectively?"

"Only if you stop patronizing me."

Ouch! Have I been doing that? Yeah, probably. "Agreed. Sorry if I've been overbearing."

She shrugged and stared straight ahead.

"One conspiracy theory has Al wanting to run for president and worried the Vermont secret will get out. So he decides to knock off the nurse and, presumably, her husband. But it doesn't work out, and now they've taken precautions against another attempt. What's he going to do now? Kill his buddies and their wives? You think he's capable of that?"

"I guess not."

I was stuck in the slow lane behind an RV and had to wait for a space to open in the next lane to pass it. With the cruise control back on, I continued, "Politics can do strange things to people, so let's assume Al has gone off the deep end and sees us as people standing in his way to glory. So he has us killed. But that leaves the Howards, who are more likely to spill the beans than we ever would be, and he can't touch them. That theory doesn't fly, babe."

I gave myself a mental high-five. Sheree's sighting notwithstanding, and that could have been anything, really, my argument was by-the-numbers cogent. My mood improved. "See any flaws in that?"

She didn't respond right away. She was staring through the windshield, frowning again.

"Honey?"

"No, not the way you put it. But as you said, it might not be Alan but someone working on his behalf without his knowing it. And this person might not know about the blackmailers, only the four of us."

Traffic flow was slowing considerably for no apparent reason, and then I saw the temporary electronic sign: "Construction ahead. Merge left." *Great!*

My aggravation was due more to my wife's astute hypothesis than the slowdown. I moved over quickly into a gap in the left lane. "You're saying the parking garage guy was a coincidence, and the boat blowing up was intentional."

"It's possible, isn't it?"

I shook my head. "Mish, we wouldn't even be thinking of an assassination plot if it weren't for the gunman in Boston!"

Her eyes teared up, and I felt like a complete ass. "Aw, honey, I'm sorry. I'll stop talking about it. Going around in circles like this isn't helping, anyway."

"I'm sorry, too, Jim. I can't think straight. Losing Sheree and Bob that way... it's put my mind in places I don't want to go. Looking for a reason to explain why... why they're gone. There has to be a reason." She looked out her window again.

I squeezed her shoulder. "Shit happens, sweetheart. Sometimes we never know why." I couldn't even see the orange cones yet, but the traffic had come to a complete stop, the stalled lines of cars in both lanes extending as far as I could see. I used the opportunity to stretch my arms and legs.

Michelle dug into her purse for some tissues. Dabbing at her eyes, she said, "There was something you said before about Al and Tammy."

"Oh, jeez," I groaned. "I thought we were going to let this drop for a while."

"Before, you said the 'us' included the Grangers, that they might be at risk, too, and I said that didn't make sense. But it would if we're dealing with some kind of revenge."

"Not by Tim Howard."

"Probably not. You said he seemed okay about what happened to him. But maybe there's somebody we don't know about. His mother's boyfriend, maybe, or somebody else Howard could have told. A wacko who decides to get retribution after learning who we all are."

The thought that had flitted through my brain without landing now found a purchase. An unknown avenger out to get us all. No more far-fetched than our other scenario but with a big difference. "In that case," I said, "you can relax. You weren't with us that night in Vermont."

"Neither was Sheree. I think they call that 'collateral damage.'"

A horn beeped behind me. The cars ahead had started moving again, and drivers who had ignored the warning sign until now were taking advantage of my inattention and moving over in front of me. I crept the car forward to close the gap.

No matter how hard I tried to tell myself we were being paranoid for no reason, it wasn't working. The possible dire scenarios—we had at least two—couldn't be ruled out. Not yet. "Son of a fucking bitch!" I slammed the steering wheel again. "We need some answers!"

We'd finally reached the beginning of the orange cones, forcing the right lane to merge now, one car at a time let into our lane.

"Maybe we should do what the Howards did, Jim. You know, the letter with the lawyer?"

"And tell whom about it? Al?"

"Who else?"

Who else, indeed. I wish to hell I knew. It kept coming back to someone we didn't know about, who Granger might not even know about, orchestrating the mayhem. I couldn't get past that. And a revenge killer wouldn't give a shit about some letter. Only someone trying to help Granger would.

"Okay, we write that letter and tell Al what we did. But if he's clueless, and I think he is, what can he do? 'Memo to staff: Be advised that killing Dr. and Mrs. Dawson now will expose my secret and doom my presidential run, so fuggedaboudit.'" I gave Michelle a mirthless chuckle. "That should work. Problem solved."

"Your sarcasm doesn't help."

"Sorry."

"There's another thing we could do."

"I'm all ears."

"Go public. Get the secret out while we're still among the living. Damn it, Jim! If what we're thinking about might be going on, how can bad publicity compare to that?"

An excellent point. Push might have finally come to shove. The debate over the pros and cons of confession had tipped in favor of disclosure. And if the revelation came from us, we might be able to control the story, put our self-serving spin on it. With the right slant, even Granger might escape disaster and survive politically. It wasn't as if such a blemish on a résumé hadn't occurred before. The teenaged Laura Bush, I recalled, had run a stop sign and killed someone. That hadn't destroyed *her* reputation or later prevented her husband from becoming president. And if Granger were even indirectly responsible for the deaths of our friends, well, he couldn't complain, then, could he? Perhaps even a vigilante might be persuaded that we didn't deserve to die for that long-ago tragedy. "We should consider that, Mish. I agree."

But do we really have to go that far? Having just decided disclosure was probably the right course to take, a trap of human nature still ensnared me. Do something wrong and the reflex to keep it quiet kicked in. Failing that, deny. And once denied, the lie must continue until it's no longer tenable. *Fuck! If only we knew the boat explosion was planned, Michelle's solution would be a no-brainer.*

With the merging behind us, traffic speed increased. Fresh asphalt was being poured on the inaccessible right-hand lane, so at least the DOT was actually at work improving the highway for us weary travelers unlike at other road construction sites I'd seen. Anyway, we were moving along at a reasonable clip now on our trip home.

Whether we could move on with our lives remained to be seen. We needed a game plan.

Meanwhile, we'd have to be careful.

Easy to say, but accomplishing it problematic. Michelle was still on summer break, but I had a job to go to, professional responsibilities…

An idea popped into my head. I didn't have to go the office yet. I still had most of my vacation time left. Michelle and I could spend it somewhere no one would know about. A safety precaution while we figured this out. The boys wouldn't be coming home from tennis camp for another two weeks. I was about to broach this great idea to my wife when she preempted me.

"How about finishing up our vacation at the beach?" she asked.

I laughed. *This woman is something else.* "Just what I was thinking, darlin'. Any place in particular?"

"Irene and her husband have been to Oak Island. She really likes it. Not one of those crowded resort areas. We wouldn't likely run into someone we knew."

Exactly! "Where's that?"

"North Carolina. We're already packed. We wouldn't even have to stop in Villanova first." She pulled her cell from her purse.

"That's a long way."

"I'll find out." She fingered the screen of her phone. "Six hundred sixty miles from here."

"Whew!" I said, but I liked her idea.

"We can do it in two or three days. What's our hurry? We need the time to sort everything out, anyway."

I flashed a smile. "North Carolina, here we come."

CHAPTER 22

Two days later
Oak Island, North Carolina

MICHELLE'S IDEA OF TRAVELING TO a distant, unfamiliar beach was a good one. We would be at the now-clichéd 'undisclosed location.' If someone had orchestrated the boat explosion, and I now considered that to be the case, the assassin could follow us as we drove to our place of hiding. I kept track of the cars behind us along the way as I changed speeds and lanes, stopped for gas and lodging. I didn't identify any suspicious vehicles.

After arrival, we found an oceanfront house to rent for a week. Height-of-the-season pricey, but after what happened at Silver Bay, we deserved a place with enough distracting ambiance to overwhelm our angst.

Michelle had chosen well. Oak Island was a low-key, largely residential beach town, a perfect place to unwind from our stress or at least put it on hold for a while.

We stocked up on supplies at the Food Lion, less than a mile down the main drag from our rental. An Eagles beach-gear store, even closer, supplied us with an umbrella, and we picked up some booze from the ABC store, also conveniently located. Less than two hours after our arrival, we were on the beach.

Michelle lay prone on her towel, facing the ocean. "Look at that."

"What?" On my back next to her, with my head in the opposite direction, I rose up onto my elbows.

"Those birds. Pelicans, I think."

Two pelicans circled lazily in the air about thirty yards offshore. Suddenly, one dove straight down into the water, emerging moments later to resume its reconnaissance.

"See that?" she asked.

"Yeah. Did it get one?"

"A fish? I can't tell from here, but they've been doing that for a while. It's so cool."

I lay back down, hands behind my head. A moderate onshore breeze kept the heat of the afternoon at bay. The sun's UV rays had to contend with the umbrella and our SPF 30 lotion. "What do you think about buying a beach place, honey? This is the life."

"What, and sell the Silver Bay house?"

I didn't know if we could ever stay there again. But with Michelle's mind now on something else, thank goodness, I wanted to avoid that subject. "How about the mountains *and* the ocean?"

I was happy to hear her laugh. "Have you come into an inheritance I don't know about?"

"I don't mean now, babe. When we're closer to retirement. The Villanova place will be paid off in a few years. We could sell that, get an RV, and cruise between our two homes, depending on the season. Something to think about."

"Jeez, you *are* relaxed, aren't you? I wish I could compartmentalize like that."

And here I thought she had. "Mish, what good does it do to dwell on what we can't change?" *Great. Now I sound like Granger.* "I mean, I'm just trying to make the best of it, take my mind off what brought us here to begin with. And it was your idea. A good one, I might add."

"Okay, you're right. Let's enjoy our stay." She reversed her position on the towel and rolled onto her side to face me. "There's just one important thing I'll bring up, and then I'll be good."

"Hold that thought." I reached into the cooler next to me. "Want a beer?"

"Sure."

I gave her a can and popped the top on mine. "Now what do you want to get off your chest?"

"The funerals, Jim. We have to go."

Of course. All those what-if scenarios had pushed such practical concerns out of my head. And four days had already passed since the disaster. "Sure we'll go. With the medical examiner and the sheriff's investigation involved, it could be a while yet. But I'll call Dad and have him let us know. We can fly out of Wilmington if we have to and return here in a couple of days.

And maybe by the time we leave here for good, we'll have some resolution of our problem. If not... I hadn't worked that out yet.

"I think Alan will make sure he attends this time," Michelle said. "Meeting with him might help."

Yes, I figured Granger would have to be there, to show he cared. That conversation with him still bugged me for some reason. A face-to-face discussion might tell me why.

———————◆⧓◆———————

That same day
Pennsylvania

Luke Elliot sat in his rental car half a block from the brick two-story house under surveillance. Only one other vehicle, a lawn-care business's truck, was parked on the quiet street. Fortunately, Elliot's car sat in front of a house for sale; otherwise, his presence could attract attention in the affluent neighborhood.

Where the hell are they? In his drive-bys the last two days and in his stationary observation of the house today, he'd seen no signs of occupation. When he'd called the man's office, a secretary told him only that he was "away," and that she could refer him to someone else if the matter were urgent. He hoped they hadn't figured it out and were now in hiding.

He'd already spent more time than he'd allocated to this project, and now his targets were missing. At least he could do the other job while he waited for them to show up, if he decided to accept the contract. And if he did, then these two jobs would be his last. He'd promised Emily a vacation in Hawaii, where he planned to pop the question. With a sizable nest egg sitting in the Caymans, he would retire from this risky business and settle down with the love of his life.

He started the SUV and drove off. He didn't yet know who or where the other potential target was, but he'd find that out in Las Vegas. And if he accepted the assignment, he'd come back here after it was done. Hopefully, they would have returned by then, and he could finish up and return to Santa Fe and Emily.

"The hospital?" Nick Poulos said into the phone. "What the fuck? Is it serious?"

"Don't know. You can't get shit from hospitals these days. Don't even have his room number."

"Well, keep on it, okay?"

"Sure, Nick."

Poulos disconnected. Standing at the window of his suite in the Paradise Palace and Casino, he looked across downtown Las Vegas. The Phoenix's edifice gleamed in the distance, occupying prime real estate on the Strip.

He clenched his jaw. *That location should have been Pop's.* He'd suspected for years but only recently confirmed that his father's death was not due to a robbery gone bad. He'd finally tracked down the man who whacked Constantine Poulos in that Vegas alley when Nick was just twelve. And now he knew who had hired him for the job. *The fucker better not die before I can kill him.*

Consulting his phone's directory, he found the listing he wanted and punched in the number.

After three rings, a voice said, "Dr. Pantelakos."

"Dino, this is Nick Poulos. I need some information."

Thirty minutes later, Poulos sipped espresso while watching the History Channel—yet another program about the danger of asteroids striking the Earth. He couldn't help it. The subject fascinated him. The ringing of his cell phone occurred conveniently during a commercial break. "Hey, Dino. Watcha got for me?"

"He's in room 412."

"What's ailing him? I've been worried."

"Pneumonia. But he's getting better."

"Oh, that's good news. Like I told you, I had a surprise lined up for my buddy, a special get-well greeting, and I hoped he'd be up to it. Thanks, Dino. I appreciate it. Are we still on for golf Saturday?"

"I'll be there."

"Okay, and thanks again." Poulos smiled as he stared at the TV screen, barely paying attention to the narrator.

"But the meteor that crashed into Arizona was a baby compared to the monster Chicxulub asteroid that struck the Yucatan Peninsula sixty-five million years ago..."

He looked at his watch. The call from Dr. Pantelakos had come just in time. In an hour, Poulos would get the call from "Bill," asking for the information his friend had just provided. In the next twenty-four hours, he'd have his revenge.

CHAPTER 23

The next day
Las Vegas

MARK ELLIOT WAITED OUTSIDE THE closed door of his boss's hospital room while the doctor met with his patient and Mrs. Logan. The heavy door didn't permit eavesdropping. He stood with his hands in the pockets of his suit pants, rocking back and forth on his heels, nervously viewing the activity occurring up and down the hospital corridor. The "cold" Logan had was apparently much more serious than that.

A radiology tech maneuvered a bulky X-ray machine into a room three doors down. Next door, a cute young nurse stood at a small ledge outside the room, writing a note in a chart. She looked over at him and smiled. He returned the smile and stepped back to give a passing gurney pushed by a scrubs-clad hospital employee ample room. The gurney, bearing a sheet-covered patient and with an IV bag dangling from a pole, headed for the elevators around the corner at the midpoint of the long corridor. Visitors stepping from the elevator alcove would first encounter the nurses' station, its long counter visible from Elliot's location.

He checked his watch. Thirty minutes earlier, he'd entered Logan's room for the morning briefing and found his boss sitting up in bed reading the paper. The nasal oxygen cannula had been removed. Though Logan remained connected to an IV, his appearance had improved significantly since yesterday's visit.

"You look better, boss," he'd said, relieved to see the improvement.

"Yeah. I should be getting outta here soon." Logan put the newspaper down and removed his reading glasses. "So what's the latest?"

"Nothing much. A rock group, the Bangers, lived up to their name last night. Had a wild party in their suite and trashed the place. I talked with their manager. It's taken care of."

"Assholes. What's with those people, Mark? Trying to live up to some perverted image?"

Elliot shrugged. "Who knows?"

"Well, that's it for those jerks and their kind. It seemed like good publicity once. Attract the younger set to the hotel with Joey and the Starfuckers or whatever staying there. But it's not worth the aggravation. Second time this year, right?"

Elliot nodded.

"From now on, unless these *musicians* make a living playing the violin or the cello, they can go wreck the Venetian instead."

"Yes, sir. Consider it done."

Logan looked past Elliot. "Here's the doc."

Dr. Kenneth Hamilton, accompanied by Mrs. Logan, came into the room. Elliot watched as the still-attractive Carole Logan stepped quickly to the bedside and leaned over to kiss her husband.

"You look good, honey."

"Thanks." Logan looked at his attending physician. "So what's up for today, Doc?"

Hamilton turned to Elliot. "Could you excuse us for a few minutes?"

"Sure. I'll wait outside." He left the room, the doctor closing the door after him.

Twenty-five minutes had elapsed since he'd been ushered out of the room. *Must be serious. I thought he was getting better.*

Just as he completed that thought, the door opened and Mrs. Logan emerged, dabbing her eyes with a tissue. She rushed past him without speaking and hurried down the hallway.

Dr. Hamilton beckoned Elliot into the room. "Mr. Logan wants me to fill you in."

Logan sat frowning, his arms folded across his chest. "Go ahead, Doc. Tell him."

"Mr. Logan's pneumonia has cleared up nicely. But then we discovered it had been hiding something else in his lung. A small spot. It could be a tumor of some sort."

"Don't pussyfoot around, Ken. Cancer, Mark. That's what he's saying."

Cancer? "He sounded like he wasn't sure, boss." He turned to the doctor. "Isn't that right?"

"Wendell, I told you we don't know that. We'll get a CT scan. It could show us there's nothing to worry about. But if it does look suspicious, we might be able to get a needle biopsy and save you an operation."

"Temporarily, you mean." Logan snorted. "Whatever. Mark, is my wife still outside?"

"She went down the hall. Hold on." Elliot stepped to the door, looked toward the nurses' station, and came back into the room. "Don't see her. She seemed pretty upset."

"Yeah, she tends to fold under pressure." He shook his head in apparent dismissal. "We all gotta go sometime, Ken, and at my age, it's natural to think about the big C. It's next after the heart, right?"

"Yes."

"So I've done some research just in case. You can do your CT scan, but that's all. If it looks like cancer, I want to go to Philadelphia for further diagnosis or treatment."

"Philadelphia?" The doctor's obvious surprise mirrored Elliot's.

"The Franklin Cancer Center."

"We have excellent surgeons and oncologists here, Wendell."

"I'm sure you do. But Franklin is nationally recognized for cancer treatment. Can you say the same for *this* medical center?"

"I'd have to check."

Logan smiled and winked at Elliot. "But I've got an even bigger reason, Ken. My daughter, Lisa, lives in the area. Carole... well, to be frank, I don't think she'd be able to cope. I could use stronger support when going through all that stuff those doctors will put me through. And Lisa works there! As an oncology nurse, no less!"

Hamilton chuckled. "Can't argue with that. Philadelphia it is, then. But before we get carried away, let's see if that trip will be necessary. I'll make arrangements for the scan."

"I'll be here."

Hamilton left.

"Happy days are here again, huh, Mark?"

"Maybe so. The doc said it might be benign."

"That's what they always do. Hold out the hope." He laughed. "But it sure beats asking about funeral arrangements. Anyway, I'll get the scan, and we'll go from there. Any official business coming up I need to do before I'm… incapacitated?"

"No, I don't think so. And I've got your power of attorney," he continued in a pitch higher than his normal voice, "if… if you're not able to sign off on something that can't wait." Despite what he thought his longtime boss could be doing for his political scheme, a feeling of sadness crept in. They had a long history together.

Logan stared at him for a few seconds. "Don't worry, Mark. I'm not about to croak just yet. Not with unfinished business. I believe I'm destined to get to the White House. All the steps along the way have gone well so far. Even if I do have cancer, it'll be just a temporary setback. I'll lick it."

"I think you will, sir."

"You say that, but I can see in your face you don't really believe it."

"It's just the shock of the news that—"

Logan held up a hand. "Let me put your mind at ease concerning your future, which I'm sure you've been thinking about the last few minutes. I got you a piece of the Phoenix in my will. You'll be set."

Elliot stared at the tycoon, mouth agape. "I… I don't know what to say." And he truly didn't. Caught up in the sorrow of impending loss, he hadn't considered what that loss would mean for his career.

Logan smiled. "'Thanks' will do it."

"Thank you." Elliot grinned. "The Phoenix has had a piece of *me* for years."

"It still does. So get back to work!"

Ten minutes later, Elliot drove out of the hospital parking lot, thinking about what Logan's death would mean for his future, inheritance notwithstanding. He glanced at the driver of a car passing him as it came into the lot then did a double take. *Luke?*

Before turning onto the street, he looked behind him at the SUV traveling around the perimeter, searching for a parking space. *He would have called me. And what would he be doing at the hospital?* Had to be his imagination. The ramifications of the recent news had cluttered his mind.

But he wondered about it as he drove to the Phoenix. When he got to his office, he called his brother's cell phone.

"Hey, bro, what's up?" Luke answered.

"You're not in Vegas, are you? I thought I saw you a little while ago."

"Really?"

Coming into the hospital parking lot."

"Uh, it wasn't me, dude."

"So you're not in town?"

After a few moments of silence, he said, "Damn, Mark, you must be psychic. I'm at the airport. Just got in."

"No kidding!"

"Some guy has a Civil War Spencer carbine for sale. He went to a pawnshop. You remember that *Pawn Stars* TV show?"

"Yeah?"

"He didn't get his price there, so he bailed. But I'm interested. Seeing him this morning."

"Why didn't you let me know? I haven't seen you in years, Luke. Jeez, man."

"I know, I'm sorry. But I didn't want to bother you on such short notice. And I'm only here for the day. Got a flight back tonight."

"Do you have time for dinner?"

"I guess so, sure."

"Great. Meet me at the Oasis Bar at the Phoenix. Around five?"

"The Phoenix?"

"Yeah. It's where I work, remember? So it'll be my treat."

"Uh, that's okay with me." Luke chuckled. "I never turn down a freebie. But are you okay? What were you doing at a hospital?"

"My boss is sick. I was just visiting."

Another pause. "That's a relief."

"I'll see you at five. Good luck with the gun purchase."

"Thanks. Later, dude."

———— ❧ ————

Luke entered the fourth-floor elevator of the Clark Memorial Medical Center, disturbed by his brother's call. *Visiting his sick boss. Fuck! It should have occurred to me!* Mark had told him years ago he worked for some fat cat who owned a hotel. But Luke had forgotten the name of the man and the hotel. He hadn't really thought of Mark when he took the contract. Las Vegas was a big place; Mark lived there. No big deal. But now the connection was crystal clear. To think he could have bumped into his brother in the hospital. *How would I have explained what I was doing there?*

But when Luke returned much later, no visitors would be around the big man then.

When the elevator opened to the lobby, his phone chirped. He read Emily's text message: *I miss you! Please hurry home.*

"As soon as I can, darlin'," he said softly and went out to the parking lot to text his reply.

———— ❧ ————

5:00 p.m.
The Phoenix Hotel and Casino

The Oasis Bar was aptly named, being a haven from the noisy casino, with its slot machines and gaming tables, adjacent to it. Luke walked down the corridor containing restrooms and a cubbyhole cigar shop toward the beckoning entrance sign that featured palm trees on the edge of a sparkling blue pond. After entering the dark bar, he paused a few seconds to let his eyes adjust. His brother waved from a small table in the middle of the room.

Mark embraced Luke when he reached him. "What are we, twins?" Mark asked, pointing to his brother's shirt. Both men, of similar height and build, wore Tommy Bahama silk shirts with tropical flower patterns and dark slacks. But while Mark's hair was thick and black-turning-gray, Luke's was thin and sandy-colored.

"Well, you know, this is Vegas, right? And I thought you'd be in a suit."

"Off duty." Mark smiled, gestured to the other chair, and both men sat. "What're you drinking?" Mark asked as a waitress materialized at the table.

"Sam Adams?" he asked the server, who nodded.

"And I'll have a Manhattan."

The waitress smiled and left.

"So," Mark said, "how did the deal go down today?"

"The Spencer?"

"Was there another one?"

"Uh, no. And it didn't work out. Couldn't get him to budge, and there wasn't enough meat left on the bone for me at his price. He thinks he'll do better at an auction."

"An empty trip, then."

"It happens." Luke smiled. "But I'm seeing you, so it hasn't been a complete waste." Luke had always liked his older brother and regretted they hadn't been closer when growing up.

"Thanks, I think."

Luke put a hand on his chest. "From the heart, man. It's been a while."

"Yeah, a couple of years. Still with that painter?"

"Artist," Luke corrected with a mock frown.

"Am I ever going to meet her? Like at a wedding, maybe?"

"Ha! Listen to the bachelor talking."

"Actually, I've been seeing someone lately."

"No way!"

"Way." Mark laughed.

Their drinks arrived and Luke took a pull from the frosted pilsner glass. *Let's make sure.* "So the guy who owns this place is your boss, and he's sick?"

"I'm afraid so."

"What's his name again? I can't remember."

"Wendell Logan."

Right! "Is it serious?"

"Yeah." Mark sipped his drink.

"Sorry to hear that. What'll you do if he doesn't make it? Would you need a job?"

"No, I'll be okay. He's giving me a piece of this place."

Good! "So you'll be okay, then. Financially, I mean."

"Looks like it. Anyway, he's doing pretty well now, and they discharged him from the hospital."

What the hell? "That's good news, huh?" he said, scrambling for an alternative plan.

"Well, he needs more treatment, and he wants to get it in Philadelphia. They're setting that up.

Philadelphia. Maybe it could still work out. "Some special hospital?"

"Yeah, he chose it. His daughter is a nurse there."

"I'm familiar with Philly. Which hospital?"

"The Franklin Cancer Center."

"Oh, yeah. Good place."

Mark took another drink. "Anyway, how have you been? Is your business doing well?"

"Can't complain. The more shooting sprees we have, the more people want guns for protection. It's a growth industry."

Mark nodded. "Like me, then, you have job security."

"You might say that."

"No qualms about the morality of it?" Mark peered at Luke as he sipped from his glass.

"This coming from a man whose job involves enticing people to gamble, maybe lose everything they have?" Luke raised his eyebrows.

Mark smiled. "Touché. We both let people make bad decisions. Freedom of choice. The American way. If lives are destroyed, it's not really our fault, is it? Not directly, anyway."

Speak for yourself, bro.

"Just coffee, thanks," Luke said when the server inquired about dessert. "Black."

"Likewise," Mark added.

"That's easy." The waitress removed the dinner plates. "I'll be right back."

Luke checked his watch.

"How's your time?" Mark asked.

"I'm good." *I'll see about getting an earlier flight. No sense hanging around now.*

The sound of an Elvis Presley song came from Mark's side of the table. Luke chuckled as Mark pulled his cell phone from a case on his belt, checked the number, then returned the phone to the holder.

"Viva Las Vegas? Cute."

"Marketing." Mark smiled.

"I thought you were off duty."

"Well, you know. Except for emergencies." He grinned. "They can't run this place without me."

The waitress delivered their coffees and left.

"So, with your boss out of commission, you're going to be busier, I guess."

"A little. But we talk every day. He's still in control, makes the big decisions."

"He's not that sick, then?"

"His condition hasn't affected his overall health yet. And if he gets his way, which he usually does, it won't."

Luke sipped his coffee. *Cancer? Prognosis?* But a contract was a contract, and he'd already been paid.

"It's great having this chance to see you, Luke. We should do this again soon, when we have more time."

"I'm for that."

Mark squinted as he looked at his brother. "I've got an idea. When my boss is back in action again, he'll owe me a vacation, and I've thought of a good place for it. The skiing out your way is pretty good, isn't it?"

Luke smiled. "Haven't been in a couple of years, but I'm willing to brave the slopes again. There's a decent place just outside of town called Ski Santa Fe." He chuckled. "I wonder how they came up with that name."

"Does Emily ski?"

"Yup, but like me, she hasn't been in a while."

"Okay, how about the four of us have a ski vacation this winter? I can finally meet that woman of yours, and you can meet Karen."

"Sounds like a plan, bro. I'd like that." Luke finished his coffee. "Speaking of Santa Fe, I'd better shove off. McCarran was pretty crowded when I flew in."

Mark came around the table. "We should keep in touch more often, man."

"I agree. Let me know when you can get away for that ski trip. Emily and I will work around your schedule."

The two men shook hands and embraced.

"Have a good flight."

"Thanks." Luke headed to the restaurant's exit.

CHAPTER 24

MARK WATCHED HIS BROTHER LEAVE and mused about the serendipitous reunion. Then he remembered the phone call. *What does he want now?* He took out his phone and tapped the number. "Mark Elliot, Governor," he said when Granger answered. "What can I do for you?"

"Mark, I still can't get hold of your boss. What's going on?"

The server returned to the table, a coffee decanter in her hand. Mark pointed to his mug. "He won't be taking any calls for a while, Alan. He's been in the hospital."

"Oh, sorry to hear that. Are we, uh, still going ahead, or does this change things?"

Mark shook his head. *No "How's he doing?" or "Will he be okay?" Just a "Are we still in business?"* "I talked with him this morning. He remains committed to the plan. Is that why you called?"

"No. I, uh, well, something's happened, and I wanted to speak to Wendell himself about it."

"Unfortunately, you're stuck with me. What's the problem, Alan?" Mark gazed around the bar, waiting for Granger to get to the point.

"Remember Bob Kretchman?"

"The football player?"

"Yes. I'm going to his funeral tomorrow."

That got Mark's attention. "My condolences. I know he was a good friend of yours."

"He and his wife were killed in a boat explosion."

"That's terrible!"

"Do you know anything about that?"

"No, I hadn't heard. Was it on TV?"

"Not that I know of." He paused. "Not yet, anyway. Mark, there's no good explanation for why the boat could have blown up accidentally. I don't have any proof, and neither do the cops who investigated, but it was suspicious."

"I don't understand. How does this involve Mr. Logan?"

"First, that nurse gets threatened, and now Bob is killed. Jim Dawson has connected the dots, and I have to admit he's got me thinking."

"Dawson is the doctor in Villanova, right?"

"Yes. He's worried someone may be trying to eliminate those who know about that secret of mine."

Christ! "I recall we've had this conversation before, Alan. By *someone*, I assume you mean Mr. Logan. I thought we'd put that ridiculous idea to rest already."

"It's hard for me to believe, too, and that's why I wanted to talk with Wendell directly, hear his side, and hopefully put my mind at ease."

"Sorry you won't be able to do that. I'll have to be your proxy, again. But I can assure you, again, that your worry is groundless." *Is it?*

"Okay. But Wendell should know that Jim thinks the explosion wasn't an accident. And right now, he doesn't know about Wendell's connection to my campaign. He suspects some unknown member of my staff was behind it. If he finds out your boss is funding me, I can imagine what he would think then."

"I get the feeling it's what *you* think now. Am I right?"

"I don't want to lose another friend. Let's leave it at that. A word to the wise and all."

The man is making a threat! "I detect an 'or else' in that."

"If anything happens to Dr. Dawson... well, I'd have to reassess my campaign plans. Running for president will have lost its appeal for me."

"So either Dawson gets left alone or you'll quit? Is that your message?"

"I think I've said what I needed to say."

Mark sighed. "I understand. I'll pass that along to Mr. Logan. Take care, Governor." Mark disconnected and put his phone on the table. He picked up his coffee mug. His hand shook slightly as he brought the mug to his lips.

Logan's handpicked, cleverly manipulated candidate is turning on his benefactor. Essentially accusing him of murder! And not without good reason. Oh, he'd tell his boss about Granger's threat, all right, but not just because he said he would. He had real doubts himself this time around that the governor's charges were ill founded. And that presented a conundrum. *What will I do about it?*

Logan would belittle the matter, of course. Laugh it off. Might even get angry, ostensibly shocked at the accusation. But if he *had* been arranging assassinations, he'd surely have to abandon that now. *What, then, would be the point of continuing?* He'd have lost his ticket to the White House.

Unless Granger was bluffing. *Could Logan take the chance the "I'll take my ball and go home" threat was an empty one? That Granger would still play along despite what he might think Logan had done?*

Yes, his boss could very well count on that. And if Logan was responsible for the football player's death, he'd already crossed a line he couldn't retreat over now. He might figure he had his man pegged; that Granger would convince himself his fantastic hypothetical couldn't be true, and that, in any case, the unfortunate deaths of his friends were not sufficient reasons to discontinue his quest for the presidency.

Hold on, there! Logan might be ruthless—no, he definitely was ruthless—but to think he'd kill Granger's buddies on the almost zero chance they would expose the secret... That was downright crazy.

As soon as that dismissive thought came, however, he knew it wasn't true. It wasn't insane to consider that possibility, because he knew Logan. Once his boss had his sights set on a goal, had made the calculations, he pursued it with all the power at his command, reducing the unknowns of the equation to the bare minimum.

Mark sipped his now-tepid coffee, pondering what had been unthinkable before the Boston incident. He'd caught Logan in a slip there, and this had made him think back to the Constantine Poulos murder. His conclusion then: his boss *was* capable of such drastic action. This latest news only reinforced that opinion. Once the last witness to that unfortunate accident two decades earlier had been removed, no other obstacles stood in Logan's way.

The blackmailers were protected now and had only hearsay evidence, anyway. They could create some exciting news for the talking heads to discuss. But that would be short-lived, soon to be relegated to a partisan conspiracy theory promoted only by Democrat extremists, similar to the right-wingers' claim that Bill Clinton had Vince Foster murdered.

Bloomberg knew of the campaign strategy but not Granger's backstory. No threat there. *Which leaves me. Maybe that was what the will announcement was all about. To keep me in line.*

Mark shook his head rapidly, as if trying to clear his mind of the troubling what-ifs sending him down wildly bumpy roads. All he really had was speculation. Logan could have hired the PI, Charley Blaisdell, to investigate the blackmailing couple, after all, and could have learned of the parking garage incident from him. Poulos could have died because of a random robbery gone bad. And an accident could have killed Granger's friend.

Doubt wasn't enough reason to leave the highway for unknown side roads that might not lead anywhere except to dead ends. Staying the course and ignoring foolish suppositions, that was the logical choice to make. The safe choice, anyway. *But the right choice?* That he didn't know. And because he didn't, he needed more information to support this crazy hypothesis before he took steps that would irrevocably damage his career.

What an eventful day, he mused, a bit calmer now. The cancer situation with Logan, the unexpected inheritance news, and then his brother showing up out of the blue.

Luke. Mark's unease returned, though he didn't know why. If he hadn't thought he'd spotted his brother at the hospital, their get-together wouldn't have happened. Luke had called him psychic, had laughed at the coincidence. *But I don't have ESP, and that was one hell of a coincidence.*

Did I actually see Luke at the hospital? If so, Luke had lied to him. *Why? And what would he be doing at the hospital?*

To see Logan.

Suddenly, Mark's attempt to keep on the straightaway hit a roadblock, forcing him into still another detour, a reason why Luke could have been there to see his boss. The incidents involving the Howard woman and the football player were coming together, much as he wanted to deny the connection. But it screamed at him now; Luke could be working for Logan. When it came down to it, Mark didn't know much about his brother's life. Their age difference growing up in Chicago prevented any real bonding. Different friends, different interests. Aside from the elementary school years, they never had classes in the same building. After high school, they took different paths, Mark off to college and Luke, five years later, parlaying a summer job he had working in a delicatessen into full-time employment. His boss owned that deli as well as a chain of others throughout the Windy City. Mark had heard the rumors about this man, Rizzo, that he had organized crime connections. By then, though, Mark was getting his MBA in California and focusing on his own career.

And then came Luke's sudden decision to enlist in the Army, where he served two tours in Afghanistan. After that, he left the service and opened a gun shop. Luke was obviously familiar with guns and with killing.

He went over their conversation, hoping to find something that would put the kibosh to that line of thought. Luke seemed to be in the dark about Logan's disease, something he would have known if he went to see him. But that could have been misdirection.

Something else, though, that Luke apparently didn't know. My boss's name. Luke didn't know much about his brother's life, either. *Maybe he didn't realize I work for Logan.* That must have come as a shock.

But then why the questions about the Philadelphia hospital? Logan would have told him that if there were to be subsequent rendezvous. *If not, why would he care?* And it didn't fit with idle chitchat. This wasn't making sense. Maybe it was a coincidence after all.

The waitress approached again, interrupting his thoughts and bringing him back to the moment. "Will there be anything else, Mr. Elliot?"

"Uh, no thanks, Debbie. Just the check."

He signed it, left the restaurant, and headed to his office. He had some calls to make.

CHAPTER 25

L UKE SAT AT GATE B10 in Terminal 1 of McCarran International Airport, surfing his iPad apps. He'd managed to get an earlier flight back to Philadelphia with an hour layover in Chicago.

Chicago. Luke smiled when the ticket agent had offered him that option, though of course he wouldn't have any time to visit. Emily had never been there, had never been east of the Mississippi, in fact. Luke had so many places he wanted to show her, but especially his hometown.

He hadn't been back since taking Rizzo down. He had no idea what became of the mobster's organization after that, and he didn't care. Except he hoped he had majorly disrupted Paulie Ryan's life. The bastard who had tried setting him up, forcing him to flee to the Army, deserved something bad to happen to him. Luke had thought about his former colleague from time to time, and if thoughts were bullets, Ryan would be long dead.

As he checked the Weather Channel for the conditions in Philadelphia, his cell phone rang. Mark. "What's up, bro?" Luke answered.

"Haven't taken off yet, I guess."

"Boarding starts in a little while. They screwed up my flight, and now I've gotta go through Chicago." He laughed. "I think I could've driven to Santa Fe in less time."

"I hear that. So you *are* going back home tonight."

"Uh, sure. Where else?"

"I was just wondering if maybe another gun deal had come up while you were here today."

Strange question. "Why would you think that?"

Mark sighed. "Oh, man, I don't want to do this, but I have to know. Luke, I'm going to be straight with you, and I hope you'll do the same."

Uh-oh. "Jeez, Mark, sounds serious. What's going on?"

"Were you at the Clark Memorial Medical Center today?"

"Still think you saw me there, huh?"

"I can find out, Luke. Trust me. But I want to hear it from you."

"I don't get it. Why is that such a big deal to you?" Luke temporized as he searched for an explanation.

"Humor me, okay? Were you there or not?"

Luke groaned. "All right, you got me. I was there."

"Why did you lie to me?" His tone held more of an angry accusation than a whine.

"I didn't want you to get all worried about me, bro. You see, I have this condition that requires a special medication. With it I'm fine, but I forgot my pills, and only hospitals carry it." He knew what the next question would be, and he didn't have an answer yet.

"What kind of condition?"

Think! Something simple but potentially dangerous. Heart... no. Diabetes... too complicated.

Someone sneezed behind him.

Allergies... yes!

"Luke?"

"I told you, man, it's nothing, really. Just some weird form of asthma."

"Asthma? Jeez, that can be rough. Sorry to hear that. But the drug controls it?"

"Yeah. Gotta take it every day, though." *Please don't ask.*

"What's the name of it?"

Naturally! Luke laughed. "I can't even pronounce the damn thing." *Will I have to spell it now?*

"So you weren't at the hospital to see my boss?"

Shit! "Mark, look at what you're suggesting. That I went to see a man I don't know from Adam, a man I didn't know was in the hospital until you told me. The logic escapes me. And what's up with these questions?"

"I said I'd be honest with you. Here goes. I have reason to believe my boss is trying to eliminate some people who could derail a plan of his."

"Eliminate as in kill? Yikes! Heavy shit, man. But what does this have to do with me?"

"What exactly was your job when you worked for Rizzo in Chicago?"

"That was a long time ago, dude. Why do you want to know?"

"Something that's just occurred to me. What did you do for him?"

"I was an account executive."

"What does that mean, exactly?"

"Managing the accounts. You know, our suppliers for the delis. Where is this going, man?" *Not where I think it's going, I hope.*

"You didn't know anything about his mob activity?"

There it is. "Uh, there was some talk, but what I did for him was legit all the way."

"Then why did you suddenly quit and join the Army?"

"I told you, bro. I thought it was the right thing to do. Fight for my country, you know? Jesus, Mark. What's going on here?"

"Okay. I have a boss I suspect has murder on his mind. I have a brother who once worked for a man rumored to be a major crime figure. He then suddenly leaves—or escapes?—for the Army. A brother who's an expert with guns, who shows up in town without telling me and then lies about being at the hospital where Wendell Logan is a patient. I connected those dots."

He's close, damn it. "Let me get this straight. You're saying I'm a hit man? Who came here to whack Logan before he could do the whacking?" Luke chuckled. "For Christ's sake, Mark, that's some wild idea you have. You definitely missed some dots along the way. If I were this hired gun, how would my employer know what the fat cat was planning? And even if he did, why would he care?"

A few moments of dead air. "That's not what I was saying, Luke. I didn't mean you went there to kill him. He's still alive, after all. I meant he could have hired you to do the hit, and that's why you were there, to get instructions."

Luke forced a laugh in response. He'd attracted the attention of a woman in the row of seats across from him, and he lowered his voice. "Who are these folks I'm supposed to rub out, if I might ask?"

"Do you know a Dr. James Dawson and his wife?"

"Never heard of 'em. I guess they don't live in Santa Fe."

"No. In Villanova."

"Pennsylvania?"

"Is there another one?"

"Beats me. I don't know anything about any Villanovas, or Dawsons, or whatever. Look, I can appreciate that you have a crazy boss who's put you into a tough spot. But my showing up and the hospital thing is all one big coincidence. I've never met Logan, and he hasn't hired me to be a hit man, okay? Me, a hit man. That's hilarious, Mark."

"Not very funny on this end."

"Sorry. I don't suppose you want to tell me why Logan wants these people dead."

"They know something he doesn't want to get out. Let's leave it at that."

"You know these people personally?"

"No, only indirectly. But I do know they're innocent, Luke. They don't deserve to die for what they know."

"Whatever you say. Makes no difference to me."

"A job is a job?"

"Man, there you go again. I have no interest in these people. None. But if you're worried about them, maybe you should warn them, you know? I'd appreciate it if you wouldn't mention my name, though, when you do."

"They're already aware of the threat. Just not who is behind it."

"Okay. They're starting to board now. Gotta go. But one thing more, Mark. I wouldn't trust this boss of yours. If he's planning to have these people whacked, you need to be invisible, man. No connection to it at all. You haven't talked to him about it, I hope."

"No. He's not aware I know."

"Good. Because you don't want to end up being his scapegoat, or worse, once the shit hits the fan."

Silence for a moment. "Right. I'll be careful. Enjoy your flight... to Santa Fe."

"Thanks." Luke disconnected. He checked his seat assignment on the boarding pass as the passengers with special needs or with small children filed through the door to the jetway.

He shook his head in amazement. *My brother. Smack dab in the middle of it. Who would've thought?*

So these Dawsons were good people, apparently. Too bad. But it really wasn't his concern.

Mark mulled over the conversation with his brother. Everything Luke said made sense, and he wanted to believe him.

Still, he could easily check something to put his mind at ease. He grabbed the laptop sitting on the credenza behind his desk and went online. After about five minutes, he found what he had hoped he wouldn't. No flights were leaving McCarran about now headed to New Mexico.

But Luke had said the airline screwed up his schedule, so perhaps he had to make a connection from Chicago. *Possible.* For completeness, he looked into flights from McCarran to Philadelphia. There it was. With a stop in Chicago. The plane Luke was now boarding. *Son of a bitch!*

Mark drummed his fingers on the polished wood of the desk as he tried to think of an innocent explanation. Luke might not be going on to Philadelphia but taking that hypothetical connection to Albuquerque, since there were no direct flights to Santa Fe. He continued his search and found such a flight. But it would mean a layover of six hours.

On a mission now, he went back to the McCarran schedule. A flight left for Santa Fe in two hours, with less than an hour layover in Albuquerque. And it was on time, no mention of any flight change. *Why wouldn't Luke wait for that one instead of the more complicated and much later Chicago connection?*

One very good reason. Luke wasn't going home. He had lied to him again. A gun deal, an asthmatic condition; they were likely lies, too. *My brother, a killer for hire?*

With mounting dismay, Mark sought another explanation, anything that would provide doubt for his ominous conjecture. Thinking of what had started him down this road of suspicion in the first place gave him an idea. He grabbed his phone and dialed a number.

"Blaisdell Investigations."

"Fran? This is Mark Elliot. Didn't expect you to be answering the phone at this hour. I was just going to leave a message."

"Hi, Mark." She laughed. "Well, you know Charley. He's on a hot case, and he needs me."

Mark chuckled with her. "That he does. Is he there?"

"Sure. Hold on."

After about twenty seconds, Charley said, "Hiya, Markie. How's it hangin'?"

"Can't complain. I'm calling about your report on the Boston case."

"Boston case?"

"Yeah. About a month ago. The Howards."

"The who?"

"Cathy and Tim Howard?"

"I'm drawin' a blank here. Haven't been to Boston in years."

Damn it! "Oh, man, I'm sorry. I just assumed it was you."

"What, is Wendell using somebody else, now? That bastard."

"No, Charley, it was all my misunderstanding. I'll check with him on that. He's been a little sick lately, and sometimes his communications aren't all that clear. He told me to find a report on these people in Boston. When I couldn't find it, I figured it was something he'd asked you to do for him. Hey, man, we're not about to waste our retainer with you."

"I would hope not. After all these years."

"Charley, my mistake, okay? You're still aces with us. You're the one I thought to call, right?"

"I guess."

"I'm really embarrassed. Please don't tell Mr. Logan about this. It could affect my bonus."

"Okay, pal. But if you want I should go to Boston, I wouldn't mind. Just as soon as I finish up what I'm workin' on. It's a doozy, but I should have it wrapped up in a day or so."

"I'll let him know and get back to you. Again, I'm sorry to have bothered you. Give Fran a hug for me."

"Will do. See ya, Markie."

Mark hung up and exhaled slowly. *That was almost a disaster.* Now that he knew his hunch had been correct, he had decisions to make. He had planned to pass Granger's threat along to his boss. But if he did that and the Dawsons were killed anyway, Logan would then know his chief of staff was in the loop.

Luke's words of caution, that he should stay out of it, came back to him. It would be the safe move, keeping off Logan's radar. But if his inaction caused the Dawsons to be killed... *Christ! A rock and a hard place.*

The same reasoning applied to his other decision, whether or not to warn those people that their suspicions were well founded, that someone was really coming to kill them. And not just someone but his very own brother.

Unable to sit still with these thoughts dashing through his head, he rose from his chair and paced. *They should be warned.* He could make the call from a pay phone and not divulge his or Luke's identity. And not tell them Logan was behind it. *Yes, that might work.* He went back to his desk, dialed Information, and got the number for the doctor's office but not a home number.

Not what he wanted, but it was something. Dawson's office would be closed now, of course, with an answering service likely fielding calls. And at that very minute, an assassin could be en route to the doctor's town, arriving in only a few hours. The office number was all he had to work with. Maybe he'd get lucky, persuade the answering service with a story plausible enough for Dawson to be contacted. It was all he could do. *Tomorrow might be too late.*

CHAPTER 26

"VILLANOVA PEDIATRICS." THE WOMAN'S VOICE over the phone exhibited no inflection, neither welcoming nor annoyed at the intrusion. Just business-neutral.

"I need to speak with Dr. Dawson," Mark Elliot replied.

"Is this an emergency?"

"Yes."

"Dr. Strasser is on call tonight."

"I understand, but Dr. Dawson said I could call him at any time about my son."

"I'm sorry, but Dr. Dawson is on vacation."

Good! I have more time. "When will he be back?"

"I don't have that information. Shall I call Dr. Strasser?"

"No, Dr. Dawson is the only one who can help. Thanks anyway." Elliot hung up the pay phone. *So the doctor probably isn't home, fortunately.* He'd try again tomorrow during office hours, speak with a nurse or receptionist, someone he might persuade to connect him with Dawson.

But the pay phone was impractical. He couldn't hang around it waiting for a callback. Then he thought of the solution: a prepaid cell phone. Still anonymous and yet convenient. First thing tomorrow, he'd get one.

The next day
Burlington, Vermont

Somehow, it didn't seem right that this sad occasion should take place on such a beautiful day, a day made for joy, for celebration. But the sunny, low-humidity weather allowed the mourners to mingle outside the Cathedral Church of St. Paul before the funeral service. And it gave Michelle and me an opportunity to have a word with Granger when he arrived, before his celebrity got in the way. As yet, he and his wife were no-shows.

We waited in front of the Episcopal church for another reason, to put off as long as possible having to face the grieving families. We, who were there at the time of the tragedy, still lived, while our friends, their loved ones, didn't. Our presence would surely be a reminder of that stark reality.

Two large men emerged from a taxi and walked up to join four men of similar size to our right. Bob's Philadelphia Eagles teammates, I surmised. I recognized one of them as the Eagles' star quarterback, now a sportscaster on ESPN. They were likely candidates for pallbearer duty.

Under other circumstances, I would have been asked to participate in that task. But our "undisclosed location" and incommunicado status precluded that, if the Kretchmans had seen fit to ask.

As we faced Cherry Street, waiting for the Grangers' arrival, Brad Stevens entered the church grounds. "Brad's here," I said to Michelle, and we intercepted him as he walked toward the church entrance. Of course, it had been many years since I'd seen him, and his struggle with cancer must have taken quite a toll on him, but I was a little taken back at how beaten down and old he looked.

A frown rather than a smile greeted us as we reached him, surprising me at first, but then I knew the reason. It had been his house on the lake. Were it not for him, we wouldn't have been there. Indirectly, he had put Bob Kretchman in that boat. His boat. So he might have some misguided sense of responsibility for what happened, and perhaps he blamed Michelle and me for being the actual agents who made it possible.

"Brad." I held out my hand.

"Hello, Jim." He shook my hand. "Michelle."

"Thank you for coming," I said.

"I had to." He pressed his lips together and, shoulders slumped, looked at the church.

"How is Linda doing?"

"She's fine. Can't get around very well, but she's not in a wheelchair yet, at least."

"And you?" Michelle's smile contrasted with Brad's dour countenance. "Are the doctors still happy with your progress?"

"So they say. There's no sign of the cancer coming back."

"That's good to hear," I said. An uncomfortable silence followed.

"So... It's nice to see you folks again." He turned to go.

"Brad, it was nobody's fault, okay?" I lied. "Your boat was in excellent shape. I had it checked out thoroughly by the mechanic you recommended. It was just a freak accident."

"I appreciate that. Still, I'll have to live with the part I played in this tragedy. If only..." He looked away for a moment. "Well, it can't be helped now. And I hope you'll find a way to get over that terrible day yourselves." With that, he left us and climbed the steps to the church.

"Jeez." Michelle shook her head. "Like we didn't already feel bad enough. Now I wish we were like your parents and didn't come today, to avoid this depressing scene."

My folks had a thing about funerals, considering them morbid spectacles. Mom and Dad had expressed to me on more than one occasion their wish to be remembered at a fun party rather than a funeral service when they passed away. They had contacted Bob and Sheree's parents to express their sympathy, but they would not be attending the funeral. Some of their attitude had rubbed off on me. Though I empathized with Michelle's sentiment, being here was the right thing to do.

"Yeah, you've got a point, for sure." I checked my watch and looked around the grounds. The football players were filing into the church, leaving Michelle and me about the only remaining mourners still outside. And I didn't want that. "We'd better go in."

"Aren't Al and Tammy coming?"

I shrugged. "He told me they were. Come on." We headed to the church steps. The time to run the gauntlet of families standing in the narthex had arrived.

As we left the bright sunshine for the appropriately darker entrance hall, there they were. Somber and, to my paranoid mind, accusatory expressions faced us. I imagined what they had to be thinking. *The Dawsons. Their boat killed my son... my daughter... my father.* We nodded solemnly, and as we continued toward the sanctuary, a hand grabbed my arm. I turned to see Bob's father, a retired cop, staring at me with the look that used to intimidate me as a kid. As it did now. A big man with short-cropped gray hair, he was an imposing figure.

"I want to talk to you later," he said.

"Yes, sir."

He released his strong grip, and we continued into the church proper.

I never did see Granger at the church, but I spotted him at the cemetery. He must have arrived at the last minute. He and Tammy stood talking with a small group of people, Pennsylvania residents, and thus potential voters for him, I concluded cynically. I caught his eye, and he gave me a small wave as the burial service began.

Afterward, as the Kretchmans passed us on their way to the car, Bob's father looked at me and said, "I'll see you at the house."

So I was now obligated to attend the post-funeral reception. He needed to talk to me, and I owed him that. But first, *I* needed to speak with Granger.

The other funeral-goers began drifting away, and we waited for Granger's acolytes to take their leave of the politician before approaching him. "Al, Tammy," I said.

Granger and I shook hands. The women gave each other tight smiles.

I was never sure of the proper etiquette of funerals. One shouldn't seem happy, of course. So glad-handing was definitely out, and I figured that any hugs should be of the consoling variety, not "good to see you again" demonstrations.

"At least it's a nice day," Granger offered, looking at the blue sky.

"Yeah. Are you going to the Kretchmans'?"

"No, I've gotta get back." He looked at his watch as if to confirm his rushed schedule.

"Any more thoughts about the assassin theory?" I stole a glance at Tammy and saw no surprise. She was up to speed, apparently.

"Actually, Jim, I do." He looked at his wife then down at the ground. He shook his head before returning his gaze to me with a sigh. "I wasn't completely honest with you the other day when we last talked. I realized there *is* someone I know who could be behind the, uh... incidents."

Finally! "Who?"

"Are you familiar with Wendell Logan?"

"Who's he?

"The Logan of Logan Enterprises, a Las Vegas billionaire."

Our conversation at the lake came to mind. "Is he connected to that PAC you were worried about?"

"Don't know, but I suspect he was behind it. I think he set me up." He chuckled but didn't smile. "If so, it was a masterful plan."

"I don't get it. That PAC opposed you, right?"

"So it appeared. But I think it was a clever scam to get me to accept Logan's offer of support. Anyway, I'll tell you about it sometime. The important thing is that Logan is now contributing to my campaign."

"I see." But I didn't yet. A campaign contributor had not been on my list of possibilities. "Okay, he's a donor. Is he also a wacko?"

"Crazy like a fox is more like it. Logan is not just *a* donor. He's offered to finance a presidential run. Whatever I need. He's made it clear he wants to see me in the White House and is willing to spend whatever it takes to make that happen."

Now I got it. "And *do* whatever it takes, as well?"

"That's my concern."

"Well, that tears it!" Michelle said with wild anger in her eyes, a look I didn't remember ever seeing before, thank God. "It all makes sense now. And what chance do we have against an obsessed billionaire? Jim, it's time we went public with that secret of yours. Before it's too late!"

"Michelle," Tammy said, "don't get carried away. Alan—"

"Carried away, Tammy?" Michelle shouted. "It's our lives at stake here, okay? Jesus!"

I looked around. We were the only mourners left, at least within earshot. Another vulnerable situation a killer might use to his advantage. I couldn't help it. My mindset now included a constant awareness of potential danger that a cemetery's peace couldn't assuage.

Granger held up his hands. "Hold on now. I've taken care of it."

I remembered those words in our last phone conversation, those words that had bothered me without knowing why. "Just how did you do that, Al?" My wife was right. It was time to end this deadly game once and for all.

"I told Logan I'd quit the campaign if any harm came to you." Granger's smug expression indicated his "bold" move had settled the matter.

Michelle wasn't having any of it. "That's it, Al?" She folded her arms across her chest in that confrontational stance of hers that *was* very familiar to me. She glared at him. "What a solution! Only problem is we'd have to be dead before you back up your threat. And then what? I can see it now. 'Oh, what's done is done. Can't bring them back now, and they would have wanted me to continue my campaign.' Ha!"

"Look, Michelle," Granger said in his patronizing talk-show voice, "Logan's invested a lot of time and money in me. He's not about to see me walk. Which I certainly would do, believe me."

"So you say. And what a noble sacrifice it would be." She grabbed my arm. "Let's go, Jim. I've heard enough of this bullshit." She tried to pull me away.

"Guys, wait a second. Please. Let's think this through first."

"We have, Al. Michelle is right."

He shook his head and actually stamped his foot. "I said I *might* have found the person responsible. But what if I'm wrong? And what if our theory itself isn't even true? Jim, you asked me before if I knew of anyone who could have done these things. Okay, I found a candidate. And then, despite having no evidence, I confronted him with it."

"But he obviously didn't fess up." Michelle released my arm.

"Of course not. Hey, let's be logical about this. If our theory is wrong, nothing will come of it, naturally. If it's right, still nothing will come of it now. Don't you see? Logan's not going to take that chance."

"Easy for you to say," I said. "It's not your life in danger here."

"Well, not literally. But in every other way, it is. Think about it. If you break the story, it will connect me with murder, and I don't just mean the Favreau woman. Bob was *there*. One of the four. And now he's killed in a mysterious explosion? How long do you think it would be before some reporter figures out the possible motivation?"

Tammy had moved so that no space stood between her and Granger as they faced us. She nodded at her husband's words of wisdom. A show of unity against the misguided doubters.

I had to admit he had a point. Some Michael Isikoff-type would wonder about that and start to dig, a Pulitzer Prize in his sights. *Why does this have to be so fucking complicated? Still, should I care if Granger's political ambition comes to an end, or even if he becomes a target in a murder investigation? What does that compare to keeping Michelle and me breathing? And what about justice for Bob and Sheree?*

As if he read my thoughts, he went on, "You wouldn't escape the bad publicity, either, Jimbo. You're a pediatrician, for Christ's sake. How many patients would you have if it comes out you abandoned a baby who could have died as a result?"

"I was just a kid, then." The excuse was itself juvenile. Granger's arguments were softening my resolve.

"We all were. But old enough to know better, as you've told me more than once."

I looked around the peaceful setting as I considered the ramifications. The coffins lay suspended in the grave openings, side by side, their polished surfaces reflecting the sun's rays. On the access road in the distance, a truck and a small bulldozer headed our way, presumably to complete the interment process, a vivid reminder of what had occurred and how all of us would end up eventually. *Some before their time.*

"Just think about it, okay?" Granger said, breaking the silence. "That's all I ask."

"We'll do that." I guided Michelle down the footpath to the road.

I introduced Michelle to some high school classmates of mine as we stood around the buffet table in the Kretchmans' dining room. The senior Robert Kretchman came into the room from the kitchen and stepped over to us.

"Jim, let's go outside for a minute."

"Sure." I gave Michelle a slight nod, put my plate on the sideboard, and followed Bob's father into the kitchen, past Mrs. Kretchman and two women I didn't know, and out the back door.

He led me to a patio table shaded by a maple tree. He took a cigarette from his shirt pocket. "I'm supposed to be giving these up." He lit it with a Bic. "But I don't think Grace will begrudge me today."

I waited for him to begin.

"Tell me what happened, Jim."

I did.

"So it was a spur of the moment decision, then? Bobby hadn't said anything before about taking the boat out?"

"No. When I asked him and Sheree if they wanted to play tennis, that's the first time he brought it up."

He took a drag and blew the smoke out slowly. "Then it was just as likely you could have been in the boat when... it happened."

"Yes, and that's what has bothered me ever since."

"Survivor's guilt. It's a natural reaction."

I made a decision. "It's more than that, sir. Did Bob ever tell you about a car accident we had when we were in high school?"

Mr. Kretchman had finished another cigarette by the time I laid out the whole story, including what I had learned from Granger at the cemetery. He was staring off into space when the back door opened and Grace Kretchman called out, "Bob?"

"Yes?"

"We need you." She closed the door.

He turned back to me. "Who investigated the attempted mugging or whatever it was in Boston?"

"I don't know. But the cops did come."

"And the sheriff at the lake? What's his name?"

"Broussard. He suspected it wasn't an accident, but I don't think he found anything to back that up."

"Damn it!" He slammed his hand on the table then rose. I stood as well. "It was bad enough thinking my boy was killed in an accident. But murdered? Christ almighty!"

I now regretted my decision. "Sorry if I've made it worse for you, but I thought you should know."

He gave a loud sigh as he shook his head. "No, Jim, you did the right thing." He offered his hand, and I shook it. "It'll give me something to do besides just sitting around feeling miserable." He started toward the house, and I followed. At the door, he turned to me. "Until we get this worked out, you need to take precautions. If the boat wasn't an accident, it was obviously done by a professional."

"That's why I was considering going public with the story, to end the motive for coming after us."

"The entire story?"

"No, sir. Only what we know for sure. The original accident." That much I'd decided. It might keep Granger safe from conspiracy rumors, not that I cared that much, but the rest of it was speculation without proof, anyway.

He stared at me for a few moments. "It's your call, Jim. You're the one at risk. But Bobby is dead, unable to defend himself now. I'd rather not have any blemish on his reputation, especially if this conspiracy thing doesn't actually exist and it would all be for nothing. I don't give a shit about Granger. He's the one who started this mess that could have ended up killing my boy."

"I understand."

"You'll need some protection, whatever you decide. Even if you go public with the story, that could take a few days. And it might not be the solution you think. It makes sense it should, but we're not dealing with a sensible person. And he would be royally pissed at you for fouling up his plan."

Stupidly, that hadn't occurred to me. *Is there no way out of this disaster?*

Mrs. Kretchman appeared at the screen door. "The Wilsons are looking for you, Bob."

"I'll be right in, honey."

She went back into the kitchen, and he turned back to me. "Do you own a handgun?"

There it was. The nitty-gritty. It could come down to us against whomever, not some intellectual exercise. The logic that had told me our escape from danger would be a simple matter, if only I could decide to do it, was hard up against a possible grim reality. Ultimately, we might have to defend ourselves from a hit man without knowing who he was or when he would strike.

Some prospect. Michelle was athletic and smart, and she certainly had guts. But I couldn't see her as a G.I. Jane. And me, a forty-year-old doctor, whose only real experience with violence had been on the football field two decades earlier. I did have a fistfight once, in seventh grade. Bruce Willis, I'm not. Oh, yeah, we'd make a formidable team against a skilled killer. I'd never even fired a gun.

Then I thought of what lay on the top shelf of my closet, hidden behind a row of sweaters. A Christmas gift from Michelle's dad in response to a recent home invasion that had occurred in my normally peaceful town.

"Jim?"

I hadn't realized I was staring at him as I thought through the import of his question about the handgun. "Uh, no. But I do have a shotgun."

"Even better, but only for home protection. And you can't stay cooped up in your house indefinitely. My advice would be to find a place no one knows about and stay there."

"We've got that covered now, but we can't just hide forever."

He nodded slowly. "No, that's true. So let's hope we can resolve this soon."

We?

He put his hand on the doorknob and faced me with a look of cold determination. "I'm going to check into this, see what I can come up with. I know some people."

He opened the door, and I followed him into the house just as my cell phone rang.

CHAPTER 27

THE CALLER ID SHOWED MY office number. I stepped back outside to the Kretchmans' deck, wondering what could have prompted the intrusion. "Hello?"

"Dr. Dawson, this is Marianne." One of our nurses. "So sorry to bother you on vacation, but a man called for you and was very insistent. He claimed you told him he could call you at any time about his son."

I quickly searched my memory bank for kids I was treating for serious conditions whose parents I might have given such an assurance. I came up empty. "Who is he?"

"That's the thing. We don't have his son in our records, and I looked up his area code. He was calling from Las Vegas. Howard Favreau."

My gut cramped. "Favreau?"

"Yes. Is this something personal, Dr. Dawson? Or is it someone trying to mess with you?"

The first one for sure, and maybe the second as well. Whoever it was, he'd succeeded in getting my attention, forcing me to respond. "I know who it is, Marianne," I lied. "I'll take care of it. Hold on a second." I fished a business card from my wallet, took a pen from my suit jacket pocket, and wrote down the number. *Howard Favreau. Clever. Someone who knows the story. But who? And what does he want?*

I went into the house to fetch Michelle. She had to be in on this. I found her talking with the Kretchmans in the kitchen. "Michelle, I think we'd better go. To get to the airport in time."

She looked at me for a second then nodded. Whether she caught an urgent expression in my face or felt no desire to stay in the melancholic environment any longer than necessary, she was with me.

"Michelle and I have a flight back we have to catch," I told Bob's dad and mom.

Grace Kretchman nodded. "Thank you for coming. I know it wasn't easy for you to do."

I didn't know if she referred to our long-distance trip to get there or the fact her son died while staying with us, but it didn't matter. "Well, we had to," I said, repeating what Brad Stevens said to me in front of the church, not knowing what else to say, as I suspected he hadn't, either. Jeez, these occasions were tough. My parents had it right about funerals.

A burly, gray-haired man of Kretchman's age approached us just as I was about to lead Michelle away. "Bob," the man said. They shook hands and hugged, then he embraced Mrs. Kretchman.

"Dick Lambert," Bob Kretchman, Sr. said, "I'd like you to meet the Dawsons, Jim and Michelle."

As we shook hands, he completed the introductions. "Dick's a retired cop, like me. Dick, Jim's a pediatrician, and Michelle is a teacher. Jim and Bobby grew up together."

"Nice to meet you folks."

Michelle smiled, and I said, "Same here." I turned to Mr. Kretchman. "We'll be heading off. We have a lot to think about."

"Give me your cell phone number."

I gave him a business card on which I wrote my phone number on the back.

"Stay safe," he said.

"We'll try," Michelle replied, and we left in search of the Stallings to say our goodbyes.

Kretchman watched the Dawsons leave and then turned to his friend. "Dick, I'd like to ask a favor of you."

"Sure, anything."

"Let's go outside for a minute." Kretchman took a shopping-list pad and a pen from a cabinet drawer and then led Lambert out the back door. As soon as it closed behind them, Kretchman said, "You still have any contacts in Boston PD?"

Lambert chuckled. "We old farts get together occasionally, and I've met some of the younger guys still active. Why?"

"I need to reach out to a cop currently on the force there, and I don't know who he is."

Lambert stared at him for a few seconds. "About Bobby?"

Kretchman forced a smile. "Once a detective, always a detective." He gestured at a chair on the deck and sat in another. "Dick, it's come to my attention that Bobby's accident might not have been one."

"Oh, shit."

"Yeah, I know. His buddy, that Dr. Dawson you just met, told me an amazing story. Bobby may have been caught up in a conspiracy and got killed because of it."

"Jesus." Lambert shook his head. "So what's with Boston?"

"An incident there could be part of this conspiracy. The cop I want to find investigated it. I was hoping you could use your contacts to learn who he is and establish my bona fides with him so he'll talk to me."

"I can do that, Bob. No problem. Shouldn't take more than a day or two. Now, what was this incident you want to know about?"

Kretchman handed him the pad and pen and told what he knew.

"I'll get on it right away."

"Thanks, Dick." He rose from the chair, as did Lambert. While they shook hands, Kretchman thought of his next move. Calling that Sheriff Broussard.

With the large number of mourners visiting the Kretchmans, I had to park the rental car almost a block away from the house. As soon as we climbed in, I said, "My office got a strange call a little while ago. A man calling himself Howard Favreau wants to talk to me."

"Howard—" Her eyes got big. "Jim!"

"I know. I wanted you to be with me when I called him."

"Absolutely!"

I had the cell phone in my hand. I tapped in the number and put the phone on speaker.

"Hello?" A man's baritone voice.

"I'm Dr. Dawson. Is this Howard Favreau?"

"That's a false name, Doctor, as I'm sure you know. I wanted to make sure you called me back."

"Mission accomplished. So who are you?"

"That's not important. The reason I called is to warn you. Someone is out to... do you harm."

I looked at Michelle, who stared back at me with wide eyes. "Because of a political campaign?"

"Yes."

"Well, whoever you are, thanks for the warning, but I already figured that."

"What you don't know is that this person is probably in your town as we speak. You're not at home, I hope."

I glared at the phone as if it were the man speaking to me. "Where I am is none of your business, *Favreau*. And why should I think you know what you're talking about?"

"Look, Doctor, you're in real trouble, okay? If you don't believe me, fine. I've done all I can do."

"You don't know me, do you?"

"I just know *of* you."

"So you saw fit to warn a perfect stranger out of the goodness of your heart?" *Who is this guy?*

A few seconds of silence passed. "I've gotten involved in this situation without my knowledge. Now that I know, I want it to stop."

What's his part in this? "To protect yourself as well, perhaps?"

"In a way. In fact, I'm taking a risk talking to you."

He knows Logan. Maybe even works for him. "Okay, I think I understand. Thanks for the heads up."

"You'll take action, then?"

I raised my eyebrows at Michelle. "Any suggestions?"

"Well, don't go home to start with."

Thanks a bunch. "Yeah, I've already been given that advice. Isn't there something you can do at your end?" *Like convince Logan to call off his hit man?*

"Impossible. As I said, I've done all I can do. Good luck, Doctor." He hung up.

Michelle and I stared at each other for several seconds. "Who do you think he is?" she asked.

"Somebody who's tied in with Logan, somehow. He's tumbled to the plot and is now worried he'll be implicated in it."

"He's in a bind. Can't go against the big man, or else somebody could then be coming after *him*."

"I think that's right. He's covering his ass without tipping his hand."

"And Granger said he'd taken care of it. What a joke!" She grabbed my hand. "Time's up, Jimmy! My God, there's a killer waiting for us in Villanova? We have to get that secret out in the open *now*."

I looked at the Kretchman house for a moment. "We might have to do that."

"Might?" She released my hand, sat back, and folded her arms across her chest. "Jesus, Jim. We *have* to. Hello. This isn't a what-if debate anymore. It's goddamned real!"

"It's not that simple, Mish. Let me tell you about the talk I had with Bob's dad."

After ending his phone call to Dawson, Mark Elliot sat back in his chair, satisfied he had done not only the right thing but also all he *could* do to help, as he had told the doctor. But now the Dawsons knew Luke would be lying in wait for them. His brother would no longer have surprise in his favor and could be in jeopardy himself. *I've warned Dawson. Now I have to do the same for Luke.* He made the call.

"Morning, bro," Luke answered.

"Did you have an uneventful trip back to Santa Fe?"

"No problems."

"Good. Say, I don't want to bother you at work. Is this a bad time?"

"Nah. I'm taking the day off."

I bet. "I just wanted to let you know that I took your advice."

"Yeah? What's that?"

"I warned the doctor that someone was coming after him... soon."

After a few moments of silence, Luke replied, "Good for you. But I hope you didn't identify yourself."

"No, and I used a prepaid cell phone."

"Smart move. Your conscience should be clear now."

"I hope so. The Dawsons will know to take precautions. Anyway, that's why I called, to thank you for the suggestion."

"Out of curiosity, do you have any idea what those precautions will be?"

C'mon, Luke, please let it go. "No."

"Well, with the hit man's element of surprise gone, that should help those people."

Yes! "That's what I figure. The assassin could be walking into a trap now."

"Yeah, too bad for him, right? Anything else on your mind, dude? I gotta get my bacon out of the frying pan before it burns."

"Bacon?"

"I'm making breakfast."

Mark couldn't help chuckling at the irony. "You need to save your bacon, that's for sure. I'll let you go."

With his warnings out of the way, Mark had one more call to make, Logan's daily briefing. In two days, his boss would be checking into the Franklin Cancer Center. And then, Mark hoped, he would focus on killing his cancer instead of innocent people.

Michelle and I flew back to Wilmington later that day. Two days remained on our Oak Island rental house. Two days to figure out what we were going to do without having to look over our shoulders constantly.

Bob's father had suggested we could be in danger no matter what we did about disclosing the secret. And then the anonymous phone call made that danger more acute. A man calling from Las Vegas, someone who *knew* we were in trouble, warned that the plan to kill us was underway, a killer already in Villanova, maybe outside our house at this very moment.

So we had two days to work things out. Not to discuss whether our jeopardy was real—that was no longer hypothetical—but to come up with a solution to keep us alive in the short term and, hopefully, put an end to this disaster. Two days.

CHAPTER 28

The next day

BOB KRETCHMAN, SR. TOOK THE cell phone number Dick Lambert had just given him out to the patio table for privacy. He hadn't yet told his wife what he'd learned from Jim Dawson, not wanting to complicate her grief. He didn't think the anger, which was helping him cope, would ameliorate her sorrow. And it might make it even worse. He tapped in the number on his phone.

"Raines," the Boston cop answered.

"Detective Raines, this is Bob Kretchman. Thank you for agreeing to take my call."

"Hey, Bob. Sure, no problem. I don't know Dick Lambert, but word around here is he's good people. If he vouches for you, that's enough for me. So you want to know about that parking garage incident. May I ask why?"

"I think it's connected to a conspiracy that got my son killed."

"Oh, jeez. I'm sorry. I had no idea."

"Now you know my interest in this."

"Absolutely. But I don't think I can be of much help. I was suspicious there was more going on than met the eye, but I didn't have anything solid to go on. Had to sign it off as a random mugging attempt."

"Anything you can tell me about the perp? Did the nurse describe him?"

"Not hardly. White guy somewhere between twenty and forty. We got a glimpse of his face from a surveillance camera, but a ball cap obscured it. The Chiefs."

"What?"

"That was on the hat he wore, the logo of the Kansas City Chiefs football team. I showed the logo to the vic, and she remembered seeing it. So that's our guy. Not much to go on, though. Didn't see any scars. The cap covered his hair. Anyway, there weren't any subsequent complaints from the woman, so that's why we essentially closed the case."

"I understand." *No help there.*

"But now you've got me going, Bob. What's this about a conspiracy?"

"It's a long story. And except for the fact this assault occurred in your town, Boston isn't involved as far as I know. I've already taken up enough of your time."

"Hey, man, it's my day off, and I'm sitting by my pool having a beer. I have the time. You came to me for info about my case. You can't leave me hangin' now. C'mon, fill me in. Cop to cop."

Raines was right, Kretchman realized, putting himself in the detective's shoes. He deserved to know. And maybe there *was* a Boston angle to this after all that could help, like what the so-called mugger looked like. "It's complicated, Sean. Do you have pen and paper handy?"

"And that's why the doctor and his wife are up against it now," Kretchman summed up after finishing the story. He'd not given any details about the secret that had started the whole mess, only that it would be bad for Granger's presidential aspirations and that his buddies and that nurse knew about it. He'd identified Logan as the probable driving force behind the conspiracy but not by name. In his mind, it wasn't out of the question Granger was doing this on his own and had blamed Logan to cover his ass. Politicians. He wouldn't put anything past them.

"Son of a bitch! All this over fucking politics? Unbelievable!"

"Power, Sean. It's an old story." He noticed a robin pecking in his grass twenty feet away.

"Have you talked to that sheriff yet?"

"Yes. Nothing there. He's suspicious, but he doesn't have any evidence."

"That's what we need. Evidence."

We? Kretchman smiled at the implication. *Looks like we've become a team already.* "You got that right."

"This talk about politics, in Pennsylvania, especially, got me thinking. There might be a way I can help you with this—and me, too. At least it's worth a try."

"Let's hear it."

"Okay, I've got this brother-in-law. Clark Munson. He works for a congressman from Philadelphia. And the thing is, the congressman doesn't care too much for Granger. Ran against him for governor, in fact, until he dropped out. For a health issue that turned out to be nothing. Clark thought something else was going on, and from what you just told me, I have a funny feeling about it, too."

"Who's the congressman?"

"Brent Marshall. Clark tells me he's one of the good guys."

"I think I've heard of him. But what're you getting at?"

"This is what I was thinking. I get Clark to put the bug in his ear about what Granger's backer is doing to protect a skeleton in Granger's closet. Marshall would have contacts, naturally, with the local cops. You got to me because of the cop network. Maybe we can do the same through Brent. He talks to somebody in the Philly PD, who talks with somebody in the Villanova PD. Somebody who can keep an eye out for the bad guy after your doctor. What do you think? Worth a shot?"

"If the congressman is willing, I think it's a good idea."

"Oh, I think he'd be willing, all right. He can't stand Granger, and this should put the icing on that cake. What's the doctor's address?"

Kretchman told him Dawson's office address and phone number from the business card Dawson had given him.

"Thanks, Sean. I really appreciate this."

"Helping a fellow cop and possibly solving a case at the same time? It's a no-brainer. I'll get back to you after I talk to Clark."

Kretchman put the phone on the table. As he thought about the new development, another robin joined the first on the grass. Both hopped around in what appeared to be a random pattern but with an obvious purpose in mind: searching for something to eat. The robins knew his backyard contained what they sought. And Villanova was where the evidence *he* sought could be found.

But assuming Raines's plan went through, it depended on one crucial thing for it to work. Dawson had to be the worm, the bait. He had told the doctor to keep out of harm's way while he looked into the matter. Now he had done that, and a solution had just surfaced. But it required Dawson to take a big risk. Making himself available as a target could not only end the immediate threat, it could ultimately destroy the conspiracy. *Will those incentives be enough to get Jim to bait the hit man? We'll see.*

He rose from the table. The robins were gone, giving the worms and insects living in the ground a temporary reprieve. But a bird would be back again, and its prey could do nothing about that. Unlike the soil's denizens, Jim Dawson would be intentionally attracting a killer to his home.

Oak Island, North Carolina

We'd talked over our options ad nauseam since coming back to our beach haven. Each one of course had its pros and cons. Calling the *Philadelphia Inquirer* had been Michelle's insistence before I told her what Bob's dad had to say about that. It might work, might not. And reputations would be forever tarnished. Still, that was at the top of our list.

Getting the Villanova police involved held the number two position. I mean, someone wanted to kill us, right? But we could tell them nothing of substance. A phone call from an unknown man in Las Vegas. Even if we laid out the whole story behind that call, I could imagine what the cops would think. Pretty far-fetched. Hell, I was directly involved in the mess, and it hadn't occurred to me that we could be targets for assassination until a couple of weeks ago. But maybe they would believe us and arrange for protective custody or something. *For how long? A week, a month? With nothing further to go on?* Even temporary protection of some kind seemed unlikely given the facts that even to us still boggled the mind. But we didn't reject that option out of hand.

Hiding indefinitely on our own, hoping it would blow over eventually, also came up in our discussion. But that was so impractical. Again, we had the time frame to consider. Michelle didn't have to return to work until late August, but I had to get back in harness soon. And our boys needed a house to come home to. Not to mention that running away from the problem struck me as the wrong thing to do. A coward's way out. I didn't consider myself to be particularly macho, but it sure got my back up to think of being forced to retreat. And it wouldn't be merely a tactical withdrawal but one that would have to last as long as Alan Granger's presidency, if he got that far. That option we did reject.

Which left us with a final choice. Face the threat head-on. At least time wasn't a factor here. Our informant said the hit man was already in Villanova, so we wouldn't have to wait long for the confrontation. And it would resolve the matter one way or the other. I could call 9-1-1 when he made his move and bring the cavalry running to my aid in the nick of time. Only my aid. No way would I let Michelle be in the line of fire. My wife objected to this plan, as I knew she would.

We were having gin and tonics, a little liquid courage to help us cope with our predicament, at the dinette in the kitchen. It was too hot for an alfresco cocktail hour on the porch.

"That's crazy, Jimmy! It's the last choice we should think about. In fact, it doesn't deserve any discussion at all. Us against an experienced killer? No way!"

"It wouldn't be *us*, sweetheart. There's no reason you have to be at risk, too. A man's gotta do what a man's gotta do," I said, trying for some levity I certainly didn't feel.

She put her glass on the table with a thump and did her arms-folded thing across her chest.

Here it comes. I sipped my drink, avoiding her eyes.

"You are not going to do anything of the kind, and that's final!"

"Honey—"

"No, James. I don't plan on becoming a widow at my age. It's a problem for the police. That's their job. Not a baby doctor's!"

Baby doctor, huh? She was pulling out all the stops. She'd never called me that before. I guessed she was trying to show how ineffectual someone who took care of babies would be against an assassin. *Or was it that I was a doctor who was really just a baby?*

In either case, I took it as pejorative, and even though I knew she meant well, it pissed me off a little. "Well, this 'baby doctor' can handle himself, okay? And I have that intimidating weapon your father gave us, remember? Besides me, this hit man will have to contend with a cloud of double-aught buckshot coming at him. And that'll be only if the cops I call don't get him first."

"No! Get real! You don't know the first thing about that gun."

"Jeez, honey, it's not complicated. I went over the instruction manual."

"Great, you read the instruction manual. You've never even fired it, have you?"

"No, but—"

"And hoping the cops would arrive in the nick of time so you wouldn't have to be Steve McQueen? That's gambling with your life, and you're not going to do it."

I sighed. My argument wasn't working, "Okay, okay." I held up my hands in surrender. "I won't do it," I lied. "But that leaves us with no decision still."

"What about Bob's dad? He was going to make some calls, right? Let's wait until we hear from him before we decide."

"Sounds like a plan." I gave her that little victory and took a drink from my glass.

One day left, and spending it on the beach seemed appropriate. Bad idea. If yesterday was hot, today was sizzling. What little breeze we had came offshore, and we sweltered despite the umbrella. Dips in the tepid surf only gave us brief and unsatisfying respites from the heat. If only we could have stayed at Silver Bay's cool, inviting lake.

After our uncomfortable discussion yesterday afternoon, Michelle hadn't brought up our quandary again. She could have been hanging her hopes on that call from Bob's dad that probably would not come in time to help us. But even so, I knew from long experience that she had made up her mind regarding my lone-defender proposal. Once she had given her proclamation, the discussion ended, and only new information could resurrect it.

That was my wife, God bless her. And I let her get away with it for the most part all through our marriage. Probably why our relationship has remained strong. I learned a long time ago that it was much easier for me to let it go than to fight, once she was convinced of her position's righteousness. And I have to admit, in those instances involving important decisions, she was usually correct. Whatever side of her brain was responsible for her reasoning, her opinions were not affected by testosterone-fueled posturing.

But while Michelle remained silent on our unresolved decision, I was thinking about how I would hunker down in the Alamo, waiting for Santa Anna to attack, and how I would get Michelle out of the way before it happened.

The heat, though, made thinking difficult. I was about to suggest to Michelle that we pack it in and retreat to the air-conditioned refuge of the house when my cell phone rang. I grabbed it from my beach bag. "Hello?"

"Jim, this is Bob Kretchman. I've got some new information for you."

I put the phone on speaker and beckoned Michelle to come closer. I hoped to hell it was good news.

CHAPTER 29

As Bob's father gave us the dope on the Boston detective's plan, I thought it was fitting we'd come full circle in a way. Congressman Marshall was again in the mix. And ultimately, he might be instrumental in defeating Granger after all.

I liked the plan, and I could tell by her nodding that Michelle liked it, too. Getting the police involved had been her first choice of action. And having a cop to call directly if needed would be an asset for what I'd decided to do.

He must have thought the same thing, because he went on, "I'll call you as soon as I hear the arrangements have been made, and I'll give you the name of the contact in the Radnor Township PD."

"That'll be good to know," I said.

"Jim, I've got an idea I'd like to run by you. Were you thinking of returning home soon?"

"Tomorrow?" I looked at Michelle.

"To a hotel!"

"Is that your wife?"

"Yes, she's listening in. My vacation is about up, and I have to get back to work. Staying at a hotel would let me do that while the cops do *their* thing." *And it would keep Michelle out of harm's way.*

"I see." He paused. "Yes, uh, that was *exactly* what I was about to suggest if you were going home."

Something sounded off in the way he said that. "Well, thanks for calling, sir. I'm really encouraged by the news and hope it works out as planned."

"I'm not sure how long it will take to set everything up. So keep your cell phone charged."

"Count on it. Thanks again." I hung up.

Michelle was all smiles. "Now we have a plan."

Yes, we certainly did. I returned her smile. "It's promising, for sure." I wiped sweat from my forehead. "Let's get out of this heat and start looking into where we'll stay when we get back to Villanova."

We left Oak Island the next morning, Thursday, for the long drive north. Six hours later, as we neared Maryland, my cell phone rang. It was Mr. Kretchman.

"Good afternoon." This time, I didn't put the phone on speaker. I had called him back in private shortly after his call yesterday. I suspected he wanted to say more than he had during that call. And though getting the killer was personal for him, he was still a cop; I wanted to get his opinion of my plan, whether or not it had occurred to him as well.

It had, and not only because it would force the issue, which was my motivation to bring to an end this deadly cat-and-mouse game. He had raised a more practical reason. Patrolling my neighborhood might result in the cops questioning a suspicious character hanging around, but without proof of an intended crime, an arrest would be unlikely. We needed to catch him in the act. So he'd agreed with my decision.

"We're all set, Jim," he said. "Is your wife listening in again?"

"No. But we're en route back to Villanova. Should be there in a couple more hours."

"Okay. The arrangements went quicker than I thought. Turns out that a cop Marshall talked to in Philly knew Bobby. He was a regular at the restaurant. And *he* knew a guy in the Delaware County Sheriff's Office who was at Syracuse a couple of years after Bobby graduated. Anyway, your contact is Detective Ron Frymoyer. I've talked with him, and he's up to speed on the situation. Unmarked patrols will be sent around to check out your street and house."

"That sounds good. I really appreciate all you've done." I smiled at Michelle and gave her a thumbs-up.

"I only wish I could be there to nail the bastard myself."

"I know."

"I've got Frymoyer's cell number."

"Hold on a sec." I grabbed a pen and pad from the door's side pocket and handed them to Michelle.

He gave me the number, which I repeated.

"Call him at the first sign of trouble, Jim. I didn't tell him you were going to be in the house. A civilian-as-bait deal would change the situation for him, and I'm sure he'd be against it. Especially since he's not divulging the true reason for the patrols at this time."

"I understand. Here's hoping the next time we talk, the cops will have the guy."

"Amen to that. I'd like to go over a few things I've been thinking about. I think he'll try for you during daylight, when your guard should be down and the home security system normally wouldn't be on. You do have one?"

"Yes."

"Well, we don't want to scare him off, so you shouldn't set it. Which means you shouldn't stay there at night. Too risky."

"Yeah, well, I can't do that anyway, remember?"

"Oh, right. Michelle would wonder where you were."

When he advised on more specifics for the operation, things I had thought about in a hypothetical way over the last twenty-four hours, the situation became very real. My hands on the steering wheel grew clammy.

"Remember, this guy is a pro. Don't take any unnecessary chances."

Unnecessary? That was some qualifier. Serious doubt about my being up to the task started creeping in. "I won't."

"Good luck, Jim."

Those were always the closing words on the self-destruct recording at the beginning of each episode of that old TV series. *Is my task going to be a mission impossible?* "Thanks. I'll need it. Bye." I slowed for a tollbooth and forced a smile for Michelle. "It's all set, hon. The cops will be checking our house on a regular basis."

She squeezed my arm. "Looks good, Jimmy."

"Yes, it does." I would let her have as much confidence in the police's ability to catch the killer before he got us as she could muster. But short of a continuous cop presence at our house, there were too many windows of opportunity for a skilled hit man. I hoped I'd be ready for him when he tried.

＊◇＊

We arrived at the Residence Inn off Lancaster Avenue at four p.m. and checked in. The unit had a full kitchen, a roomy sitting area, and a separate bedroom.

"Will this be okay for a week or so?" I asked as I checked out what utensils, cookware, and appliances came with the place.

Michelle sighed. "It won't be our home away from home, exactly, but it'll do. The bathroom is nice."

"While you're getting our stuff organized, I'll go pick up some supplies. How about we have a drink here and then go out for dinner? There's an Olive Garden just down the street."

"Well, I'm not in the mood for cooking tonight, but do you think it'll be okay to go out?"

"Honey, we can't stay cooped up here twenty-four, seven. I don't think our hit man will be cruising all the restaurants in the area looking for us if we're not home. And we're pretty far away from our neighborhood."

"Okay, that makes sense, I guess."

I grabbed my car keys and sunglasses from the kitchen counter and left. I had to visit the supermarket and liquor store, but first a little reconnaissance was in order. After reaching Newtown Road, I parked about a quarter-mile from our house and proceeded on foot, wearing my shades and a ball cap. A block away, I saw a big, black SUV parked across the street from our house, facing away from me.

I knew my neighbors' cars, and the vehicle in question did not belong. I got close enough to see the driver's head through the back window. Looked like a man. In case he was checking me out in the rearview mirror, I checked my watch, made like I'd forgotten something, turned around, and walked back the way I'd come.

At the end of the block, I glanced back to check the SUV. It was still there, its occupant apparently waiting for... what? *To pick up my across-the-street neighbor for a late round of golf or something?* Possible. *But why not park in his driveway?*

Then I remembered the Woffords were in San Diego for an extended visit with their son and his family. After reaching my car, another non-threatening possibility for the presence of the SUV occurred to me. I pulled out my cell phone and called the number Bob's dad had given me.

"Frymoyer," the cop answered right away.

"Detective, this is Jim Dawson."

"Are you okay?"

"So far. Just checking in with you. We got into town a little while ago. Have you been by our house yet?"

"Went over there this morning. Place is locked up tight. Didn't see anything or anyone suspicious. You're not there, are you?"

"No, we're at a hotel. But I need to get some things from the house, and I was wondering what kind of car your people would be using in case someone pulls up while I'm there. So I'll know it's one of you guys."

"Not a good idea, Doctor. You should stay away from your house. I've got a dark blue Crown Vic, and I'll be driving by this evening on my way home."

"You live in Villanova?"

"No, West Wayne. An unmarked unit, I think it's a white Dodge Charger, will be checking your place out during the night, but we can't be there constantly. We've got a county to cover."

In the distance, the SUV pulled away from the curb and drove off. I couldn't get the license number, unfortunately. "Okay, I understand. Thanks, Detective. I appreciate your help."

"Protect and serve, Doctor. It's what we do. Stay safe, and I'll call you when we get the guy."

"I hope it's soon. Thanks again. Goodbye."

We had just finished breakfast in our Residence Inn suite the next morning when I told Michelle that Detective Frymoyer wanted to see me at the sheriff's office. "He called when you were in the shower. He has a suspect they picked up hanging around our neighborhood, and he wants to flesh out the story of what's been happening with us so he'll know what questions to ask in the interrogation."

The excuse I had invented to get me back to the house sans Michelle sounded good to me. I was getting good at lying to my wife lately, I realized with regret. But the rationalization of the end justifying the means gave me some solace.

She perked up at my canard. "Really? Boy, that was fast!"

"Yeah. Maybe it's a dead end, but we'll see. At least it shows the cops are on the job."

"When does he want us there?"

Didn't think of that. "Uh, he wants *me* there as soon as possible. I asked him about you, but he specified only me. He didn't say why. Must have his reasons."

"That's weird."

I shrugged. "Anyway, I don't know how long it will take but hopefully not long. And then maybe this whole thing will be over."

"And meanwhile, I'll be sitting here waiting and worrying, with nothing to do." She shook her head.

"You could go down to the pool, catch some rays before it gets too hot."

She sighed. "I'll try calling the boys. Haven't heard from them in a while. Tell that detective I'm part of this, too, okay?"

I smiled. "I will." I kissed her pouting lips and left.

This could be it. I started the car. A feeling of impending doom threatened to overwhelm me while I went over my strategy, simple as it was, one more time. I had already put Frymoyer's number on speed dial just in case.

I took a deep breath, backed the car out of the parking slot, and headed to my moment of truth.

Lancaster Avenue heads west out of Philadelphia to the suburbs of Ardmore, past Bryn Mawr, then to Villanova, Berwyn, Paoli, and beyond. At the Villanova section of the highway, Luke Elliot sat in a diner having breakfast. He was about to begin his final day of the stakeout. The *Philadelphia Inquirer* lay on the table next to his plate.

As he ate his last piece of bacon, he thought of the conversation with his brother two days earlier. *Saving my bacon?* He smiled and shook his head. Mark's ploy, while clever, had been so transparent.

The server refilled his coffee and took away his now-empty plate. After reading the headlines, he turned the newspaper over to scan the stories below the fold.

And there, he saw something that told him his stakeout would be a waste of time.

> *Paoli residents Nathan Cohen and his wife, Rachel, were killed yesterday when their private plane crashed shortly after takeoff from Orly Airport in Paris. There were no other passengers. The pilot of the Cessna aircraft, who had filed a flight plan to Zurich, Switzerland, was also killed. Cohen was an accountant in the Philadelphia firm of Cross & Spencer. According to an official of the firm, Cohen had been on an extended leave of absence.*
> *Salvatore ("Sonny") Gianelli, a client of Cohen and owner of Gianelli Imports, also of Philadelphia, was recently charged with racketeering under the federal RICO statute. According to a source in the U.S. Department of Justice, Cohen had been sought for questioning in the matter.*
> *The cause of the crash has not been determined. NTSB and FBI officials are assisting French authorities in the investigation of the incident.*

Luke sipped his coffee, pondering the implications of the story. One of his two remaining contracts was now over. As far as the mobster Gianelli would know, Luke had been responsible for the death of the crooked accountant, what he'd been paid to do. He smiled, thinking of the money he'd just made without really earning it. His last contract certainly wouldn't be that easy.

He grabbed his wallet after calculating the tip and placed some bills on the table. He was about to take the check to the cashier when a man at the service counter made him freeze in place.

Paulie! Luke quickly sat down and watched around the edge of a menu as his nemesis from the Rizzo days, Paul Ryan, paid for a large to-go cup of coffee and left the diner. *What's he doing here?*

The black SUV was parked where it had been the day before. So far, so good. *Or so bad?* My lawn care service was busy with mowers, edgers, and blowers as I slowed for the turn into my driveway. Just a normal summer day in the neighborhood. If only they knew. With a furtive glance at the SUV, I saw a man's head drop down below the driver's side window. He was waiting for me, as I figured.

As soon as the car hit the driveway, I pressed the remote button and then drove into the garage before the door was fully open. House key in hand, I quickly exited the Lexus, ran up the small stoop, unlocked and opened the door. I turned off the security alarm, now buzzing its warning.

I ran to our bedroom, making it in time to look through the street-facing window. A man wearing a baseball cap climbed out of the SUV and crossed the street. It was happening. What I had been seeing in my imagination for the last two days was unfolding for real. And there was no time to call Frymoyer.

In the walk-in closet, I pulled the shotgun and box of shells from the hiding place on the shelf and quickly loaded the weapon, pumped it once, and turned off the safety. I hurried to a short hallway that led from my kitchen to the dining room, where I waited, pulse racing, out of sight from the door to the garage, the entry he'd use. A large, stainless-steel saucepan hung from a pot rack over the kitchen island, and its reflective surface gave me a view, though quite distorted, of the door. I was as ready as I could be.

The 12-gauge was getting heavier by the second in my sweaty hands, so I rested the stock on the floor. And then I heard a slight rustle from the blinds covering the door's window. Hefting the Remington again, I saw in the pot's reflection the door slowly open.

My cell phone rang.

I lost my grip on the shotgun but caught it before it could leave my hands. I looked down reflexively at the giveaway on my belt, cursing myself for the lapse. When I looked up again at the reflection, a man's shape filled the doorway. Too late to do anything about my ringing phone now. I peeked around the corner and saw the man from the SUV at the same time he saw me.

He raised the weapon in his hand, and I ducked back just as the gun's muffled report reached my ears. A chunk of plaster flew past me, and there was a *thud* against the wall to my left. My heart was beating like a jackhammer. He'd be coming for me now, surprise gone. This was it.

With the shotgun at waist level, I took a deep breath and held it. I stepped back into the short hallway, waiting for him to appear around the corner as my phone's distracting ringing finally stopped. Hatred of this man who had killed Bob and Sheree overcame paralytic fear, and I stood ready to send the killer into the great beyond.

But he didn't appear. I listened, trying to separate lawn-machinery noise from kitchen movement, but nothing helped me know where he was and what he was doing. I took a chance and stepped to the corner so I could see the pot's reflection again. The man still stood in the doorway. *Why isn't he coming after me?*

He'd turned around, looking toward the open doorway to the garage, his gun trained in that direction. *Have Frymoyer and the cavalry arrived?* If so, the cops would catch the killer in the act, and my derring-do would not only be unnecessary but unjustified. *What should I do?*

I stepped back into the hallway, hoping I'd hear shouts of "Drop your weapon" and the like. But all I heard was the wail of a leaf blower. *Should I call Frymoyer? But what if he and his men are already outside?* A call to him now might interfere with his imminent takedown of the assassin. *Shit!* Indecision had replaced my plan of action, so clear only moments earlier.

There still was no other sign the cops had arrived, putting doubt to that desperate hope. Maybe a member of the lawn crew working on the side yard or an AC person coming to service the neighbor's unit, whatever, had spooked him. The what-ifs were stampeding through my head. The only thing I knew for sure was that a killer stood in my kitchen and wanted me dead. I'd prepared myself before for this, and I needed that courage back. Him or me. It boiled down to that.

Another peek told me he was still focused on the garage. I stepped into the kitchen.

He was swinging his gun toward me when I pulled the trigger.

CHAPTER 30

THE FORCE OF THE SHOTGUN blast knocked the killer backward and partway through the open door. He lay on his back, not moving or uttering a sound. I stood in shock, staring at the man lying on my kitchen floor, his gun a foot away from his outstretched hand. The front of his shirt had been blasted away, and bloody, torn flesh surrounded a softball-sized hole in his sternum. Though I had envisioned this possible outcome, it seemed so unreal. And less than an hour had passed since I put in motion the actions that led to this moment.

"Hello in the house," came a shout from the garage. "Don't shoot! I'm coming in."

"Frymoyer?"

"What?"

"Are you a cop?"

"No."

"Then who the hell are you?"

"I'm a friend. Can I come in?" A man with hands raised and holding an automatic pistol in one of them showed himself in the doorway.

"Put your gun down, then keep your hands raised as you come in. Slowly."

The man tucked his weapon into the pocket of his cargo shorts and climbed the stoop. He held up his hands as he looked at the hit man's face, the dead eyes staring at the ceiling, then at the gaping wound in the center of his chest, before looking up to see me still aiming the shotgun at him. "Please point that thing away from me, okay?"

"Is he dead?"

"Oh, yeah, he's dead, all right. Nice shooting."

"So who are you?"

"I'm the brother of the man who called you from Las Vegas to warn you"—he looked down at the body—"about him."

I leaned against the counter, knees weak, adrenaline strength dissipating. "I don't understand."

The stranger maneuvered past the hit man and approached, hands still raised. "Better put the safety on."

"What? Oh, yeah." I engaged it but kept the weapon in my hands, still kind of pointed in his direction. "What are you doing here?"

The man, who looked to be in his mid-thirties, lowered his hands. "I followed him here. I figured out what he was going to do."

"You were going to help me? Why?"

"No offense, Doc, but my motives had nothing to do with you. I wanted to keep my brother out of trouble, and, well, I had a score to settle with that fucker." He pointed to the dead man.

Suddenly exhausted, I ran a hand across the top of my head. "Oh, shit. What do I do now?"

"Simple. Call the cops. Home invasion, self-defense, bad guy shot. No problem."

"Is it over?" I was still trying to cope with what happened. A man lay dead on the floor of my kitchen. A man I had put there.

"It is for him." He crouched in a spot on the floor free of gore, next to the body. He went through the pockets of the man's jeans. "No cell phone, damn it." He lifted out a wallet and opened it. "Fake ID. Good."

"Good?" My brain struggled with paralysis.

He started to wipe the wallet with his shirt then apparently changed his mind and stuffed it into his back pocket. He stood. "Yeah. Now I don't have to ditch the car."

"What are you talking about?"

"If Ry... this guy... gets traced back to the man who hired him, my brother could be in a shit-pot full of trouble."

"Your brother works for Logan?"

He arched his eyebrows at me. "You know about that?"

"I guessed." It was much quieter now. The background noise of the lawn crew had stopped. "Do you think he'll try it again?"

He stared at me for a moment. "By the time Wendell Logan can find out that his boy failed and think about making new arrangements, he won't be in any condition to do it."

"How do you know this? From your brother?"

"In a way."

I looked down at what only moments before had been a person, a living human being. Already my mind had transformed him into an object, mere evidence that something horrific had occurred but was now over. And I was still alive. Soldiers walking through a battlefield in the aftermath of combat must feel the same combination of detachment and relief. "What about fingerprints?" I asked.

"You shot him, your fingerprints on the gun. So what?"

"I mean his." I pointed at the hit man. "You don't want him identified and connected to Logan, right?"

"Gotta have prints to compare to, though. He wasn't in the service. He's got a Missouri driver's license, so no fingerprint requirement. He could have been busted over the years, so that's a possibility, though. The cops could get lucky and ID him, I suppose. But if he's been careful, the trail should end there, if I can find his fucking cell phone. He's a contract killer, a hired gun. I doubt he and Logan actually knew each other."

"You seem to know a lot about this stuff." I glanced at the pocket of his cargo shorts, where I could see the top of the gun butt. *Who is this guy, really?*

"Yeah, whatever. Look, I gotta go. Take care, Doc." He stepped around the body and avoided the blood. He bent down to pick up the man's ball cap. "Kansas City Chiefs." He showed me the logo on the front. "No sense giving the cops a clue." He stuffed the cap into the pocket opposite the one that held his gun. "Do me a favor. I'm going to search for his cell phone in the car. If you look through a window, I can signal you when I'm done. Wait until I'm gone before calling 9-1-1. And I was never here, okay?"

"Okay. Uh… thanks."

He smiled. "You did all the work, dude." He descended the steps and walked out of the garage.

I went to the dining room window. He crossed the street to the SUV, put the ball cap on his hand to open the driver's door, and climbed inside. After less than thirty seconds, he emerged, held up a cell phone, and walked away.

CHAPTER 31

I WAITED AT THE DINING ROOM window after calling Detective Frymoyer. I wanted to put some distance between the gruesome scene in my kitchen and me, but I didn't want to step around the body to get to the garage. In less than ten minutes, an unmarked Crown Vic and a patrol car carrying two uniformed deputies arrived at the house within seconds of each other. An ambulance followed shortly thereafter. As the man from the dark blue sedan led the crew of deputies and EMTs up my driveway, I returned to the kitchen and stood at the island counter.

A tall, forty-ish man wearing a sport coat and slacks appeared at the door, the two deputies behind him. He glanced at the body at his feet then gave me a pissed-off look and shook his head. "Dr. Dawson, I presume?"

"Yes. You're Detective Frymoyer?"

"Unfortunately." He said something to the uniforms, who disappeared from view. He took a pair of disposable gloves from his sport coat pocket then slipped them on, stepped around the body, and approached me. Behind him, the EMTs checked the body for signs of life. "Didn't I tell you to stay away from the house?" Frymoyer looked at the shotgun on the counter.

"I had to get some things, as I told you."

He shook his head in annoyance again and pointed at the shotgun. "Good thing you were prepared, though, huh?"

"He's dead, Detective," one of the EMTs announced as he watched the EKG tracing on the defibrillation device.

"The ME will be here soon, guys. Stand by."

The EMTs left the scene. Frymoyer crouched down next to the corpse, in almost the exact place where my would-be rescuer had done the same thing. He, too, went through the man's pockets, coming up empty. "Stinson," he called into the garage.

"Sir?"

"Get me a large baggie, will you?" He took a pen from his pocket and, as I'd seen done in countless cop shows, used it to pick up the hit man's gun by the trigger guard. A deputy leaned into the doorway, holding a plastic bag open, and Frymoyer slipped the weapon into it. "Thanks." He grabbed the bag, sealed it, and stood. "Is that his SUV across the street?" he asked me.

"Yes."

A man in a suit and also wearing gloves appeared in the doorway.

"Hey, Carl," Frymoyer said. "This one shouldn't tax your forensic acumen much."

"You think?" the middle-aged man, who I surmised was the medical examiner, replied with a wry smile. He beckoned to someone in the garage, and a younger man holding a camera came up behind him.

Frymoyer gestured to the hallway behind me. "Let's find a comfortable place to sit, and you can tell me exactly what happened, okay?"

I led him to the living room. I related the sequence of events to the cop, leaving out the parts that involved the stranger "friend" and my intentional trap, of course. And that made me think of Michelle. With the relief of having survived the life-and-death ordeal, and then the confrontation with Frymoyer, I had completely neglected the thought of my wife waiting for me at the hotel. Until now. She had no idea, of course, what her husband had just done. What I would have to tell her and then suffer the consequences. I couldn't begin to think what those could be.

But as bad as that prospect was, something potentially worse occurred to me. Michelle thought I had gone to the sheriff's office because that's what I had told her. She could blow my cover story if Frymoyer got to her first. He wouldn't have a reason to question her now, though... *Would he?*

He answered my question when he said, "Keep yourself available, Doctor. This case needs to be sorted out, and I want the whole story from you *and* your wife. Have you called her?"

"Oh, man." I shook my head. "I'm not thinking straight yet. But it would be better if I tell her in person. Her reaction... well, that should be some scene."

"Yeah, it's gotta be a shock. Okay, I'll let you have a little time for this to simmer down, and then I'll need your statements for the record." He headed back to the kitchen, and I rose from my chair to follow him.

The environment had changed. Gone were the medical examiner, his assistant, and the EMTs. And so was the body, along with the entranceway carpet. In their place were two newcomers. A twenty-something woman dressed in jeans and a white golf shirt with *Sheriff's Office* printed on the back was sweeping the tile floor with a mini-vacuum cleaner. A man of about the same age and similarly attired was scraping some dried blood off the floor with a knife.

Yellow tape stretched across the open doorway. "What's going on?" I gestured at the activity.

"Gathering evidence."

Evidence? I had been naïve to think it would be so simple: man invades house with a gun, owner kills him to protect himself. *But Frymoyer doesn't have all the facts yet, so he's just being thorough.* "Does this mean we can't move back in yet?"

"Not until we've cleared it. Shouldn't take long, though. I'll call you tomorrow. I'll need your house key."

I frowned. "House key?"

"We'll lock up when we leave, and if we need to come back to check something, I don't think you'd want us breaking in."

"Oh, right." I went to the bedroom to get the keys I had tossed on the bed in my earlier haste. Returning to the kitchen, I removed the house key from the ring and handed it to him.

"Where are you staying?" he asked.

"The Residence Inn, off Lancaster."

"You can go back to your hotel now. Your wife must be wondering what's happened to you."

To put it mildly. "Thanks." I headed automatically for the kitchen door, but the technicians blocked the way.

"Use the front door, Doctor," Frymoyer said. "I'll call you tomorrow."

I left the house for the garage, where I climbed into my car and then headed to the Residence Inn to face the music.

As expected, Michelle was not happy. "You idiot!" she yelled. "Were you out of your mind?" She thumped my chest with both fists. "What in God's name were you thinking?" She paced around the small sitting area. "And you lied to me!"

"Honey, it was the only way—"

"Stop." She held up a hand. "I don't want to hear your excuses now." She collapsed into an armchair. "I can't believe this. Jimmy, you could have been killed. I was worried you might try something like this. That's why I called you." She started to cry. "But you didn't answer." She bent her head and covered her face with her hands.

I had seen that missed call when I used the phone to get Frymoyer. I didn't think it would be a good idea to tell her it could have done me in. I knelt on the floor beside her chair and put a hand on her knee. "Sweetheart, I'm sorry. But Bob's dad and I decided it was the only way to end this. The hit man had to be caught in the act. I was hoping to get the cops there first, but there wasn't time. It happened so fast."

She looked at me with tears in her eyes. "You didn't tell me you were going to do this! Because of what I would say, right? Damned straight! I could have been a widow, and our boys could have lost their father."

"But you're not, and they didn't. And it's over finally, Mish."

The hope in her eyes was a welcome change in mood. "Really?"

I told her about the other man with a gun who had shown up and what he'd said about Logan.

"Do you think that man in Las Vegas sent him—his brother—to help us?"

"I don't know, honey. But that's the only explanation that makes any sense. That guy who works for Logan must have changed his mind and decided to intervene, after all."

"Is this brother of his another hit man?"

Ah. She had just put her finger on what had bothered me about the mysterious stranger, another man with a gun at the ready. *Could he really have been sent to get the killer before he could get us?* And that raised a troubling thought: *Could I have avoided my Rambo act altogether and let one gunman take care of the other, and be spared all that trauma?* Trauma that I would keep reliving the rest of my life. But that question was moot. The arrow of time always moves forward, not to the past. *What's done is done.*

"Jim?"

"Sorry. I was just thinking. I have no idea who he is, Mish. And I don't know if he wanted to save us or just protect his brother's interests. I doubt we'll ever see or hear from him again."

She wiped her eyes and looked at me, shaking her head. "My stupid hero."

It was just as well we were forced to continue our stay at the Residence Inn over the weekend. I had to pick up some clothes suitable for my return to the office on Monday, and I was curious about what, if anything, the sheriff's people were doing at the house. So on Saturday morning I took Michelle's key, promising her up and down that I would be back within half an hour. When I got there, a steady stream of cars was driving slowly down the street, their occupants staring and pointing at my house. The news in the paper and on TV had made my home a tourist attraction.

I parked at the far end of the curved driveway, past the garage and out of sight from the street, and used the patio entrance to get into the house, which was empty. I grabbed my clothes, surveyed the kitchen briefly, saw with chagrin that there was some blood to be cleaned up, and left.

Detective Frymoyer called late Saturday afternoon to give us an update on the investigation and to get some answers. "No ID on the guy yet. We found a rental agreement in the Suburban—Avis, at the Philadelphia Airport. Their records showed a Missouri driver's license, but that turned out to be bogus. His MasterCard used to secure the car sends his bills to a P. O. box in Independence, Missouri.

So no real name and no address to work with. All we know is the shooter is probably from Missouri. No hits on the fingerprints."

"Could be a dead end, then?"

"You're sure you have no idea who he is?"

"None. Sorry." I shrugged at Michelle, who was listening to the conversation, a glass of chardonnay in her hand.

"But you do know who hired him."

"Not exactly, Detective. It's only a theory." I swirled the ice cubes in my glass of bourbon, anticipating what would be coming next.

"Look, Doctor, I went out on a limb for you based on some convoluted, politics-based conspiracy that my buddy in Philly took seriously. Unlike him, I didn't know Bob Kretchman personally, but I knew *of* him. Anyone at Syracuse around the time he was there did. And I wanted to get the bastard who killed him. But now I've got a dead man—a man you killed, let's not forget—and questions need to be answered, a lot of questions that might get our DA interested in digging into your self-defense claim. Do you get what I'm saying?"

I certainly did. Push had come to shove. "Yes. I'll tell you everything I know."

"Good. How about moseying down to the office now and we'll talk."

"Uh, I'd probably pass a breathalyzer test, but I've had something to drink. Can this wait until tomorrow?" *And give me time to rehearse my story?*

"You've already ruined half of my weekend, and I'm not going to add Sunday morning to it. I'll be there in twenty minutes." He hung up.

Michelle put her wine glass on the coffee table and picked up newspaper sections strewn about the couch. On her way to the kitchen to dispose of them, she asked, "Are you going to tell him everything? About Logan? And about the Favreau woman?"

I took a sip of my drink. "I don't think we have any choice."

—⊷⊷⊶⊷—

I laid out the whole story, including the original Vermont incident and Logan's subsequent role in the conspiracy, to Detective Frymoyer, except the parts involving the two brothers who had tried to help me. That one of them could be about to send Logan to his reward didn't bother me in the slightest. Logan deserved to reap what he had sown. After the cop left our hotel suite, apparently satisfied with our narrative, I realized I needed to inform someone else of the hit man's demise. I would let Granger know, but he could wait. I called Bob Kretchman's dad.

"Mr. Kretchman, this is Jim Dawson. I've got some news for you."

"Did you get him?"

"Yes."

"Thank God! Is he talking?"

"He's dead, sir. He came after me as we figured he would, and I shot him. I had no choice."

"Oh, Jesus. Are you okay?"

"Physically, yes. Mentally... well, I'll have to see how I feel over time. It's hard to deal with right now. But I have no regrets."

"It's never easy, Jim. In all my years on the force, I only drew my gun a handful of times, and one of those times, I killed a man. To this day, I can still see it go down plain as day. But he was a bad guy, and he would have shot me if he could have. So I have no guilt over it, and neither should you."

"Okay. I think I'm good there."

"What about the story that led up to it? Do the cops know about Bobby and you and the others... about that accident?"

"Yes. Their main concern now, though, is trying to track down who the hit man was. He hasn't been identified yet, and they want evidence against the man who hired him."

"This Logan character."

"Yes."

Kretchman sighed. "If they prosecute him, the story will have to come out."

"I know. But better that Logan gets nailed."

"Yes, I agree, Jim. I've thought about that. Anyway, you did good. Thank you. Knowing Bobby's killer didn't get away with it helps a little. And now you and Michelle can get back to normal."

"I hope so. It all depends if Logan wants to try again." *And if I misinterpreted what the brother said.*

"Don't worry about that. The heat's on him now. And I'm going to apply some of my own. He won't risk another attempt. Too many people now know what he's done. If you hear anything more about the case, you'll let me know?"

"I will, sir. Goodbye."

Two days later
Franklin Cancer Center
Philadelphia

At two a.m., Luke Elliot stepped through the hospital entrance, and a security guard immediately confronted him.

"Where's your ID badge, Doctor?"

Luke wore an open white lab coat over jeans and a Philadelphia Eagles T-shirt, a stethoscope draped around his neck. He looked down the front of his coat then patted his pockets. He gave the burly guard what he hoped was a sheepish look. "Oops. I must have left it at home." He yawned and scratched a bristled cheek. "Sorry, chief. I'm barely awake. Was called out of bed to see a patient. I'm Dr. Lewis, and I do have other ID." He reached into his back pocket and pulled out his wallet.

The guard waved his hand in dismissal. "Okay, Doc, but remember that badge next time."

"I will. Thanks." Luke put his wallet away and walked through the lobby, past an empty information kiosk. He turned right at a long corridor, and a few more steps brought him to the open doorway of the Admissions office.

All the cubicles except one were unoccupied and dark. He approached the one clerk on duty. "Morning," he said and smiled. "I'm Dr. Lewis, Dr. Kraft's new associate?" It had taken a number of trial and error calls to the offices of the oncologists on staff listed in the Center's website, but he finally found Logan's attending physician.

"Yes?" The plump, middle-aged woman smiled back at him.

"Dr. Kraft got sick suddenly and asked me to cover for him tonight. His patient had an issue about something, the nurse called Dr. Kraft, and he told me to take care of it." He grimaced. "The problem is, I can't remember what room he's in, and I don't want to bother Dr. Kraft again."

"What's the patient's name?"

"Wendell Logan."

She tapped some keys then scrolled down a list of names as Luke looked over her shoulder. "Here he is. Room two-ten."

"Thanks. I hope the rest of *your* night is a quiet one." Luke smiled again and headed for the elevator down the hall. He knew the layout of the floors of the Center, similar to the Las Vegas hospital's design, having scouted them out earlier in the day.

The room should be out of sight of the nurses' station. He'd lucked out, but he figured the billionaire would have insisted on the best room they had and not close to the floor's busy nerve center. He fingered the syringes in his lab coat pocket as he stepped off the elevator.

He reached the corridor that circled the floor around the nurses' station and rooms used for supplies, coffee breaks, and conferences. Patient rooms were situated off the opposite side of the corridor like gates at an airport terminal.

A nurse looked up from whatever she was doing at the station's counter. He nodded at her and turned right, just a doctor checking on a patient.

At the closed door of two-ten, Luke checked up and down the hall. Another nurse turned in to a room at the far end. In the opposite direction, past the nurses' station, the corridor was empty. Quiet time in the oncology unit. No visitors, no scheduled meds or procedures, light nursing staff. Just what he'd counted on.

Satisfied, he pushed the door open, entered the room, and let the door close automatically behind him. A nightlight provided enough illumination for him to identify his target, who lay on his side in the bed, apparently asleep. He didn't see an IV stand, complicating his plan, but he had prepared for that possibility.

His experience with junkies during his Chicago years and later in the army taught him how to inject a vein. That was why a hospital hit had appealed to him when the Greek tycoon, Poulos, had given him the news about Logan. That opportunity had come to nothing, but now he had a second chance. And his subsequent Google research about cancer patients told him about the possibility of an even easier way to accomplish the mission. *Maybe he's had a Port-A-Cath inserted.*

Luke switched on the fluorescent fixture above the head of the bed. He gently squeezed Logan's shoulder. "Mr. Logan?"

The patient squirmed, grunted once, but did not awaken. Luke shook him again. "Mr. Logan?"

Logan turned onto his back and opened his eyes then immediately squinted in the light at Luke. "What? What's going on? Who are you?"

"I'm Dr. Lewis, one of Dr. Kraft's partners."

"What time is it?" Logan rubbed his eyes and looked at the clock on the opposite wall. "Two-thirty? Christ, don't you guys keep me busy enough during the day? What's the problem?"

"Sorry, Mr. Logan, but Dr. Kraft has scheduled a special test of your lung function in the morning, and you need a pre-test injection so he can do it."

"He didn't tell me anything about that. I'm supposed to see the surgeon tomorrow—I mean later today!"

"Yes. In fact, the surgeon's the one who requested it." Luke pulled the stethoscope from his neck. "Can you unbutton your shirt, please?"

Logan sighed and unbuttoned his pajama top. "I'll never get back to sleep now." He groaned. "Doctors!"

"I'd rather be in bed now myself." Luke smiled. He went through the motions of listening to the patient's heart and lungs. That was when he saw it. He stood and replaced the stethoscope around his neck. "At least I won't have to hunt around for a vein."

"Yeah. That thing is convenient. It keeps my arms free so I can punch out a doctor who wakes me up in the middle of the night." Logan gave a humorless chuckle and shook his head.

Luke laughed, too. "This won't take long, sir."

A YouTube video had shown Luke exactly how to access the Port-A-Cath device. *Piece of cake.* Luke removed an alcohol swab packet from his pocket, tore it open, and wiped the swab over the lump in

Logan's upper chest. Then he took out the smaller of the two syringes and removed the needle cap. Holding the Port-A-Cath between his thumb and index finger, he inserted the needle into the center of the lump. When the needle struck the back wall of the chamber, he withdrew the plunger. The presence of blood in the syringe immediately rewarded him. He then injected its contents and backed out the needle, replacing its cap.

Soon, Logan half-closed his eyes. "Jeez, Doc, I'm feeling kinda dizzy."

"That's normal. It will only last a few seconds."

As the morphine coursed through Logan's bloodstream, he closed his eyes and his breathing slowed.

"Mr. Logan?" No response. Luke shook him. Still no response.

Luke took out the large syringe from his pocket and withdrew the plunger, filling it with air. He injected that into the Port-A-Cath. His research indicated that the amount of air needed to produce a fatal embolism was not a precise number, so he repeated the process five more times to be sure.

Then he observed his "patient." Despite the morphine coma, Logan thrashed in the bed, gasping for breath. Wild eyes opened briefly then closed. His breathing slowed again and finally stopped.

Luke checked for a carotid pulse and didn't find one. With both syringes back in his pocket, he picked up the alcohol swab and its packaging and put them in his pocket as well. After re-buttoning Logan's shirt, he turned off the light and left the room.

He stepped into the elevator. *There might be an autopsy. They might even diagnose air embolism and suspect murder when they learn of the late-night doctor's visit.* He walked through the lobby to the hospital entrance.

"Everything okay, Doc?" the security guard asked.

"Couldn't be better." Luke smiled before going through the automatic door. He walked to his car, pondering the aftermath. If they suspected Logan was killed, the nurse on the floor would likely be questioned. And the security guy, and maybe the admissions clerk. Many ifs. But granting all that, an investigation would have to end there. There would be nothing else to go on.

After reaching his car, with a mud-daubed license plate preventing identification from a security camera, Luke opened the door and took off the lab coat. He threw it onto the floor of the back seat and climbed in. *Before the cops start looking for the mysterious Dr. Lewis, I'll be on my way back to Santa Fe.*

Luke took off the horn-rimmed glasses with clear lenses and put them on the seat next to him. He removed the fake mustache and hairpiece and stuffed them into his jeans pocket. They would all end up in a Dumpster on his way to the airport. He applied his seat belt harness, started the motor, and drove slowly out of the parking lot.

He thought back to the question Dawson had asked him. *Yes, Doc. It's over.*

CHAPTER 32

I DIDN'T KNOW WHAT TO EXPECT when I arrived at the office Monday morning. *Will I be avoided as some kind of alien life form? Or will I be treated as a celebrity of sorts?* Either way, I wondered how my notoriety would affect my practice.

Marianne greeted me, all smiles, after I came through the back door. Our receptionist, Peggy, stood behind her, also beaming. They must have seen my car as I drove to the staff parking area and been waiting for my grand entrance.

"Welcome back, Dr. Dawson!" Marianne said.

"Thanks. It's good to *be* back." No shunning by the employees. So far, so good. *But what about my partners?*

Steve Bryce appeared in the hallway. "I see you've survived your vacation, Jim." He winked and held out his hand.

I shook it and gave him a tight smile. "Yeah, well, it did end up in an unexpected way."

"I should say so! That must have been scary. How is Michelle taking it?"

"She wasn't home at the time, thank goodness. But she's fine." *Relatively speaking.* I could see him searching for what to say next. *How does one chitchat about such an event?*

"Look, Jim, I'm sure your scheduled patients will understand if you need the day off." He raised eyebrows at Peggy.

"No problem. I can start calling now."

"And I'll cover any that slip through today," Bryce said.

"Thanks, Steve, but I need to get back to work. I need something to occupy me, you know?" As if on cue, the front door chimed as it opened, and Peggy left.

"I understand." He looked at Marianne. "Dr. Dawson will have a busy schedule today?"

She rolled her eyes. "All week!"

I chuckled. "That's the trouble with vacations. Even normal ones."

"Well, it's good to see you back, Jim. If you ever want to talk about... you know... feel free."

"Okay." We shook hands again, and he went back to his office.

"Give me a few minutes to check my mail, Marianne, and then we can start."

"You got it, Doc."

It *was* a long day, giving me no time to dwell on hit men, cops, and when Michelle and I could move back to our house. That was a good thing.

With my last patient seen and only fifteen minutes of office hours remaining, I put my feet up on the desk next to a pile of charts accumulated during the day. About a quarter of them represented new patients, and some of those would need letters dictated. But I didn't have the energy for that now. And Michelle was waiting for me at the hotel.

My intercom buzzed.

"Yes, Peggy."

"Dr. Dawson, a Detective Frymoyer is on the line." I could hear the excitement in her voice.

"Okay."

"Line one."

"Dr. Dawson," I announced.

"Doctor, I just wanted to let you know that we're done with your place. You can have your house back."

"That's good news." I made a note to clean up the kitchen before Michelle saw it.

"Do you have a spare key you can use until we get around to returning the one we have?"

"Yes. No problem. Any progress in the investigation?"

"Not really. Still haven't identified your intruder."

Intruder? The euphemism was likely meant for any prying ears. "What about Logan?"

"Las Vegas PD tried to question him but found out he was getting treatment at a hospital out of town, our neck of the woods, actually. Franklin Cancer Center in Philly."

Cancer center. *Is that what the cryptic comment from my mysterious visitor meant? That Logan was dying?* "I know the place."

"So I called my buddy in the Philly PD. He's going to see if Logan is able to answer some questions."

I heard muffled voices over the phone.

"Hold on a second, Doc. That's him on the line now."

He put me on hold, and I waited an anxious five minutes for the report. "Uh, I'm afraid Wendell Logan is no longer with us. Seems he died suddenly during the night. Heart attack or something."

I tried to stay calm as this fantastic news lifted the one remaining burden from my shoulders. It still depended on Frymoyer, but there was a chance the story would stay buried now. Then I thought of the gunman's prediction again and wondered if Logan's death was more than just fortuitous. I felt compelled to ask, "Will there be an autopsy?"

"The wife refused one. Said she didn't want him disrespected by having his body cut up, and what difference did it make if his heart, or the cancer, or the drugs they gave him for it killed him. She wasn't going to sue anybody." He paused. "Why do you ask?"

"Just a doctor's natural curiosity."

"A real doctor, that is."

"What do you mean by that?" I had a queasy feeling in my stomach.

"Seems there was a strange visitor to Logan's floor last night. Somebody pretending to be a doctor."

So he did do it! "Do you suspect something?" I asked in what I hoped was a level voice.

"My buddy sure does. And he's not going to let someone who would be on the suspect list obstruct an investigation. He's going to talk with the DA to get a court order. Despite Mrs. Logan's money, I think he'll get that autopsy."

"I see. And *your* investigation? Is that over now?"

"Looks that way. Unless we can find out who that guy you took care of was. We're showing his picture around the Kansas City-Independence area. But if he ends up leading us back to Logan, that would close it."

"Detective, you're not going to release the, uh, story I told you to the press, are you?"

"I don't see the point, now. As far as I'm concerned, it's irrelevant."

"Thanks."

"Oh, and we'll return your shotgun when we drop off the key."

"Does that mean the DA isn't coming after me?"

Frymoyer chuckled. "I'm not going to arrest you, and he's shown no inclination to butt in. You're home free, Doc."

"That's good to know."

"Take care." He hung up.

Home free. After the turmoil of the last year and a half, it was a great feeling. As long as I didn't think about the second death now on my conscience. I would try to take the advice Bob's dad had given me about considering it justified as self-defense and, well, he was a killer, after all.

I was taking off my lab coat when the intercom buzzed again. *Frymoyer?* "Yes?"

"Sorry to bother you again, Dr. Dawson. I was just about to call the answering service to sign out when this call came in for you."

"Who is it?"

"He wouldn't give me his name. He said he was the guy who took the Kansas City Chiefs hat, and that you'd know who he is. Should I tell him you're gone for the day?"

The mysterious gunman. "I'll take it, Peggy."

"Okay. Line two. Goodnight, Doctor."

"Have a good one." I pressed the button and lifted the handset. "I didn't think I would ever hear from you again."

"I thought you'd like to know that the man you were worried about is dead."

"I heard."

"It's made the news already?"

"I doubt it. The cop looking into his involvement told me a few minutes ago."

"So you told him about... my brother's employer."

"I had to. The detective was making noises about charging me with something. But how did you know he was dead?"

"Let's just say he died of unnatural causes."

Oh. My guess was confirmed. "Your brother should be out of trouble, then."

"Yes, if you didn't mention him to the cops."

"No, just that an anonymous caller told me about the hit man. And I kept you out of it, too. But the Philly cops suspect foul play in Logan's death. Seems there was a bogus doctor seen in the hospital last night. They're trying to get an autopsy."

"Yeah, that makes sense. But that'll go nowhere. As they say, Doc, this case is closed. Have a great life."

I sat in my now-quiet office building, mulling over the end of the turmoil that had occupied Michelle and me for so long. I had told Bob's dad that I had no regrets concerning my part of the resolution, and that was true. Yet I had killed a man, and the vision of him lying on my kitchen floor would likely continue to haunt me. Michelle, thankfully, had not witnessed that, but I wondered if her knowing what I had done would change anything between us. Only time would tell.

Then I thought of the one person without whom none of it would have happened, and who probably was in the dark about the previous two days' events. I picked up the phone and called his cell.

Granger's response surprised me at first, but on reflection, it shouldn't have. Instead of joy that Michelle and I were out of danger— he gave cursory acknowledgment of that—he voiced out loud what this could mean for his political ambition. That was it, as far as I was concerned. My former teammate, the fun-loving guy I used to get a kick out of, had become an insufferable, egocentric ass. He likely always was, but the others and I had gone along with, even admired, I guess, his big-man-on-campus, life-of-the-party persona. I wasn't that callow teenager any longer, thank God. Even more important, though, every time I'd see him, I wouldn't be able to ignore his part, though unwitting, in Bob and Sheree's deaths.

Finally, I owed it to the Howards to tell them they were no longer in peril. I had played a role, after all, in the event that put the whole mess into motion so many years ago.

"Hello?" he answered when I called him.

"Tim, this is Jim Dawson."

Silence ensued for a few moments. "Oh, hi."

"I called to tell you that the man who assaulted your wife in the parking garage is dead."

Silence again. "Who was he?"

"I don't really know."

"Then how do you—"

"The same man later killed my friend Bob Kretchman and his wife and then came after me. I was able to get him before he got me."

"Jesus! That means... he was going after everyone who knew about the accident."

"Yes."

"Did Granger put him up to it?"

"No. But the man who did is also dead."

"Holy shit, Doc! I wouldn't have guessed you could be a... a vigilante."

"No, I wasn't responsible for that one. He died of apparent natural causes. But he was the one behind it all. As you suspected, he didn't want Granger's political career threatened, but Granger wasn't a part of it. His mistake was having this man on his team."

"I see." His voice was low. "Kind of."

"Bottom line is you and your wife now have nothing to fear."

"Thank God for that."

"So have a nice life, Tim."

"Doc, wait a second. I have news for you, too. Cathy and I are expecting."

"Congratulations!"

"Yeah, we're real excited about it. And I'm thinking, well, you're a pediatrician. And we do have a significant history together, don't we?"

I smiled as I looked around my office, realizing where he was going. "Yes, we certainly do."

"After the baby comes, would it be all right if we could call you for advice if, you know, the kid gets sick or something?"

I laughed. "It would be my pleasure. I didn't take care of you when you were a baby, and I should have, so consider it payback. Send me a birth announcement."

"I will. Thank you."

"Goodbye, Tim. I wish you and Cathy the best."

Later that year, in November, the big news on Wall Street was Logan Enterprises being taken public. The IPO caused quite a stir, including the news that Carole Logan, the tycoon's widow, would control fifty-one percent of the shares in the new corporation. "Another Joan Crawford" was a common line heard in business circles, especially when her background came to light.

Thanks to Detective Frymoyer, I learned that the autopsy performed on Logan had been inconclusive, and no evidence supported suspecting his wife of murder. The large universe of those who would be happy to see Logan dead kept the cops busy for a while, but they had charged no one to that point. An intense hunt for the mysterious night visitor came to nothing.

Alan Granger easily won his gubernatorial re-election that same month. But with Logan's funds now controlled by a board of directors with no interest in bankrolling a presidential candidate, and with the Democrat currently in the White House looking to be a formidable incumbent, he decided to end his dream of becoming president. A victim of term limits, he left politics after his second term and returned to his law firm. Brent Marshall succeeded him as governor of Pennsylvania.

Michelle and I still exchanged Christmas cards with the Grangers, but that friendship, such as it was, had ceased. Al must have understood the reason; he never called me on it.

Two years almost to the week after our adventure, Michelle accompanied me to a medical convention in Chicago. On our first night there, we got tickets for a Second City show, which we usually did when we visited Chicago. We enjoyed the skillful improv artists and wondered if any of them would, as several other famous alumni of the troupe had done, move on to the next level of comic celebrity.

We had just left the theater after the performance when a man said, "Dr. Dawson?" behind us. I turned, and blue eyes stared back at me. I had seen his face for a total of a few minutes two years earlier, but I would never forget it. "You're... well, I never did get your name," I said.

He chuckled. "That's right, you didn't." He stuck out his hand. "Luke Elliot."

I shook it. An attractive blonde stood next to him as other theatergoers maneuvered around us on the sidewalk.

"Dr. Dawson, I'd like you to meet my wife, Emily."

"That's Jim." I offered my hand, which she shook. "And this is my wife, Michelle."

"Nice to meet you," Emily said.

"I met Dr. Dawson a couple of years ago on one of my business trips, honey," Luke explained.

"Do you live in Chicago?" Michelle asked.

"No," Emily replied, "just visiting. We both love this city."

"So do we."

"Well, it was nice seeing you again... Jim." Luke took Emily's elbow. "Michelle, I'm sure Jim has told you all about the circumstances surrounding the time he and I first met. I often think back to that day myself. Have a nice evening, and enjoy your stay in Chicago." With that, he and his wife turned and walked up North Wells Street into the night.

Michelle was staring after them with wide eyes.

"Yup, that was him," I confirmed.

"The man who showed up right after... and then..."

"One and the same. Now I finally know his name."

"Well, isn't that something?"

I tried to find him on the Internet when we got back to our hotel room, using all the variations of *Elliot*, but none of my hits seemed appropriate. "I guess he'll always be our mystery man," I said as I shut off the tablet computer.

"It's probably best he stays that way, for his sake and ours." She kept her attention on the TV screen, feigning a nonchalant attitude.

I smiled and pointed a finger at her. "I think you're right about that. What do you say we go down to that fancy bar in the lobby, have an overpriced drink, and talk about old times?"

"And times to come?"

I gave her a meditative nod. "Especially those." I held out my hands, which she took, and helped her stand. "Some things should just stay in the past." I encircled her waist and drew her to me. "We have the rest of our lives to create memories we *will* want to relive from time to time."

ACKNOWLEDGEMENTS

I COULDN'T HAVE PUT THIS NOVEL together without lots of help. I am indebted to my fellow authors who gave of their time and knowledge to read the entire manuscript and offer suggestions for making it a better product. D.A. Amberson, Nathan B. Childs, C.J. Driftwood, Ann Everett, Irene Hamilton, T.M. Hobbs, Erin Landers, Karen McDaniel, Audra Middleton, Janet Reid, Janet Taylor-Perry – I owe you many thanks.

My two eagle-eye editors, Alyssa Hall and Jenn Loring, cleaned up my miscues and suggested changes to make the story flow without speed-bumps from beginning to end. They held my feet to the fire to avoid superfluous passages and add needed ones. But editors can only do so much. At the end of the day, the finished product is my responsibility, and any errors can only be laid at my doorstep.

Finally, my publisher – and I'm talking about the actual person who runs the company, Lynn McNamee – deserves a huge thank-you for her hands-on approach every step of the way from manuscript draft to sale-ready book, and for hiring the right people for her staff.

Thank you all for your support.